From Diana Hun... her first night in New York.

> "Dear Diana,
> ... you don't have to go looking
> for love; the love is there for
> you if you'll just let it in!"

And, goodness, she had already
let a lot of love in via...

> Angelo O'Shaughnessy—the golden
> haired cab driver whose perfect
> proportions and performance
> prepared her for his sexy sideline.

> Rod Peters—the "African god of
> lust" who spoke with an English
> accent and produced porn flicks with
> an elegant expertise.

> Muffie Free—her old friend from
> Beavertown, who offered Diana bed,
> board, and body too.

It was only the beginning
for as Muffie put it...

> "Oh, Diana, goddess of the waking
> moon, you're so magnificent, you
> turn everybody on!"

Diana's Desire

LYTTON SINCLAIR

WARNER BOOKS

A Warner Communications Company

WARNER BOOKS EDITION

Copyright © 1983 by Warner Books, Inc.
All rights reserved.

Cover photo by Bill Cadge

Warner Books, Inc.,
666 Fifth Avenue,
New York, N.Y. 10103

 A Warner Communications Company

Printed in the United States of America

First Printing: April, 1983

10 9 8 7 6 5 4 3 2 1

To Lynn,
the Contessa

Diana's Desire

PART I

Chapter One

The whole way into New York City on that Grey-
hound, I kept telling myself to turn around and go back
to Beavertown, Pennsylvania, where I had just quit a
nice, secure job as a waitress at the local Howard
Johnson's. But, of course, it was too late. I was, as they
say, stuck on the bus, and before long, little ol' me, Diana
Hunt, the original kid from the country, had arrived at
the Port Authority Terminal at Eighth Avenue and
Forty-Second Street, smack in the middle of half the drug
pushers, muggers, and twenty-dollar hookers in these
United States. New York: the dream and the nightmare
rolled into one. I was overwhelmed—and absolutely
thrilled. I couldn't wait to explore Life in the Fast Lane.
The minute I stepped off the bus, I could taste Manhattan's special energy, and I knew at once, instinctively,
that here in this city of stone and steel I would find men
who would appreciate me—warm, physical men, hustlers
with hard cocks, exciting, creative entrepreneurs who
weren't afraid of money and success, who liked to keep
their hands (and their mouths) full of pussy.

And I hoped that meant me. Even in Beavertown I
had always been told my cunt was second to none.
I was like a happy drunk fantasizing about my destiny.
I couldn't wait to show off my incredible figure in a
sheer, clinging gown I had designed myself to be worn
without underwear, something I never dared do in
Beavertown. The silky, chenille garment was, by design,

the exact color of my labia, a special coral-pink blush, and in the "backless" back it draped casually over the top of my ass. As far as that part of my anatomy goes, I am extremely lucky; even though I am one hundred percent Anglo-Saxon, I am blessed with a black woman's ass. It stands out high and proud and drives men wild. I wondered how long it would be before I'd be invited into New York's glittering night life with its fabled film directors, clothes designers, international businessmen and the most beautiful women on five continents.

But for the moment, as I walked into the main terminal, I found myself completely alone, except for one suitcase roped together and the phone number of my best friend in the eleventh grade, Margaret "Muffie" Free who, according to her mother, was now a top New York model, although I must confess I had never seen Muffie's picture in any fashion magazine. Muffie and I had eagerly made plans over the phone for me to stay with her for a few weeks until I could get a place of my own. Muffie faithfully promised to meet me at the terminal when I arrived. But on this particular day, as Fate would have it, the friggin' bus was four hours late, thanks to a broken axle on the New Jersey turnpike, and by the time I finally arrived, the sun had long since set and Muffie was nowhere to be seen. I couldn't blame her. I figured she was probably having supper with her boyfriend Rod Peters, who she claimed was the "king of erotic film producers." I decided to hail a cab, schlep down to her Greenwich Village apartment, and wait. Muffie had mailed me a key, thank God, so I wasn't worried where I'd sleep that night.

As I was lugging my overstuffed old suitcase to the main entrance on Eighth Avenue through the scaffolding of a remodeling job, past begging "nuns," and teen-age prostitutes of several sexes and colors, suddenly, from out of the shadows, comes this jet-black dude in an open gold trench coat, a wide-brimmed white fedora, and a three-piece camel's-hair suit so tightly fitted in the crotch that from a block away a blind man couldn't miss his bulging cock, which ran halfway down his thigh. Now, I may be a country girl, but I have always watched television, especially "Kojak;" I think I know a pimp when I see one. This incomparable Nubian prince comes right up to me, puts his hand on my shoulder as if I was a long-lost friend, and says in an impeccable English accent, "I say there, are you the girl who's looking for Dick?"

I was dumbstruck. "Looking for Dick," I stammered. "What do you mean?" thinking how unbelievably handsome he looked with his hooded, almost Chinese eyes.

"Yes," he continued, "I thought you might be looking for Dick. I can help you find him, if you like. Dick, that is."

"Dick?" I protested, "no, I'm waiting for Muffie."

He looked at me and winked. "Muffie, hm?"

I was furious. What was this man suggesting? "No," I said, "I mean, I'm waiting for my girlfriend."

He laughed uproariously. "That's what I thought you said." His smile was admittedly dazzling—it did not stop, and as he stared at me, I could see that his super-intelligent light-gray eyes were sparkling like diamonds. And when he accidentally-on-purpose brushed my breast with his chiseled black hand, I felt an unexpected shiver of joy go straight up my spine. But what was I to do? I was so young, so inexperienced (sort of), and at this point so terrified of strangers, especially black men dressed like pimps who made sexually suggestive remarks, that I blurted-out, "I can't stop to talk! I have an emergency medical appointment. It's a matter of life and death. Maybe I'll see you again." Oh, what racist hypocrite I was! I was so ashamed, especially since I could

13

feel that incorrigible cunt of mine aching for the kiss of his ramrod cock.

He must have sensed my ambivalence. Like a magician pulling a bouquet of flowers out of a hat, he flashed something under my nose. "My card, madame." I grabbed his card, and, without looking behind, ran straight for the revolving doors to hail a taxi, leaving my Othello in the dark, and my poor cunt without the company it craved. But fortunately, Fate had not finished with me; little did I realize the surprise lying in wait for me later that night. The truth is, I would see my ebony emperor again.

In the meanwhile, as I was wrestling with my old relic of a suitcase through the revolving door, the ropes broke and the luggage opened up the second I hit the overcrowded street. Much to my absolute horror, my lingerie and panties, much of which I hadn't had time to wash, were blowing in all directions all over Eighth Avenue, and already several ragamuffin panhandlers were picking them up and smelling them, and, I might add, grinning from ear to ear. You must realize I had always designed and made my own underwear, because I loved the look on a man's face when he saw me in my ultrafeminine, ribbon-and-lace, perfumed panties, many of which sported see-through panels in front. You can imagine my extreme embarrassment as I witnessed in horror my most intimate apparel scattering all over the intersection of two of the dirtiest, most sordid, trash-strewn streets of a city known all over Middle America for its rampant vice and unnatural wickedness.

And to think that I was adding to the evil! I wondered what my grandmother, a devout deaconess, would think if she saw me now! But Grandma must have been praying for my soul, because at that moment, the gods intervened. Suddenly, in the middle of heavy, congested midtown traffic, almost from out of nowhere, a battered yellow cab made a rip-roaring U-tern in the middle of

14

Eighth Avenue and drove headlong towards the front of the Port Authority Terminal. Like a kamakaze pilot, the Yellow Peril skipped over the curb and headed straight for me. I was frozen in terror. With a loud squeal of the brakes, the car stopped dead at my feet with about eight inches to spare. I thought, "This is where I get shot dead."

Not quite. A six feet tall copper-headed hunk with a black shirt open to his naval, exposing a muscular sun-burned chest matted with curly red-gold hair and wearing skin-tight, bleached jeans with a torn crotch and brand-new cowboy boots jumped out of the driver's seat, screaming, "Hey, pussycat, I'll get your panties! I'll get your panties!"

And sure enough, he did. It was like a miracle. Within the space of a minute, he had tracked down and collected every piece of my precious underwear, even though he ripped my lavender lace bikini briefs in half, grabbing them from some bum who refused to give them up. But there he was, standing in front of me, both hands stuffed with my panties, his cornflower-blue eyes staring intently at me with unmistakable hunger and anticipation, his sexy voice slow and husky.

"Hey, babe, I'm your driver. I'll drive you anywhere you want." At that moment, looking at this magnificent sun god, I completely forgot my British-tongued blacka-moor. My crotch felt a familiarly delicious ache, my vaginal juices began to flow, and I thought, "Oh my God!"

To think that only the night before, in Beavertown, in a searing and semitragic domestic scene, I had said good-bye to my One True Love, our family's beloved dentist, who was unwilling to leave his wife and children to follow me, and here I was, less than one day later, like some kind of no-good tramp, staring into the most beau-tiful masculine eyes I had ever seen. I knew this man wanted me. That's what really turned me on—his look of

15

absolute desire. My heart leapt, and I praised all Creation, knowing I would not have to be alone in what seemed the most terrifying city in the world. When I took my panties from him, I found myself stroking his large workingman's hands. I just couldn't help myself. His hands were hard, muscular, and covered with fine gold hair, just like his spectacular chest.

My feelings overwhelmed me. I wanted to take his rugged fingers and work them slowly and deliberately into my pleasantly aching cunt until the juicy lips opened up, ready for the rest of him, but I restrained myself, thinking he might not like a girl to be too forward on the first meeting, especially before he knew my name. And, of course, I was afraid of getting arrested. So I just looked at him and said, "Sir, I'm going to Greenwich Village." I proceeded to step into the back seat of the cab like it was my private limousine, knowing my man would finish repacking by suitcase and put it in the trunk, which he then proceeded to do.

Inside the cab, I was surprised to see that besides lacking the traditional sliding glass door partition between the front seat and the back, the seats were upholstered in a soft, glove leather, a blood-red burgundy which framed my lean, tanned legs to the best advantage. On the tape deck, mood music was playing the seduction sounds of an oversexed saxophone. I sat there feeling languidly at home as I watched my Lancelot hurriedly pack my suitcase, the muscles of his hard, athletic legs bulging through his jeans. And when he turned around with my suitcase, he was grinning sheepishly at me, a thatch of gold hair hanging over his forehead like a little boy's. The all-American Dream.

There was something else. I could not help but notice at least eight inches of engorged hard-on pushing furiously against the prison of his too-tight jeans. I knew my gorgeous rescuer must be in great pain, all on account of me, and my obviously crazed impulse was to bolt the

16

cab, unzip his fly, and pop what I fantasized must be a plum-sized glans into my drooling lips to relieve him of so much discomfort. But again, my inner voice spoke up just in time, warning me to wait until we could be alone, or surely I would land in the observation ward at Bellevue.

With that, I found myself suddenly politicized, as we used to say in our high school history class, so mad at the present system of sexual repression that I wanted to stand naked in Times Square screaming, "Give me your tired, your poor, your huddled masses yearning to breathe free, and I'll give them a blow job they'll never forget!"

But, of course, I could never do it. I'm basically an old-fashioned girl. Indoors has always been my favorite place for sex. Behind me, I could hear the cab trunk slam down hard as my rescuer put my suitcase in place. As he started back for the driver's seat, a couple of Hispanic hookers in hot pants and four-inch heels had noticed his flagpole erection and were pointing at it, making lewd remarks like, "Look, honey, see that! There's a man with three legs!" and "Hey, baby, can I fly my flag from your flagpole? Oh Say Can You See, America!"

I didn't think those girls were one bit funny, and even though I must admit that I secretly felt proud that I was the ultimate cause of all the excitement on the street, as my savior leapt into the driver's seat, I stammered, "I'll do anything to make it up to you!"

He turned his head around and said, "Come here, darlin', I'll tell you a secret."

In my innocence I leaned forward. In a flash, he had stuck his thick, warm tongue into my mouth and was exploring every crevice of my soft pink orifice, his lips hungrily and passionately sucking mine. I was so overwhelmed by such sudden friendliness in what I had always heard was a tough town that I found myself gasping "Yes! Yes! Yes!" with at least a dozen cars and buses honking angrily on Eighth Avenue. His right hand was already inside by dress fondling my breasts, stroking my nipples with a practiced hand. All of this in the space of fifteen seconds, with the whores that I mentioned taking in all of this X-rated activity, hootin' and hollerin'. They were bent over from laughing so hard.

But suddenly, my golden-headed god, realizing that we were headed for disaster, was back on duty at the wheel screaming, "Christ! I better get out of here!" We took off like a rocket up Eighth Avenue with the hookers screaming at me, "Good-bye, pussy, make sure you get your two dollars!"

My driver spoke again. "Where do you want me to take you?"

I stammered, "My girlfriend's apartment. It's on Chambers Street. I have the key, but I don't know where she is. My bus was four hours late."

His voice was so soft in its own gravelly way. "I hope I don't make you nervous," he said. "You're the sexiest broad I've ever met. I want my cock to dive into your cunt and stay there for the next hundred years!"

With that, I guess I became possessed, and I blurted out, half in tears, "I love you! I'll do anything for you." I couldn't believe what I was saying, but frankly, my main strength is that I have always trusted my instincts for being able to "read" another human being immediately, and I now felt in the depths of my soul that this stranger was golden to the core. Diamonds are some girls' best friend, but to tell the truth, I've always been mad for gold.

In short, I wanted to fuck my brains out. I whispered, "My name is Diana Hunt, and I'm in New York for the very first time. I have always heard New York is such a cold place."

Without turning around he spoke again. "I can make it warm for you. Every time I picked up one of your panties back there on the sidewalk, I was going out of

18

my mind. I could feel your pussy. I could smell it. I crave you, Diana, I want to eat you out. Please, Diana. Pulleaze!"

By now, he was driving me wild, and I was fondling my clitoris. I couldn't help myself. My vaginal juices were flowing and I was beginning to sweat, imagining my cab-driver Tarzan on top of me, weighing me down with his hairy, muscular bulk.

He must have known what I was doing in the back seat, because he kept it up—the conversation, that is. "I want to mouth you, Diana, between your thighs, I want to kiss your pussy lips."

I must have started moaning, but then, with a start, I realized that the bright lights of Broadway were around us on all four sides. Crowds of smartly dressed people were going into the theaters right outside the cab win-dow, so I stopped masturbating, knowing it was just a matter of time before we'd be alone together. "Darling," I insisted, "please stop talking before you turn me into a nymphomaniac. We'll have plenty of time together in a few minutes."

He apologized and shut up. There was a long deathly silence. Looking out the window, I wondered what my destiny would be—would I end up on the Broadway stage or in a burlesque house—or would I always be a waitress? My future stretched ahead of me like the end-less avenues of Manhattan as we sped south from Times Square toward "the Village" with its promise of artists, designers, dancers—creative types I had heard about but never seen in Beavertown. Caught between desire and fantasy, I must have been in a daze, because I sud-denly realized I did not even know my new Adonis's name.

"Please," I said finally, breaking the silence, "tell me your name."

I was hardly prepared for his response. "Angelo O'Shaughnessy," he shot back, "Italian-Irish." Full of

19

wine and poetry—and magic. Wait till I show you." And then, with the full-bodied joy of a self-confident male, he laughed, throwing back his sculpted head with its magnificent lion's mane. "I'm an actor," he continued.

"You've got quite an act," I retorted.

He countered with, "I like to think I'm a leading man."

And I came back with, "You can lead me anywhere you like. As they say in show biz, take my hand, I'm a stranger in paradise."

The man obviously knew what he wanted. "Well, as a matter of fact, I'd especially like to help you unpack your suitcase," he said, adding, "I'm good at that, among other things."

And then I, ever the romantic schoolgirl, with absolutely no sense of propriety, which is at once my greatest weakness and my greatest strength, said, "I could model some of my panties for you, if you like," and then no longer being able to control myself, reached over the front seat and bent down to feel the hardness in his crotch, and, to my utter amazement and delight, discovered his mammoth rod had escaped its confining cage and was sticking straight up in his lap, bigger and redder than I dared imagine. Unbeknownst to me, Angelo with his strong left hand was jerking himself off, working the thick outer flesh of his shaft up and down over the marble-hard inner core, breathing heavily and whispering my name.

Looking at his magnificent piece of meat, which told me so much about my rescuer's loneliness and his need to be loved, I suddenly felt a hunger so deep that I hurled my entire body over the front seat. In a flash, my greedy hands had encircled his cock, which was already oozing little drops of glistening lubricant. I took him into my mouth. With my free hand I dug down into his briefs and reached for his oversized testicles, which were nested like eggs in their hairy sac hanging between his loins. I began stroking and fondling them as I moved the soft inner muscles of my mouth up and down over his plum-sized glans. He began moaning so loud I thought I must have accidentally gouged him, but I hadn't.

"Oh Christ, you're so fantastic," he cried out. "You're so unbelievable I could die and go to heaven." And then, he shuddered and heaved and thick gobs of white come exploded into my mouth like waves in a heavy sea breaking against the rocks. Needless to say, with his strong orgasm, he lost control of the wheel, and the cab skidded violently and threw me on the floor, fortunately uninjured.

We had missed the crosstown bus on Fourteenth Street by about two inches. The bus driver was scarlet with rage and was spewing obscenities out the window at my beloved Angelo. Horns were honking. Passers-by were shouting, and I heard sirens in the distance coming closer and closer (which, thank God, turned out to be an ambulance headed for nearby St. Vincent's Hospital). Angelo, thinking it was the cops, screamed, "Diana, stay down! We better get to your friend's apartment quick!"

All I remember is that the next ten minutes were a succession of stops and starts in the dark, with me crouched down on the floor, not knowing if the police were on our tail or not. And all the while Angelo was chanting in his low insistent voice, "I love you, Diana, you're the best thing that ever happened to me. My cock will never forget you. I'll help you in any way I can. Oh please, don't send me away, Diana, I'll do anything you want if you let me eat your pussy. I can see it now, it's fat and pink and it's aching for me. Right?"

"Yes, yes," I cried, again putting my fingers down between my thighs, separating my cunt-lips, wishing his mouth and tongue were already there inside me, exploring me, licking me, kissing me. I could feel the inner muscles of my vagina begin to heave, and I was transported into such an orgasmic high that I barely heard

Angelo park his cab on Chambers Street and open the door on my side. Bending down over me in the dark twilight, he kissed me repeatedly on the back of my neck and then lifted me up, whispering over and over again, "I love you, Diana. I love you."

I could barely contain myself, knowing that in a few minutes I would be in Muffie's bed, and I only hoped the key she had sent me fit the lock. Muffie's street was filled with brownstone townhouses that had been converted into apartments. Angelo carried me up the worn stone steps in the dark. The fat brass rails on either side were polished and glinting under the streetlights, and once we had opened the outer oak door with its etched glass panels, the small vestibule inside was a masterpiece of dark mahogany paneling freshly oiled and shining, with a note for me taped to Muffie's brass mailbox which read, "Dearest Di—Welcome to New York. I'm out having dinner with someone you'll love. Will bring you home a present. Can't wait to see you. *All* my love (and more!). Muffie. P.S. There's food in the refrigerator."

How divine of her! How loving! My romantic interlude continued without cease as the burly Angelo seized me and carried me in his strong arms with their sinewy, ropelike muscles up three flights of narrow stairs carpeted in blood-red velvet pile to Number 69, Muffie's apartment, with its ten-foot tall mahogany front door. The key worked beautifully. Inside was an unexpected sight— the most extraordinary living space I'd ever seen: two interconnected, adjoining rooms that looked like a first-class suite on an ocean liner. The walls were cherry paneling, dark with a hint of red, and there were warm brass fittings everywhere: sconce lights, doorknobs, hinges, rails. The chesterfield sofa along one side of the living room was upholstered in a bittersweet tangerine suede. Everywhere was total luxury. Oriental vases turned into lamps with pleated silk shades, plum damask draperies, nineteenth-century oil portraits of English aristocrats riding to hounds, end tables of drum-shaped Chinese brass gleaming dully under an antique crystal chandelier. The room adjoining it, the bedroom, I blush to say, was almost masculine in its strength, as if there were some guiding male presence behind the scenes telling Muffie what to do. This room, much to my surprise, had a mirrored ceiling, the first I'd ever seen, and the bed, or more accurately, the sleeping platform, which was double-size, took up most of the room. It was so enormous I figured it must have been custom-made—it could sleep at least six people. The fitted bedspread was red satin with a big monogrammed M in black smack in the middle. On the bed was another note from Muffie which read "P.S. There's champagne for the two of you in the refrigerator."

I thought to myself, "She has some nerve. She must think I'm some kind of a pick-up or something." But I couldn't stay mad at her, especially since I knew my feelings for Angelo were grounded in as deep an affection as I had felt for anyone, including my dear departed dad. Without saying a word, Angelo pulled back the bedspread and lay me down on the pink silk sheets. Then he left for the small kitchen off the living room, presumably to fetch the champagne.

I had work to do. By the time I heard the pop of the champagne bottle, I had slipped out of my clothes and was lying completely naked on the pink silk sheets, feeling their tingling smoothness against my back and thighs—and needless to say, I was stroking myself and dreaming of Angelo.

We must have had mental telepathy. By the time he returned, carrying the magnum of champagne, white foam oozing out around the top of the bottle, he was completely naked, his broad cock half erect like a python hanging down from a tree in the Amazon jungle. His bush was dark red and seemed to spread luxuriantly

23

over most of his lower abdomen like a smoldering fire around his magnificent tool, which began to stiffen and thicken the minute he caught sight of me lying there with my cunt spread wide open waiting for him. And I, of course, as I looked at my warrior, was stroking myself, as I love to do, to let men know how badly I want them and how welcome they are to take over the job of bringing me to the heights of ectasy.

Angelo laughed and said, "The booze can wait. You're stimulant enough." And with that, he dove for me, his face almost immediately buried in my cooze, the bristles of his day-old beard tripping the nerve-ending wires of my clitoris, as wave after wave of small explosions broke within me. He looked so happy, slurping me up, his rough hands kneading my golden buns. He kept saying, "Oh baby, Oh baby, Oh baby," over and over again. Then we went sixty-nine, and at last I was free to enjoy him without fear of the Gestapo, and I eagerly stretched my mouth over his swollen purple knob, which sat on top of a shaft as thick as a baby's arm. His hands guided me, taking hold of the back of my head, bringing me up and down, up and down, up and down.

Then, suddenly, Angelo was on top of me, his mouth in my mouth, exploring me with his insistent tongue, which I sucked on voraciously, exploding inside whenever he touched me, the matted hair on his chest arousing my nipples in such a way that every time he moved it was as if a thousand tiny gold wires were stroking my most sensitive parts.

Like many women, I can be brought to full orgasm by having my nipples stroked. There seem to be invisible wires connecting my breasts with my cunt.

Angelo wanted genital connection like few men I have ever met. "I want to fuck you, baby! I want to fuck you!" he cried out, and finally I heard myself screaming, "Fuck me! Fuck me! Yes! Yes! I want you! I want you!" and I reached down with both hands and lifted his

24

massive equipment into my most secret recesses. I have had longer cocks than his, but never one thicker, combined with such massive balls. It was like being reamed by a pile-driver. If it had been anyone else I would have been terrified, but because I could feel such intense warmth in his cock, and his heart seemed to beat in the enormous pulsating blue veins that roped around it, I felt like I was connecting with a profound and ancient soul that the gods—and surely there were still gods; there had to be—had sent to comfort me on my first night in the Big Bad City.

Angelo started moving in and out of me, except that each time he moved out, the whole force of me, spirit and flesh, moved with him, my vagina like two sensuous lips holding onto him, sucking him with the primal rhythms of my own blood-beat. This was the kind of fucking I had never dreamed was possible back in Beavertown, where even the best of men seemed a little embarrassed by their own passion. Maybe it was the combination of Irish and Italian blood, but Angelo was my first lover who was a poet-beast. We rode together to a point where we were one being, crying out with pleasure and pain. I say pain only because we had not as yet had a full orgasmic release together.

And then it happened. I could feel his stout rod within me begin to thicken and the glans grow as big as an apple pounding against me. Then, the dam burst. He cried out with an animal cry, like a jungle beast that has been mortally wounded. I felt the gush of warm sperm flood into me, and I clung to him, this wild horse, this bucking bronco, my nails gouging into his back, my teeth biting into him until I felt the warm salty taste of blood in my mouth. He bucked and screamed for a minute, and then he lay still as his sperm, thick and honeyed, dripped out of my secret cave, matting our thick bushes with nectar.

I reached down and began to massage his ultrasensitive balls, coating them with his sperm, a natural lubricant, and squeezed them gently as he moaned some more in delicious ectasy. And then I, too, lay still for a moment, thinking we could at last sip some champagne, and, in a few minutes, start all over again.

I looked at my stud. "I never knew New York contained such a jungle animal," I said lovingly.

"You ain't seen nothin' yet, you Queen of the Jungle," he said. "When the men of New York discover you, you'll have your Tarzans coming down out of the trees."

"That's very nice of you to say so," I cooed, "but for the moment, there is just you and me."

And with that reassurance, he gently opened my legs and poured some champagne into my cunt and began to lick open the shimmering lips of my ever-so-delicate labia, saying "Ooh, babe, this is delicious!"

I was a little miffed, and said so. "I suppose I'm supposed to drink my champagne out of a glass or something."

With that, he lay me on my back and poured some champagne on his chest, telling me, with a lopsided grin, "This is best I can do at the moment," as I slurped the delicious juice from the indentation between his rib cage and his chest, stroking his wet nipples with my pointed tongue, hoping to make them stand out stiff and straight. Few men are aware of how sexually stimulating their nipples are, but then again, few men have experienced me.

With that, I had one of the biggest surprises of my young life. The front door opened, with barely a sound. And who should be standing there in a full-length mink but my old friend, the raven-haired, violet-eyed Muffie Free; and right behind her, much to my horror, was the tall black "pimp" from the Port Authority Terminal.

Muffie was grinning from ear to ear. "I hope you enjoyed Angelo, my darling. He's the top porn star in New York at the moment, in case you hadn't already guessed."

Angelo, needless to say, lay on the bed playing with his cock, looking like the cat who swallowed the canary. Muffie continued, "I so wanted you to feel at home on your first night in New York."

"But, but—who's that?" I stammered, pointing to the "pimp." "That man tried to pick me up at the bus terminal!"

"But you see, darling," Muffie explained, "I had no idea what you liked, so I sent both my favorite studs. This is my special boyfriend, Rod Peters, producer and star, *and* the biggest dork in the city."

With that I jumped right out of bed. "Oh, Mr. Peters, I'm sorry I misunderstood your intentions. I thought you were some kind of pimp!"

"You little bigot," he laughed, "just because I'm jet black, and just because I dress like a pimp . . . and the mere sight of your luscious breasts. . . . Oh God, Muffie, I'm losing my mind. Look at those tits! I don't know what I'm going to do!"

"Well, I know what *I'm* going to do," said Muffie, as she slipped out of her mink coat and shoes and stood there stark naked except for her black lace bikini panties, which she stepped out of in less than ten seconds flat. Rod, who apparently didn't wear underpants, had his pants and shoes off, revealing what I had already suspected—a cock as big as a crowbar, long, straight, black, strong, and ready to get to work. He still had that know-it-all grin on his face and said, "Our stud Angelo here takes at least twenty minutes to get it up again, so the question at hand is, 'Have you tried dark meat?' "

To tell the truth, I hadn't, and although this man did not strike me as being as warm as my Angelo, I knew that despite his joking he wanted me desperately, and so I thought, "Why not?"

I don't believe in impersonal group sex, but let's face it, this man was a person. After all, he had gone out of his way to make me feel welcome, and I had rejected him. I started to kneel down to glide my eager tongue over the surface of that fabulous crowbar to make him feel especially wanted, but I had another surprise: Muffie. She was now stroking me and kissing me on my buttocks and on the back of my thighs. "I want you to be so happy here, my love," she sighed

Now, I have never considered myself a lesbian, nor do I necessarily approve of such immoral activity, but with some special women I will always make an exception to the rule. And Muffie was always at the top of my list. Even at the age of eighteen, in the shower room of Beavertown Central, her breasts had hung like ripe pears from her lithe athletic body, and I remember how much I craved them then, but of course in those years I was young and almost flat-chested, and so insecure I had no idea how I could possibly get her to let me touch her.

I looked at Rod and said, "I'll be right with you," and then turned to Muffie with such indescribable gratitude I thought I would burst into tears. I blurted out, "Oh, Muffie, I never thought..." and then I took her raven head in both hands and guided her to my tender nipples which craved her so much they were already taut with expectation. Then I dove for her fabulous muff—she was well named—a luxuriant thatch that drove me wild with desire as I fantasized about that ruby clit that lay there in its pink nest of throbbing flesh waiting for the touch of my lips.

And with equal excitement, my new friend and former enemy, Mr. Rod "Crowbar" Peters was on my back running his wondrous black tool between my buttocks. I shivered with delight, knowing he would fuck me up the ass, something I had never before experienced. He must have carried his own supply of lubricant, because he had already greased his long black pole with some ointment that made it feel like a smooth glass rod. We were one happy trio on those pink silk sheets, and it wasn't too long before Angelo, my angel of the hour before, joined us with his godlike hulk to participate in what became for me the most unbelievable sexual thrill of my entire life: Mr. Rod Peters entered me at last!

I watched in the overhead mirror as his warrior's spear cleaved into my ass, with him first pulling apart the halves of my buttocks with his strong steady hands, as if he were splitting a peach in two. At first, I moaned in fright because I was constricted, but as he simultaneously pinched and massaged my sensitive nipples until I thought my tits were going to take off into outer space, and Muffie unashamedly mouthed my hanging fuck-flesh in front, licking and sucking me like there was no tomorrow, something happened! I let go. I spread my thighs and elevated my ass; I let him in.

I let everybody in! I could feel the full length of his prick gliding up my anal track, a black anaconda devouring me from the inside out. I was the white virgin being consumed by the ancient powers of the jungle, and I willingly gave my body to the serpent god. Then, Rod turned me on my side, where Angelo was facing me, his muscular legs entangled with Muffie's arms, his huge cock once more stiff and scarlet tinged.

Angelo spoke to me like an innocent little boy who wanted to play. "Hello," he said, "can I come in?"

"Honey," I responded, "you can come in anytime you want!"

In the meantime, Muffie had found a way to pleasure me even more, positioning herself above my head in such a way that her glorious vulva, that delectable fuck-nest, was right on top of my hot and gleaming face. What a treat! I reached down with both hands and guided Angelo's heavy member straight into me, whereupon my two wonderful, sweating studs began to fuck me, one up the ass, one in my sex-crazed cunt, with only a thin membrane separating one cock from the other.

They were so aroused they made only animal sounds.

Grunts. Gasps. Slurps. Moans. I was electrified! Angelo, in the meantime, was licking and kissing Muffie's ass, his red muscle of a tongue probing the nerve-endings of her little pink asshole, tasting the forbidden remnants of chocolate cream lingering there; he was breaking all taboos, real and imagined.

Muffie simply went wild, and I was there to taste her excitement. Lucky me, my whole face was buried in her mink muff, my lips pursed around her prick-hard clit, fondling it, tasting it, the top of my tongue able to send her into ecstasy, her love-juices streamind down my face. I could feel her body begin to heave in continuous orgasm. As for myself, since I was in a sense held in place by two stout penises, the shock waves of my own orgasm went from the tops of my toes to the farthest reaches of my brain, wave after wave of release. I lost all control, all sense of time and place. I no longer remembered names: Peters, Muffie, Angelo, Free, it was all one. Whose penis, whose balls, whose clit belonged to whom I no longer remembered. I no longer cared. I was being made love to by something larger than a single personality. I had been seduced by the god of Love, the god who ruled the Amazon and the city streets, the hermaphrodite he/she god with magnificent knockers and more than one cock. The god who is painted black and white and pink and gold, who comes to orgasm in several voices like a choir of angels, moaning and whispering in highs and lows.

Rod came like a fireworks display. At the crucial moment, he pulled his big black cock out of me and splattered a starburst of come over the three of us, which we greedily licked off each other's bodies like it was the finest *crème anglaise* in the finest French restaurant. Such fantasy. We loved the make-believe, because the sex was real and our bodies were hot. But by now I was so tired I just had to sleep, and, as I stretched and yawned, I was tucked in by what seemed a hundred pairs of lips and tongues. I went to sleep dreaming of a heaven filled with cocks and cunts.

My first night in New York! What a wonderful welcome in the City of Strangers. I guess it just isn't true. This can't be the Age of Anxiety.

As I later wrote in my diary, "Dear Diana, You don't have to go looking for love; the love is there for you, if you'll just let it in!" Little did I imagine, however, my first night in New York, just how much love was out there waiting for me to let it in, little did I dream how far that tide of love would carry me; little did I suspect how deeply I would be desired.

Chapter Two

The next afternoon, when I awoke from my intoxicating twelve-hour dream journey, I was still half-conscious. My naked flesh felt warm and tingling against the pink silk sheets. Muffie's bedroom was dark, and full of perfume from the night before. Through the little slits and openings of the casually closed plum damask draperies with their heavy, sensuous folds, the late afternoon October sun peeked through with its dying golden light. I felt like a mistress in a royal bedchamber, so completely protected, so wrapped in luxury, so deliciously secure. But then, imperceptibly, almost as soon as I awoke, my old "problem" returned; yes, my terrible fear of being lost and abandoned. It seems that no matter how much reassurance I receive, especially at night, from one or more of my various lovers, in the morning, when I awaken, it's as if the harsh, dog-eat-dog workaday world were beginning to make its inroads all over again. Even in Muffie's spectacularly comfortable bed, I somehow sensed that beyond the Oriental rugs and the priceless luxury antiques and the romantic mood music, the good ol' twentieth century was out there in the streets waiting to get me. Even today with all my success, I'm always in need of comforting, desperate for someone to hold me at night when the lights go out, and again in the morning when there's no place to hide.

It's not that I would mind so much being raped or murdered—at least there's some distinctly human contact there, if not an actual one-on-one relationship—but to be left alone, to be told no, to be abandoned—that's worse than death. I have always been eternally grateful for people willing to give me simple companionship, sexually or otherwise. I have discovered that most people, whoever they are, are generally at their best in bed, making love. What's a woman like me supposed to do when a deeply feeling, incredibly handsome, and well-hung gentleman approaches me—say "No, thank you, please leave me alone"? You've got to be kidding. Besides, most of the successful major religions back me up. "God is love and love is God."

At another point in my story, which I consider a courageous account of my admittedly courageous arrival in New York City, I will present my deepest feelings about certain sexual activities that our present hypocritical society considers unnatural and obscene, such as incest, bestiality, and sado-masochism; when, in fact, these so-called perversions give millions of frustrated human beings the only pleasure they have ever known.

In any case, when I was finally fully awake in Muffie's luxurious apartment, I realized with a start that both my African God of Lust and my pornographic cab driver had deserted the scene. For a moment I felt so terrified that my dear old school chum Muffie had also deserted me that I began to breathe in short, asthmatic gasps, and my eyes welled up with tears of fright. But no, thank God, she was still with me, behind me in bed; in fact, that dear sweet slut was brushing the back of my ass with the hairs of her thick black bush. I could even smell the intoxicating musky odor of her never-to-be-forgotten cunt. Then, to make certain I felt desired, she pressed her thick warm lips on the back of my perpetually tense neck and began to suck on my tight muscles there with her open mouth, massaging me and making me feel it was good to be alive. Needless to say, everything about me turned her on. I could feel her heavy breath and her little sighs. I was so profoundly moved by her devoted love for me that I turned around and embraced her.

That's when I began feeling aroused. I couldn't help myself. There was just something about the feel of her labia brushing against mine—a dry feel, except for the hint of moistness in the magic slit, that almost hidden seam that can be teased open to reveal the treasure trove inside.

"I want you, Diana," she pleaded. "Can I have you?"

I didn't answer her. Instead, I stuck my tongue in her mouth. Delicious! Muffie was such an uncivilized animal, her mouth had the taste of a wild, exotic fruit.

"Ohhh!" she moaned, in her husky little-girl sound. That drove me absolutely crazy. She reached down and caressed my ass, thrusting her delta of mink closer and closer until our cunt-lips were kissing with a life of their own, and I could feel rays of splendid fire explode within me and begin to spread from my vagina throughout every fiber of my body. "Muffie, Muffie," I whispered, "I want you; you're so good to me. I don't deserve all your attention, but . . ."

"But what?" Muffie responded, sighing. "I couldn't stand for you to be alone."

"You don't have to stand for me ever," I said, teasing

33

her. "Especially when I'm lying here in your big warm bed waiting for your pussy to come lick my face."

"Meow," she purred.

And with that, I lay back and locked my legs around the back of her neck and with my hands gently guided her gorgeous face with its luxuriant raven mane onto the outer lips of my pink-red labia, glistening wet and awaiting penetration, which she gently coaxed open, gliding the tip of her well-practiced tongue up and down my slit until it finally opened up like the petals of a lush, ripe rose. No one woman in my entire life, not even my devoutly religious mother, had ever addressed herself so simply to my basic need for sex. I was so overwhelmed by the pure goodness of Muffie's intention to give me the sense of security and the simple ectasy I craved so much that, half-crazed with sheer joy, I thrust my furry mound up into her eager face again and again. My back arching with convulsions, I clutched onto her head for as long as I could, groaning with intense pleasure as she tongued my inflamed clit, teasing it with her teeth until it grew hot and hard, a pink pearl bursting in its nest of pulsating flesh. "Oh Muffie Mama, Muffie Mama," I cried. "Eat me! Please eat me!"

For the moment, Muffie had other things in mind. Hers was a practiced hand. Her fingers reached up and groped for my breasts. They found their mark, my nipples, sore from the night before, but aching to be fondled and nibbled and sucked by my girlhood idol. As I teased and pulled her hair, she began to knead my nipples and pinch them and twist them until they became almost numb from a kind of pleasure-pain. I have never been officially indoctrinated into what is called "S and M," sadomasochism, but I have to say that just this side of terrible pain is an exciting danger area, a secret garden where most lovers dare not go. I dared. I always dare.

Muffie buried her face in my cunt, biting my clitoris

34

just to the point of tearing the skin. I screamed out, "Don't hurt me!", hoping in my heart of hearts she'd continue to bear down on me with her vampire's teeth. At that moment I did not care if I began to bleed and she drank my blood and I died on the spot. I was in total ecstasy. I was alone with this savage animal. I couldn't get enough of her. Who could? She was too much for any one person to handle, too much perfection, too much mouth, too much soft, yielding flesh, too much spirit, too much soul. Her breasts in particular drove me wild with desire; they were neither pointed nor fat, they were merely perfect—full, globular, and proud. They hung from her body with a ripeness reserved for certain kinds of cocks, especially the uncut ones that hang with a sense of heaviness and yet are not heavy, just ripe—ripe, tropical fruit begging for hands and mouths to taste and suck their delicious flesh.

Muffie's breasts had been a temptation to me for almost five agonizing years, and the night before, with the two gorgeous studs, one fucking me and the other one reaming me up the ass with their almost legendary instruments, I had been too distracted and having too much fun to concentrate on another woman, even Muffie. But, Now Was the Time!

I cried out in exaltation, "Muffie! Ready or not, I'm coming!" and immediately reversed my position so I could ram one of her delicious breasts into my hungry face and fondle the other one at the same time. I felt drowned in her flesh, drowned in milky-white weight, drowned in soft sexual heat, and I loved it! Her flesh suffocated me, and I was in a religious ectasy!

But Muffie was not altogether pleased. "Diana, my love, I absolutely crave your cunt. I've got to have your cunt!" she said, insistingly. "I want your pussy-wussy. Please, Diana, please! Sit on my face. Please! Please! You don't know how long I've waited for you to get off the bus from Beavertown!"

"What are you talking about?" I said, feigning ignorance.

"It was the first time I ever saw you, in the girls' locker room back at Beavertown Central..." she began to explain.

"No, no," I interrupted. "That was the first time I saw *you*." I remembered for the nine-thousandth time my first excited glimpse of her perfect, voluptuous breasts.

"No, no let me finish; it's my turn," Muffie wailed.

"You can turn anywhere you like," I cooed. "You're beautiful from every angle."

"You're the one with the angle, right where your legs come together," Muffie insisted. "I remember you were sitting on a bench in the locker room," she continued, no longer joking. "You were wearing your cheerleader's uniform. You were putting your socks on, and you weren't wearing any panties. I walked by on my way to the shower room and you asked me the time of day, knowing full well I wasn't wearing a watch or anything else. You wanted me to come close to you, didn't you, so I could catch the barest glimpse of your ravenous little pussy?"

"But Muffie," I said, "if I forgot to put on my panties, how could I remember I'd forgotten—oh my goodness, maybe that's what everyone was screaming about in the gymnasium at half time when I jumped up in the air to lead the cheers! Imagine, all this time I thought all the boys were crazy about my personality!"

Of course, I pretended I had forgotten. The boys at school were one thing. I loved it when they caught me with my proverbial pants down and practically went on a rampage. I loved what they called the "gang-bangs." I loved being what they called the "town switchboard." I loved being called a "tramp." I loved the married men, especially the doctors and the teachers and the ministers circling my house at one and two in the morning after my parents were asleep, knowing that sooner or later

I'd come downstairs and crawl in the back seat with one of them. I loved all of this because I was the center of attention, and I got all the physical pleasure I craved.

But Muffie, you see, Muffie was always my secret desire. When I think of all the countless times I deliberately left my panties off and sat for hours on that cold locker room bench, hoping Muffie would come into the locker room and pass me by on her way to the showers so I could ask her the time or the weather or what was playing at the local movie houses. If I had only known that she, too, was in love with me. Why hadn't one of us spoken up?

"Diana," Muffie continued with her exciting revelation, "I used to walk back and forth of where I hoped you'd be sitting, praying you were looking in another direction so I could catch a quick look of your plump pussy, that sunken treasure of pink and coral, all covered with the most delicate peach fuzz. Oh dear, am I mixing metaphors?" she asked.

"You can mix anything you want," I replied, taking her hand and finger-fucking myself with it.

Muffie was beginning to sweat. For a moment, she tried to continue telling me her oldest and best-kept secret, her passion for me. "Oh Diana," she continued, "I wanted to dive into you like a fish and nibble at you, suck at you, suck your sweet nectar. . . ." And with that, poor Muffie lost the power of speech and the ancient art of self-control. She dove for my cunt like a madwoman and began to lick me, mouth me, and kiss my infinitely soft center of desire, so that for the first time in my life, if only for a minute, I truly felt that another woman actually didn't want me dead. I decided that as long as I had a cunt, Muffie was to be my ardent admirer. How wonderful for me! I knew now I would always be blessed with a kind of security. I was so happy, if only for a time.

Because then it struck me! Whammo! The truth! How horrible! Yes, I must be a lesbian! A pervert! Yes, I must be one of those sick degenerates who was responsible for the decline and fall of Western civilization, not to mention the American Way of Life, according to all those absolutely fantastic and dramatic television ministers who are desperately trying to save our beloved country from weirdos and sickos like me. All this hit me with the revelation of pure and ancient religion.

Muffie could see my tears, and she lovingly brushed them away with her long, tapering fingers. She held my face and kissed me where my tears had fallen. She was so motherly, so understanding, but I could smell the evil on her voluptuous lips as I, in my inner confusion and torment, kissed her again and again, drinking in her mouth with its infinite pink warmth for what I knew must be the last time if I was to save myself from a life of perversion. Finally, I could take no more of this, neither her love nor my own inner revulsion, and I pulled away. "Oh Muffie," I blurted out, "this is so wrong."

"What's so wrong?," she said, shocked.

"Oh, Muffie, I do so adore your breasts and I do love to put my tongue in your fantastic pussy," I cried. "I can't lie about it, but Muffie, we've got to stop kidding ourselves."

"Who's kidding who, you magnificently gorgeous piece of ass?" Muffie replied.

"Oh Muffie," I cried, "face the truth. We're perverts! We're nothing but a couple of dykes!"

Muffie was wide eyed. "Di, you and I, dykes?"

"Yes, yes," I screamed. "We're living a lie. We're unnatural women."

Muffie looked like I'd slapped her in her beautiful face. "Oh Diana, come here. You're so upset. Let me hold you. Let me comfort you. I can't stand to see you so upset."

And so, in my shame and weakness, I surrendered to her again. We cradled each other in such a way that the outer lips of our vaginas rubbed against each other and our clitorises grew hard with warmth and desire and pressed against one another as we spoke. Our nipples touched, too, as we brushed against each other, hoping to make them touch. I could feel Muffie's hot breath on my mouth, and I could smell her many smells, the acrid morning mouth I wanted to taste because it was private and forbidden, the sharp sweetness of her breath mints, the trace of lipstick with its cheap waxy perfume, the clean smell of her perspiration, the sourness of her under arms blended with what was left of yesterday's deodorant. And as I gazed into the sad intensity of her violet eyes, I could even smell her faraway cunt with all its mysteries, its sweetness, its saltiness, and I could not stop imagining at every instant its own ragged beauty, like an orchid that has fallen into the sea and become, in time, an animal, cousin to oysters, related to scallops with the suction powers of an octopus, all these things meant to be eaten raw, if possible. But for the moment, I wasn't interested in sex. I just wanted Muffie to hold me and talk to me and explain to me the new meanings of love and affection that I had read so much about in the women's magazines.

"Darling Diàna," she said, embracing me as closely as she could, "the most highly sexed people in any society have always been attracted to other highly sexed people, regardless of their sex, if you follow me. Other people, who aren't so sexual or emotional, whose economic and emotional stability depend on a one-to-one male/female relationship, are jealous of women like us. They call us whores and tramps if we make love to too many men, and they call us bull dykes if we make love to those few special women in our lives. The truth is, most of the critics are afraid to let themselves go."

"So what are you saying?" I said. "That everyone's a little bit bisexual?"

"No, Di, I'm saying that everyone's sexual to a greater or lesser degree, and, as they say, 'like attracts like.' My body's ripe and delicious, Diana; I have many treasures to give. What honest woman wouldn't be attracted to me?"

"You mean a lesbian or a heterosexual woman?" I said, still puzzled.

Muffie was so patient as she continued to explain to me the mysteries that had been kept hidden from me. "I feel as sorry for so-called lesbians or gays as I do for so-called straights. The strict lesbians are avoiding the pleasures of the opposite sex as much as the "straights" are avoiding the pleasures of their own sex. Oh Diana, goddess of the waking moon, you're so magnificent, let's face it, you could never be a lesbian any more than I could. We're just two ravishing women; we can't help it if we turn each other on; we turn everybody on, men and women alike. There's just something about us, my love. When we walk down the street, little old ladies who go to Mass every morning look at us and think sex. Children look at us and think sex. Even fags look at us and think sex. Diana, there are a certain number of women in each generation, and men, too, with bright shining skin, ripe asses, oversized genitals, cunts and tits and cocks that stick out and make a big statement. The way I figure it, we came into this earth-plane to have sex. If the gods had wanted us to be angels, they would have kept us up there, imprisoned in the clouds, away from body heat, away from desire. The way I look at it, you gotta go with what's been given, and baby, let's face it, we've been given."

"I know," I blurted out. "I agree with you!" But of course, I understood practically nothing of what Muffie had said and had so many more questions to ask her. But she was talked out and had other things in mind.

"Oh Diana, you're so maginficent, let's not talk anymore."

And with that, I surrendered to her, and she to me. We became one flesh, our genitals locked in embrace, the hills and valleys of our flesh moving up and down in their own grooves, a human landscape on the cutting edge between earthquake and tidal wave. And when it happened, our orgasms, I convulsed in ecstasy with triple-barrelled waves of pleasure, my pelvis moving up and down with the force of a summer storm. I experienced spasm after spasm of delight, then lost all muscular control as Muffie and I melted into each other with absolute happiness.

Hours later, we were still in bed. We had fucked and sucked and fallen asleep many times. Now Muffie looked at me longingly and spoke in quiet, almost reverential tones. "I do love you, Di. I hope it isn't just physical attraction between us. I want to see you well fed, beautifully clothed, and living it up in a first-class East Side apartment, perferably in a penthouse with a full-time maid. What I'm trying to say, is I want to see you happy."

With that, inexplicably, I burst into tears. "Oh Muffie, you've been kinder to me than my own mother, God rest her soul, or either of my stepmothers, both of whom accused me of making it with my father, which is an absolute lie, even if he did love me more than any person alive, and please let's not discuss the subject ever again. But Muffie, I can't stay here with you forever. For one thing, I just can't go to bed with every person you bring into your bedroom. I mean, sooner or later, you'll be involved in some kind of personal relationship with one special person and you'll be needing some privacy, right?"

Muffie was so sweet as she listened. With one hand she stroked my hair and with the other she fondled my blood-engorged labia. "What are you worried about, my dearest Diana?" she cooed.

I was getting very upset. "I don't know how I'm going to make a living!" I sputtered it out, but at least it was out. "I never got more than a C-plus in English," I continued. "I can't do math to save my life, except count money, and I haven't got any money to count. Furthermore, my boobs are too big for me to be a fashion model, which has always been my greatest ambition."

When it came to harsh reality, Muffie could be as cold as the iceberg that sank the *Titanic*. "You're right," she said. "Face facts. You're too oversexed for designer clothes. When you walk out on the runway, no one but an enraged designer will be looking at his clothes."

If Muffie hadn't been coddling me in her strong athletic arms and stroking me with such practiced care, I think I would have despaired. Instead, I told her about the only thing that gave me hope. It had happened the year before, on my birthday, when I went to a fortune teller in Philadelphia, a gypsy woman who read my palm. She told me that before the year was up, I would go to New York and within a short time become very famous. "But doing what?" I cried. "Will I become a Broadway star? How is that possible? I can't sing or dance."

The gypsy said Broadway wasn't what she had in mind. "It has something to do with photographers and publicity, and I see you known all over the world within ten years."

Muffie snapped to. " That's what I want to talk to you about," she cried. "I agree with your gypsy!"

"What do you mean?" I said, as puzzled as ever.

"Very simple," Muffie announced. "I'm going to make you famous."

"But doing what?" I cried for the second time.

Instead of answering me straightaway, Muffie sauntered into her stainless steel kitchen with its glass shelves and lacquered black walls to make breakfast. I followed her around the kitchen as she cooked scrambled eggs for the two of us. The eggs were moist and hot in no time, and they slithered down my gullet like come. Well, I'm sorry, but it was impossible to be around Muffie and not see sexual innuendo in everything from her special tapioca pudding to the framed photographs of porn stars in action in her guest lavatory. Like she said, some people are just naturally oversexed. Her breakfast conversation was more of the same, although, typically, she was clearly leading up to Something Big.

"Do you remember when they used to censor movies and television?" she began. "I mean, even ten years ago, you weren't supposed to see a woman's navel on TV."

"Yes, I heard about that," I admitted.

Muffie kept pressing on. "Not too long ago in this country, certain things were considered evil and sinful, whereas the truth was they were just sexy, and today we think nothing of seeing a woman nude in a magazine, right?"

"Right," I said. "Muffie, what are you getting at?"

"Do you want some cheddar cheese in your eggs?" she she said, as she stirred a new batch, a thick yellow mass, with a long wooden spoon that reminded me of my father's cock.

"Sure, I like cheese," I said, wondering what Muffie was trying to tell me. She wasn't exactly spelling things out.

"Did you know that in the nineteen-fifties, which wasn't so long ago, the Church's Legion of Decency condemned a picture called *The Moon Is Blue* just because it used the word 'virgin'? And did you know that when Lucy Ball was pregnant on 'I Love Lucy,' she wasn't allowed to use the word 'pregnant,' she had to say 'expecting'?"

"Yes, yes," I said, "I think I heard about some of that stuff." But the truth was, no one had to tell me beans about censorship. I remember the time I innocently forgot to put on my panties before going out to lead a few cheers when Beavertown Central played St. Rose's of Carbondale for the championship in basketball, and when I jumped up for those cheers, my skirt fell off. I practically got arrested and thrown out of the school, not to mention Beavertown itself. "Yes, Muffie," I said,

"I happen to know there are still a few prudes around, so what do you want me to do for the cause, yours and mine—pose in the nude?"

"Diana," she said, holding me by both shoulders as her long wooden phallic spoon dripped half-cooked scrambled eggs in pale yellow clots all over her left breast, "last night you met my boyfriend, Rod Peters, the king of porn producers, and you met Angelo O'Shaughnessy, who's also known as Big Boy Dorkoff, the hottest property in erotic films today."

"I know who they are," I cried, as frustrated as hell. "Didn't I thank you, Muffie? What's going on, anyway? Didn't they know I was really happy to meet them?"

"What I didn't tell you," she continued, "is that I'm the hottest female in love films today. They call me Lisa Pink."

"You're Lisa Pink!" I said, gasping, shocked out of my wits. "*The* Lisa Pink?"

"Would I lie?" she answered.

"No," I retorted, "but you'd probably lie down with anything that had two legs and something between them. I'm sorry, Muffie, I didn't mean that; I just can't believe you're really Lisa Pink."

"I'm really Lisa Pink," she said, "obviously without the pink wig, which is in my front hall closet, since I don't want to be raped by the delivery boys now, do I?"

"No," I stammered.

"And by the way," she said, "how do you know about Lisa Pink? Don't tell me you go to porn films to see Lisa Pink!"

"No, no," I tried to explain. "Once a boyfriend of mine took me to Scranton to see you in *Desire Under Elmer*. I remember thinking how much Lisa Pink reminded me of you, but it never . . . oh Muffie . . . !"

"Listen, Di," Muffie said, "they make up your eyes with about a pound of eyeliner, and they put wigs on you, and nobody would ever think it's you—I mean me."

"But Muffie," I babbled, "I thought you were a high fashion model for *Vogue* and *Harper's Bazaar* and the only reason I never recognized you is because you probably had to lose about fifty pounds, because high-fashion models are supposed to be scrawny, if you know what I mean."

At this point, Muffie was on her naked knees in her black lacquered kitchen trying to eat me out, except I wouldn't stand still, because I think I know a con job when I see one, especially when it's Muffie, the original Cunt Job. The time had come for basic information. "Muffie, I know you're trying to tell me something, so would you please take your tongue out of my cunt before I come, because if I come, Muffie, I'm really going to be upset with you."

"You can see right through me, can't you?" she said in an exasperated tone.

"I just want to know what you're trying to tell me," I said.

"Look," she stammered, "both Rod and Angelo think you could be a bigger porn star than any chick in this town since Marilyn Chambers, and they want you to go in with them, in business, I mean."

I was flabbergasted. "Muffie, I somehow feel I'm going to have some kind of career in the fashion world."

"Darling," Muffie whispered, trying to calm me, "I promise you, love-making will always be in fashion."

"And what about fucking strange men?" I commented, thinking that would get her.

It didn't. After all, Muffie Free was now Lisa Pink, a woman of considerable expertise in the area of startle and shock. "No, no, darling Di," she went on, "they never make you fuck anyone you don't want to fuck. Besides, all Roddy wants now, really, is for you and Angelo to make a picture together, and maybe if you're good, I'd come in, too, for a cameo fuck scene."

Now I was really shocked. I mean, I may have been

the Beavertown free lunch when I was young and idealistic, but even I have my limits. "You mean," I said to this person I decided I must not know at all, "that Rod wants you and me to make love on camera for the benefit of paying customers?"

"Well?" answered Muffie.

"Well, what about my career?" I said.

"My dear," she said, incomparable bitch that she was when she chose to be, "I hate to sound negative, but what career are you talking about?"

There was a very long, very uncomfortable silence. That's when the cold, harsh truth finally dawned. I really didn't have a career, did I? I was just another small-town girl with big ideas and a nonexistent bankbook. And Muffie, businesswoman that she was, went on to warn me that if I didn't take a chance at becoming a "love star," I might end up a high-priced hooker, and I'd have even less choice about who I made it with. But still, I kept thinking that if I became a porn star, that someday, if I ever decided I wanted to be a judge or a surgeon or a Congresswoman, I'd be in big trouble when pictures of me fucking Angelo O'Shaughnessy and Rod Peters were revealed to the general public. "I d-d-d-don't kn-kn-know," I stammered.

Muffie looked at me wtih those enormous violet eyes of hers as she took a large bottle of Chanel No. 5 from her bedside table and poured about an ounce of it on her breasts and started massaging them, giving special attention to the nipples, which stood out like little knobs just waiting to be turned on. She did have a way of hypnotizing me.

"Diana, won't you just be broad-minded enough to come with me?"

"Muffie," I said, "I've never been anything else but broad, and as for coming with you, I've been coming with you ever since I got off the bus from Beavertown."

Muffie laughed and I laughed. Then we took the phone

46

off the hook and spent the rest of the evening in bed making love. Then it was time to sleep. We had an early morning appointment with Venus Productions.

Chapter Three

Early the next morning, Muffie and I walked south from her apartment through the SoHo district, which means "south of Houston Street," where many struggling and sexually liberated artists live in huge lofts. SoHo had once been a factory district, but after World War II, many factories moved out of the city to New Jersey and Connecticut, abandoning their warehouses and leaving empty space behind. That's when the artists and the small filmmakers, like Rod Peters, moved in, thankful for the relatively cheap space. New York has so much history and so many fascinating intellectual and international leaders, some of whom, I have since discovered, are also warm human beings. But for me in those early days in the Big Apple, or as I like to call it, the Big Clit, even walking the streets, if you know what I mean, could be an absolutely first-class education.

I can still remember my first morning in SoHo, my first experience of the raw hustle and bustle of the world's most important real estate. There I was, the kid from the sticks, the small-town cheerleader, the ex-Howard Johnson's hostess, looking for the Big Career, wearing what I thought at the time was a hot snaz outfit: a hot-pink French angora sweater I had purchased in a duty free shop in Martinique on my wonderful visit there with our saintly family dentist, plus my little sister's red satin "hot pants," which I had mistakenly decided would look good with the sweater, a particularly dumb move since the "hot pants," which were originally her gym shorts, were about four sizes too small.

Unfortunately for me, Muffie and I had a seven a.m. sharp appointment with Rod Peters at his Venus Studios. I say "unfortunate" because I did not realize until it was too late to turn back that the slit in my vulva was provocatively accentuated by my hot pants, and that people of both sexes were staring at my crotch. Not only that, but to make matters worse, my tits were bouncing up and down under my sweater. The reason for the bouncing, as I explained to Muffie, is that in New York, people walk much too fast. In Beavertown, whenever I wore a tight sweater without a bra, I always made a point, no pun intended, of walking a little bit slower so that my breasts wouldn't jiggle up and down in front of all the undisciplined young men in sexual heat standing around idly on Washington Avenue wishing they could feel me up, lay me down, and shove their hot, thick cocks into what they called my "fantastic cunt." You see, I always could read a dirty mind from a block away, especially when it led straight to a visibly bulging erection. I mean, like any well-brought-up American girl, I believe in a strong code of modesty, but here in New York, with Muffie racing me along the streets like some kind of show pony, I must have looked like a twenty-dollar floozie out for an easy lay. Especially with my four-inch high-heeled shoes and my 1945 nylon stockings with the black seam up the back of my leg that stopped midway up my thigh, and the black lace garter belt I wore outside my gym shorts, I mean my hot pants.

I guess I have only myself to blame. All I was trying to do was start a new style. Doesn't every girl in every generation? Isn't that what America's all about? Muffie said my outfit looked terrific, and that the film people would

48

love it. I kept saying I hadn't decided about the film yet. I steadfastly maintained that if I ever did do a porno film, they'd have to use a double for the nude parts, like Brooke Shields does in all her movies. I remember exactly what I said, and Muffie kept reassuring me, "Don't worry. The important thing is they get to meet you."

Muffie sure was a puzzle. Nobody, male or female, had ever had such a hunger for my cunt. You would have thought my clitoris was the key to the Fountain of Youth or the original cure for cancer, diabetes, and night blindness combined, yet Muffie maintained she was "pan-sexual." So it surprised me as we walked along West Broadway with all its wonderful avant-garde art galleries that sell neon-light sculpture and paintings on linoleum that she kept muttering about all the gay men who supposedly live in the Village and SoHo, as if homosexuals were the natural enemy of beautiful women. But I decided that if all the men in SoHo and the Village were gay, then I couldn't figure out how come every time we stopped at a corner for a red light, some strange guy would accidentally walk right into my ass and say "excuse me" while accidentally rubbing his rapidly expanding crotch against my derriere. This happened three times in a half hour. I have to say that like the story of the princess and the pea, I can always feel a cock, even though it's under five layers of denim and polyester.

Then, it happened. My first love affair of the day. We were at some intersection. I think it was West Broadway and Broome. We had to ask this traffic cop for directions. He was a large, burly man with a muscular Slavic face, high cheekbones, and a large gash of a mouth with sunburned skin from being out in the air all day. I could just imagine the rest of him, the sinewy body of a tough guy from the Polish ghetto in say, Wilkes-Barre, a real macho stud from ten generations of coal miners with an overeducated wife who had probably pressured him to surrender his soul to the upkeep of law and order.

But clearly some part of him would never surrender. I could see that at a glance. I knew that he and I belonged naked together wherever we could get it, or, if not naked, at least just fucking our brains out, somewhere, anywhere. I wanted this larger-than-life, would-be revolutionary hunk to rip my stupid clothes off and take me roughly into his arms and growl, "Diana you're a fucking piece of ass; welcome to New York!"

And without warning, without apology, I wanted him to fuck me standing up, right there at the corner of West Broadway and Broome. Sometimes, under certain circumstances, despite what my hearts-and-flowers friends say, foreplay is for little old ladies and emotional cripples. Sometimes, I can't help myself, I crave to be ravished by strangers in uniform in broad daylight before my vaginal juices have begun to flow, and believe me, I'm not some neurotic puppy dog who has to be petted twenty-four hours a day. I'm wilder than that. Sometimes, I lust for the smell of spit and sperm and blood and the madness of our times. That fuckin' traffic cop was just my speed. I wanted to grab his hard ass and feel the back of his muscular thighs as he split into me and pumped me back and forth . . . but where was I?

Wait a minute. Yes, I was at the intersection of West Broadway and Broome. The policeman. The hunk. Was I insane? Was I drowned in fantasy? Not quite. God must still be in his heaven. My policeman was a madman, too. As I said, Muffie and I were asking directions on how to get to Canal Street to Venus Productions, Rod Peters' studio. Since Muffie supposedly worked at Venus Productions, I'm not quite sure why she needed directions, but of course, asking directions from an attractive stranger does not always mean we are asking directions, does it? So, in pointing out "directions," he accidentally-on-purpose brushed his large workman's hand against my nipple, which was under my hot-pink angora sweater, of course, but still pretty apparent. Then, while he was incanting, "Oh, I'm sorry" for accidentally touching my nipple, he accidentally brushed his other hand on my tummy just above my crotch. What a brutal, sensitive hand. And what a stroke! Yes, he was actually stroking me. So I stroked him back. On his ass. It was hard, devastatingly hard.

"Hey, what is this?" he said. "Cop a feel or feel a cop?"

"Both," I shot back. I pretended to be angry, but how could I be angry with such a victim of the modern age as the traffic cop? Especially one who with a different set of parents would probably have become a general and led us to victory in Vietnam. He looked at me with those beautiful alcoholic gray-blue eyes, so full of sadness and evil and pity, all of that, and I said, "Hello." And only then when he, out of embarrassment looked down at his crotch, I looked down at it, too, and saw the bulge. What a bulge! A huge bulge, an imprisoned jackhammer, full of the longing that can only come from watching so many beautiful women drive by without being able to follow them. "I'll be back," I promised him.

"Please," he said, "I know we have a lot to talk about."

"We do?" I asked, continuing to stare steadfastly at him.

That's when it happened. My officer turned to Muffie, who had been pulling on my arm, insisting we were late, and said, "Would you please excuse us for five minutes?"

I asked Muffie to wait.

"This isn't funny, Diana. Rod doesn't like to be kept waiting, and for that matter, neither do I."

"Don't worry, Muffie," I implored. "I'm sure you'll find some woman, I mean some person to talk to."

"Hey Muff," said my hunk in uniform, "I've got a better idea. Do me a favor and watch the traffic for me."

"Where are you going!" wailed Muffie.

"Nowhere," shot back the cop.

"But where is nowhere?" pleaded Muffie.

My coppo just pointed to a black limousine parked across the street on West Broadway.

"That?" screamed Muffie. "What is this, the nineteen-fifties?" she said, as she almost got clipped by a speeding bakery truck.

For the next five minutes, Hunko and I never looked back. We had created our own private idyll, and we were determined to live in it before the relentless world came and took it away from us.

The limousine was a twenty-year-old Lincoln Continental in perfect condition. Shining black enamel with classy wire wheels. The side windows were smoked glass. I figured some nice person had given it to my man for his disposal. Well, the truth is, I didn't know and I didn't care. Certainly, he'd used it before. I mean, as much as I like to kid myself, I wasn't the first girl who'd taken off her hot pants for this fantastic piece of Polish prime meat.

He lay down on the back seat, pulled me into the car on top of him, and shut the door behind us. He tried to pull his pants down, but he couldn't, because his zipper was stuck and his erection functioned like a clothes hook. The more he pulled, the more it stayed.

"Be patient," I whispered, trying to free his cock.

"Be patient?" he replied. "Honey, we're in a truck zone. All I need is for some trailer truck from Kansas City to run a red light while I'm not there and crash into some fucking garbage truck from New York!"

Well, with great difficulty I managed to work his pants down over his never-say-die reproductive muscle which, when it was finally freed from its bureaucratic cage, was quite impressive. It stood at attention like it had been carved in marble. And by this time he'd gotten his massive red peasant hands under my angora sweater and was squeezing my big breasts for all they were worth.

"We don't have time for formalities," he said. He lifted me up with both hands directly above his waiting cock, which was already glistening with lubricant, and ordered, "Put it in."

As ordered, and feeling secure in my obedience, I spread the blood-marshalled lips of my cunt with the fingers of my right hand and guided his bone-hard tool into the middle of it with the other.

For five minutes we fucked like jackrabbits with the sound of the early morning rush-hour traffic whizzing by outside. My tits bounced up and down like water-filled balloons until his huge meaty hands closed around them, much the same way my tight sucking cunt-flesh closed around him. "God, you're great. I adore you. Fuck. Christ. Jesus. Fuck," my hunk said with religious devotion. But most of it was silent and fast. I loved the danger and the disobedience of what we were doing. I guess in our own way we were making a statement, which is how people do everything in New York. We were saying that sex is more basic than traffic lights, right?

Our climax came fast. Hunko began to moan. So did I. I could feel our sexual energies rise to a crescendo; the traffic outside seemed to join in. As we climaxed, my whole body was suffused with a tingling white light. I was aglow in every pore, and that man-mountain was repeatedly arching his pelvis into me as he came. I felt like we were in the middle of a volcanic eruption. I literally heard the crash of the explosion. It seemed like all the world was screaming. The heat of the fires was not to be believed. I think I finally knew the true meaning of sex.

But then, abruptly, Muffie opened the car door screaming bloody murder and pulled me off my Cossack lover and out into the streets with my hot pants around my ankles. There was smoke and burning everywhere. I could barely breathe. "But Muffie," I screamed, "I'm naked!"

"Pull your sweater down!" she screamed back. I stepped out of my hot pants and left them where they were on the street. Thank God angora sweaters stretch.

And thank God for Muffie. She dragged me around the corner and down the next block where the smoke thinned out and the commotion was not so great. "Don't look back!," she had yelled.

But I had looked. My officer had been psychic. Half a block from where we fucked our brains out, a fuel truck had run a red light and crashed headlong into a pretzel vendor crossing the street with his little cart with its smoking charcoal fire. Since this account is primarily meant to be about me, I won't belabor the obvious: the blood and guts and property damage. As for my own guilt in the matter, nobody saw me, and the traffic officer I've described in such intimate detail was able to claim he was taking a piss. I can't blame him. A red light is a red light. I have always had the greatest respect for America's policemen, because in my experience, whenever I needed them, they have always gone beyond the call of duty. Indeed, before this very day was out, I was to experience firsthand the true meaning of the phrase, "New York's finest."

Chapter Four

After two more blocks of art galleries showing American versions of African tribal masks and "twenty-five silkscreen lithographs of recent assassinations" and health food restaurants featuring broccoli with bean dip, baked acorn squash with bean curd, and soybean steak with black bean sauce, we arrived at the right address on Prince Street. There it was: Venus Productions—Fourth Floor. But Muffie, ever watchful for sex and/or danger, took one look across the street and muttered, "Oh my God!"

"What's wrong?" I whispered, fearful that we'd been followed down the street, especially since I was having trouble keeping my angora sweater pulled down over by bare pubes.

"Across the street," she whispered back. "But don't stare. Just keep walking."

Well, I had to peek. It was a black Cadillac limousine the size of a hearse parked across the street. Like the limousine I had just been dragged out of, this one also had windows of dark glass, but this one was definitely occupied. Someone was sitting at the wheel, waiting, and a squat, dark man wearing a white polyester leisure suit like my uncle used to wear in Fort Lauderdale was leaning against the back of the car, his arms folded across his chest, obviously waiting for someone, too, and at the moment staring at Muffie and me.

"It's the mob," Muffie whispered, as soon as she got me inside the building. "Don't look. They'll see you looking."

"I don't understand," I said under my breath.

"The mob is trying to control the sex industry. All of it. They want one-third of Rod's profits right off the top. They claim he owes them half a million dollars already. They've threatened to start breaking legs if he doesn't pay up."

"Is the mob the Mafia?" I asked.

"Is the Pope a Catholic?" she replied.

"I don't understand," I said. "I thought the Pope was Italian, or is he still Polish?" You may have noticed that I frequently play dumb in the face of imminent extinction, but I really was worried about Rod's health.

Admittedly, our only contact had been a little sodomy, so I barely knew him, no pun intended, but I really did care whether he lived or died.

At this point, with my heart pounding and all of SoHo but a big blur around me, Muffie pulled me into the dark lobby of the Venus Productions office building. Before you could say Jack Robinson, or for that matter, Marilyn Chambers, we were inside a rickety elevator painted my favorite shade of cunt-pink. Going up, considering everything that had happened during the previous fifteen minutes, Muffie really had her royal nerve. She stuck her greedy, oversexed hand through my two arms that were trying to keep my angora sweater down over my vagina, and she began to run the side of her palm up and down through my slit, playing with my thick bush. Muffie loved to stroke and pet my luxuriant thatch. She loved being able to get my juices going. She was so perverse. That's what I loved about her behind closed doors. Then, without warning, she knelt down on the elevator floor in front of me and lunged for my clitoris with her fat pink tongue. In shock, I blocked her way with fists clenched around the front of my sweater and pulled it down in front of me, almost to my knees.

That was exactly what she wanted. My rear entrance was completely exposed. Before I knew it, she had encircled me with both arms. With one voracious hand she was stroking my buns, and with the index finger of her other hand she had entered me and began to fingerfuck me. The truth is, it felt wonderful, but at that moment I had a lot of things on my mind, not the least of which was my survival in the world's toughest city. "Muffie," I gasped, "what do you want me to do, have an orgasm in the reception room of this film studio or what?"

"As a matter of fact, pussy-lips, that's exactly the idea," she said.

I was really mad. "Muffie," I said, "I don't care if

you're Burt Reynolds, I would really appreciate it if you'd keep your cotton-pickin' hands out of my cunt when we're in public."

But of course Muffie was older and stronger than I, and she knew how to get my juices going whenever she felt like it. She'd cup her hand over my plump outer lips, knowing I liked to be held there. Then, she'd caress and stroke my labia until the blood rushed to them. Then, she'd kneel in front of me and find my clitoris and kiss it. Yes, Muffie knew all the spots. I have to admit I loved it. It was something I could never get my mother to do. Like I always told her, "Muffie, if you had a penis, you'd be dangerous."

But some women, I've decided, have as many psychological problems as men. So, of course, as we're standing in the elevator, or I should say, as I'm standing and Muffie's kneeling in front of me with her face in my pussy, the elevator door opens and we're facing the main production room of Venus Productions. New York lofts are funny that way. Just as the door opens, I couldn't stand up any longer, and fell down, with Muffie's face pinioning me to the floor as I bucked like a wild horse, heaving my pelvis up and down in waves of orgasm unleashed from deep inside my dark interior.

I was really embarrassed, as well as just plain bareassed. I mean, I was as red as my clitoris. We had to be pulled apart by Rod Peters, who had, apparently, been jacking off watching the shooting of his latest production, *Y'all Come*. Then, on the floor of the set, under arc lights in front of a mousy little director, with a handheld camera, was my beloved Angelo O'Shaughnessy naked on a white fur carpet in front of a fake fireplace with a fake-red, flickering fire, tit-fucking a redhead with lustrous globes like milk glass, so delicate and lovely, the aureole as pale pink as my tongue. You could see the faintest blue veins coursing through those spectacular jugs. The colors were subtle and teasing as she held her breasts together, creating a deep crevice for Angelo to enjoy with his thick, hard prick.

Under the bright lights, in fact, all the colors seemed especially alive and seductive. Angelo's corona on the end of his marble column was a bright shade of lavender. Stunning. Even their sweat glistened like diamond dust. I couldn't wait to see what his come looked like under the lights. I began to fantasize about come. I was so embarrassed to be introduced to the film world this way that I pretended I was in another place. I imagined yellow come, pale yellow like lemon pudding. And come that was glacial blue, like ice. And come that was almost transparent, like royal jelly. I began to fantasize I was back in Beavertown with my beloved family dentist, in some quiet place in the dark like his examining room after hours. I never saw his come in the light. I only remember it was the most wonderful lotion, which I rubbed all over my fuck-flesh, front and back.

Rod Peters brought me out of my reverie. Like I said, he was standing there, buck naked, crowbar cock in hand. To his credit, he didn't bat an eyelash. "You'll have to excuse me," he said, sounding like an Oxford barrister, "but you see, this is the only way I have of knowing if our material will sell. It has to pass my jack-off test."

"I've always loved tests," I teased. "They're so challenging."

Muffie, observing all this, acted like she was at a church social. "I brought Diana over to see what I do for a living," she said, cryptically.

"Has she agreed?" Rod asked.

"Agreed to do what?" I asked back as he, ever so nonchalant, pulled loose hairs off my sweater and stroked the back of my ass with his large comforting hand. I could sense these people were practiced pros. If I gave in to every demand of theirs, I decided, the next thing would be they'd want me to become a call girl in some

58

stable on the East Side. Rod would make the perfect pimp.

But I had to check myself. I was feeling a little angry and was allowing myself to wander into racial stereotypes, one of which features a tall black pimp, hung like a stallion, with his harem of blue-eyed blondes. But that was about the extent of my hostility. Being so young and from such a small town and having been raised in so strict a religious sect, the Tabernacle Witnesses, I was eager to explore life and not to pass judgment on anyone too quickly.

But I have to say, at first glance, I was disappointed by this "film studio." It seemed more like some cluttered-up old warehouse with stacks of film piled on the bare wooden floors and several humongous cameras parked on the edges of the room. The windows of the loft were blacked out so that the light could be better controlled inside. Most of the ten or so assistants were young men, wearing faded jeans and ripped T-shirts, and I noticed there were a few hard-ons. The main cameraman was an aristocratic Latin type. He was very tall and incredibly built. His T-shirt said "Lucky" on both front and back.

I thought to myself, "How lucky can you get?" and couldn't resist flirting with him. "Does that mean you get lucky?" I said, referring to his shirt.

"No," he answered, looking at me with his penetrating olive-black eyes, which drew me toward them with the force of two black holes. "That means you get lucky, if you want to," he said. Then, from deep in his jeans pocket, he pulled out a clear lucite disc with a four-leaf clover imbedded in it. "This is to remind you of me," he said.

I was deeply touched by this man's generosity, so I took the lucky charm. But I'd forgotten I didn't have any pockets. "You'll have to excuse me," I said, "but I'm afraid I haven't any pockets at the moment. You'll have to keep this for me."

"Does that mean I'll see you again?" he asked politely. Christ, what a gentleman! I'd forgotten they existed. I was also so charmed I forgot to keep my sweater down over my pubic hair and the little bit of labia that starts peeking out of me when I get the least bit excited.

Lucky bent down like a perfect gentleman and kissed me gently on my vulva. What an incredible diplomat he was! I was really impressed by his sensitivity. It was just like Jesus kissing the paralytic, or one of those stories. "Lucky, I'll never forget you," I said, with tears in my eyes.

"I've got to go," he said. "I'll see you later." And off he went down the elevator with some of the other cameramen and electricians.

Maybe by flirting with Lucky I was trying to make my beloved Angelo jealous. Why not? Here was my Great New Love, my fabulous Fuck, my sensitive, endearing cab driver of the night before tit-fucking some broad with the biggest pair since the invention of mother's milk. What was I supposed to think? I had caught my boyfriend red-handed, or should I say red-handled? Angelo, bless his heart, turned around when he realized there was another center of activity in the studio, namely me. With his "co-star," whose name I later discovered was Desiree Bernstein, stage name Desiree Bee, I must admit they looked like a couple of classical statues with their pale white alabaster skin and their coppery red bushes. They looked perfect together. I realized that with my gold skin we could never be cast in a pornographic movie together, presuming, of course, I even wanted to. I'd make Angelo look like a Halloween ghost.

"Hey, babe!" he said, as if he'd been clipping hedges. "What are you doing here?"

"I'm taking a tour!" I waved back, as if I were at Disneyland. Angelo seemed a little annoyed. I couldn't have been more delighted. His co-star Desiree just lay there yawning. She was some hot number, ha!

Angelo shouted to Rod, "Hey, how come Diana's here?"

"Who do you think Diana is, the Virgin Mary?" Rod shot back.

In an instant Angelo, devout Italian that he was, was at Rod's throat. Well, almost. I think their oversized erections got in the way. Angelo was livid. "I told you I don't want Diana fucking in front of a camera; she's planning to become a fashion model. What the fuck is fucking on cue going to do for her except fuck up her fucking career?" he raged. Rod, at that moment more imperially British than black, looked at poor Angelo with utter disdain. With the British, black or white, apparently, an open display of anger is considered more obscene than fucking Mrs. Astor's pet pony at Madison Square Garden.

"This woman has a mind of her own, hasn't she?" clipped Rod with a selectively arched eyebrow.

"She has a cunt of her own, too!" screamed Angelo. "Hey, babe, we got to get you out of here. This over-educated jungle bunny's going to fuck up your career."

"Look, I'll be alright," I sighed. "I'm a big girl now."

Angelo was insistent. "You don't know what you're talking about. Your modeling career won't be worth two cents if it turns out you were a fuck-film star. Look what happened to Marilyn Chambers and the Ivory Soap ads. I mean, after America found out she had a cunt to go with the kid, how could anyone wash their face with Ivory Soap?"

"I don't understand!," I blurted out, half in tears.

"I don't understand either," bellowed Angelo, "but that's the way it is!"

Rod was beginning to get testy. "What do you think this is, white slavery, man? You think I'm some bad-ass nigger, don't you? Come on, say it."

Angelo was adamant. "Rod, I don't trust you any farther than the length of your cock, which, by the way, has always reminded me and everyone else of a black-snake."

Rod was fuming. "What's that supposed to mean?"

"Draw your own conclusions," said Angelo, who then went way too far. "Face facts, the only thing that turns this nigger on is the prospect of a dollar bill."

With that, Rod landed a left hook on Angelo's perfectly chiseled jaw. With that, the grips and cameramen rushed over to break up the fight, but Rod was too quick for them. He hadn't built up his mini-empire without staying one step ahead of everyone else. He began to laugh and proclaimed in his booming imperious tones, "I'm sorry, man," and stuck out his hand to make peace with Angelo.

Angelo's Irish was getting the better of him. "What's that supposed to mean?" he asked.

"A truce," intoned Rod.

Angelo was clearly not about to yield.

"Only when Diana leaves the building."

"My dear man," said Rod, still gloriously buck naked, "I promise you I am only giving her a tour."

"A tour of what?" said Angelo.

Rod thought all this was very funny. "Would you please get back to work? You're losing your million-dollar erection. By the way, you are still working for me, aren't you?"

Angelo looked at me with soulful eyes. "As soon as I come, I can take a coffee break," he said. "Please wait for me."

I was so overcome by his impetuous little-boy caring that I went over and kissed him softly on his cock. I guess I revived his manhood. His drooping organ nodded, woke up, and began to reach for the sky. "I love you very much, Angelo," I said softly. I meant it. He almost started to cry.

"Just remember," he said, "you're a great lady and you're going to be a great model."

"Hey," I said, "did you say great lady or great lay?"

"Hey, both!" he said.

"Hey, I'll see you later," I said.

"Hey," he shot back. "There's a lot of hay in here. Maybe there's a hayloft where we can fuck."

"No," I rejoined, "the hay is for horses."

"Don't I qualify?" he shot back.

"Hey, I said I'll see you later," I called out. "Get back to work, you bum!"

I had to get out of that studio fast. Desiree Bernstein had just lain there for fifteen full minutes on that white fur rug with her humongous tits and her perfect alabaster skin, slowly fingering herself in her pastel-pink pussy and not saying a word. I didn't know whether to kick her in her frankly sensational cunt or kiss her right on her little jewel of a clitoris. Believe me, it was love-hate at first sight.

And Muffie! My God! She kept circling Ms. Bernstein like an arctic wolf around a campfire, eyes riveted on those delicious hot-pink labia, whereas I, for all my fascination with big-breasted, pink-pussied women, am really into men. I don't really care about height, weight, muscular development, or cock size. What makes a man masculine to me is the extent of his involvement in the world outside himself. This may sound heavy, but I had it all worked out by the sixth grade. It's true, I was fourteen in the sixth grade, but the bottom-line truth is, I like a man who likes life. That's why I was so attracted to Angelo.

Muffie and Rod were beckoning to me, so I rejoined them. They led me out of the main studio into Rod's office in the back of the building. The office was singularly dramatic. All white: white tiled floor, white walls, white furniture. The only things not white were large black and white photos from fuck films which Rod had produced.

What photographs! There was raw passion and hunger in them. I was really impressed. Rod could see the admiration in my eyes. "I see you like my visual records of love and desire," he commented.

"Oh Rod," I chimed. "That's it. There's love there. There's desire. There's a quality—I don't know exactly how to describe it."

"Could it be the word you're looking for is 'spiritual'?"

"That's it! They're spiritual, Rod. Why, they're almost religious."

"They are religious," he explained. "That's the whole point. They show how sex is the link between the gods and man."

"And women," added Muffie, unnecessarily.

"See," Rod said, pointing to a mammoth close-up of a big-headed cock swollen to the point of bursting just at its moment of entry into a wide-mouthed, flesh-furrowed cunt that seemed to be screaming "Fuck me! fuck me!"

"That's not just a cock about to ram a cunt," I said. "He's caught the passion of the moment."

"That's right," said Muffie, as she simultaneously stroked my ass and kissed me on the back of my neck, "that cunt is a mouth that's screaming for love."

My head was swimming. Here I was, in a major studio, almost, where an erotic film was being shot right in the next room. Not only that, between the still-naked Rod Peters gleaming like a Masai warrior with his lean and chiseled warrior's form and his still rampant cock, which showed no signs of lying down and calling it quits, and my sometimes-best-friend Muffie Free, who was able to seduce me any time she wanted, I wasn't sure what my next move should be.

I guess, as usual, Rod was one step ahead of the game. Rod was so charming in his own offhand way, like a king cobra dancing in an Indian bazaar. But who was kidding who? Finally, he got to the point. "Muffie, you must show Diana Studio B," he ordered.

"Why? What's in Studio B?" I asked.

"We have another little epic being filmed, this one with a new Swedish discovery you might enjoy."

"A Swedish discovery?" I exclaimed, putting on my dumb act.

"His real name is Solvig Hansen, but we're going to call him Johnny O'Toole," said Rod. "He's a perfect human specimen."

"I'm so happy for you," I said. The truth is, I didn't know what to say. I wanted to back out onto West Broadway, back to that intersection where I'd had so much good clean fun earlier in the day, and see if I couldn't make a dinner date with Officer Hunky, or whatever his name was. I wished Rod would shut up, but he wouldn't. Forever the businessman, he was trying to make some point about his latest discovery.

"Yes, Johnny O'Toole's got the handsomest face since Gary Cooper went to the Happy Hunting Ground. His body is better than Burt Lancaster's. And the cock, for once, looks like it belongs on the body instead of a third leg that's been grafted onto the Pillsbury Dough Boy. I really think you...."

With that, I'd had enough of his filthy mouth and I decided to give him some of mine. I'm not sure why. These things come over me. I just can't resist taking advantage of a black stallion. Besides, it was the only way to shut him up.

His cock took at least two hands to hold it steady. I had the hands in question, although I was unable to completely close them around his ebony chair leg. I worked the wet meat of my inner mouth over the head of his cock and was able to swallow about five or six inches of him. He made no attempt to stop me and moaned, "Diana, yes, oh blonde baby, yes, I been wanting you nonstop fantastico." Then his hands were on my pussy. He was possessed. He was trying to fist-fuck me. Rod was losing most of his British accent and every bit of his British reserve. The force of his penetrations in my mouth as he began to pump me like a piston all but knocked the breath out of me, and his hands were making inroads into parts of me that had never been touched by anyone.

Muffie, of course, had to get in on the act, and after my initial resentment that she was again intruding with her tremendous sexual power and appetite, I surrendered. I decided that if she was perverted, that was her problem. As for myself, I wanted to take advantage of her fantastic tongue. Lying on her back, she wedged her head between my legs, and forcibly removed Rod's exploring hands. "You've had enough," she shouted. "I want her. She's a cup of honey in my life and I want her, so get out!"

Rod had no choice, so intense was her commitment to eating me out. She glued her mouth to my slit, forcing apart the passion-thick lips with her insatiable tongue. She wanted a hot wedge of my pussy meat; she began to lick every fold and crevice, her mouth sucking out my pouring cunt-juice with greedy little swallows. I felt as if a mighty concrete dam somewhere inside me was about to burst. My flesh was on fire and it began to rumble, threatening to explode. "Hey," Muffie groaned, "don't shake so hard; you're going to knock out my fuckin' teeth." She buried her tongue in my cunt, all the way to the cherry, sucking my labia into her mouth. I couldn't stand it any longer. I came harder than I had in months. And kept coming again and again. I was sweating like a pig and feeling weak in the knees. My body glowed and tingled. I felt light-headed and began almost against my will to say, "Yes, baby, yes, yes yes!"

And then there was Rod, his cock still in my mouth, taking advantage of every involuntary spasm of my orgasmic tongue. Rod Peters. His body ignited me. Maybe it was his blackness. It reminded me of the finest tempered steel, the world's most powerful machines. And would you believe Rod's imposing physique worked like the finest machine, his piston cock a miracle of minute reflexes? It had a mind of its own, and a power that begged to be respected. Did I see Rod as a person? Who knows? Do I see filet mignon as a person, or the finest champagne? Or cocaine? What is appetite, anyway? I only wished my mouth and throat were adequate for the full scope and profound sophistication of Rod's incredible cock. I mean, you can't expect a stallion to fuck a pussycat and get much fun out of it, can you?

But thank God for my basic humility; I never pretended to be more than a great piece of pussy. Like everybody else, as far as sex is concerned, I can only do my best. "Rod," I begged, hoping to satisfy him, "give it to me up the ass! I want you to be happy! I'll give you whatever you want!"

The Venus Studios were so drenched in animal sex that even the air smelled of cunt-fish and male musk. I was beginning to get carried away. I wanted Rod to fuck me in my ears, on the backs of my knees, on the palms of my feet.

"We haven't time, darlin'," he gasped. "We're behind in Studio B. Just give me more of your sinfully effective tongue around the crown of my sceptre and let your hands do the rest."

"Yessir," I responded, eager to please. I wrapped one hand around the base of his pole and worked his shaft up and down while I slid my lips up and down on his glans, drawing his cock deeply into my throat, then backing up, then stuffing him down deep into the soft wet back of my hard palate. I dug my hands into the black leather sac that contained his oversized balls, but they were too big and full; I couldn't handle both at once, so I played with them, stroking them and fondling them as I sucked the head of his cock, faster and faster, plunging the dark plum into the wet meat in the back of my hungry mouth, using my throat muscles to contract around his stout dick.

The next few minutes were a sexual ballet in slow motion, with me wrapped around Rod, and Muffie wedged into me, all of us about to come and no one able to stand up or kneel because of the full force of the three-way orgasm. Rod's cock started to explode. His sperm-spray shot across my fevered tongue, splashing against the back of my throat and oozing down my gullet. At that very moment, I snatched the black instrument out of his mouth and used it as a vibrator on my breasts, rubbing it back and forth over my hypersensitive nipples as I, too, began to explode in a series of orgasms, as the three of us, like a house of cards, fell slowly into an orgasmic heap, and then wound down, tingling, sore, and completely relaxed. Finally, even Muffie stopped, because she, too, had come, and she needed her hands free to attend to herself, Imagine! America's porn queen, Lisa Pink, getting off on herself! She gave new meaning to the phrase, "To each his (or her) own."

By this time, I figured I'd had enough sex for a while. I wanted to go shopping for a badly needed skirt. How much longer could I walk around New York with a loosely knit sweater pulled down around my pubes? Earlier in the day I'd seen a Mexican wraparound skirt made of raw cotton in a shop window on Prince Street. I had an overwhelming urge to go try it on.

But Rod Peters had, apparently, made other plans for me. Studio B. He insisted I meet Mr. Swedish Meatballs. When I finally arrived at Studio B—it was a full two steps across the hallway from Rod's office—I was unprepared for what I saw. Studio B itself was no larger than the average Levittown living room, and the "set" for the newest production, tentatively entitled *One Night At A Time*, was clearly somebody's idea of an upper-class patio. Cardboard french doors which opened to nothing were nailed against the cardboard back wall, which was painted-on bricks. In front of that was a round white table with its familiar beach umbrella. The most extraordinary piece of "patio" furniture, custom-made, no doubt, was a double-width chaise longue, a clear invitation for two people to take the sun together, or anything else that same to mind. The "swimming pool" was an illusion, a fake tile-boarded metal trough about ten feet across, three feet long, and two feet deep. Its inside was painted aquamarine, and needless to say, the thing was filled with water. It looked like a perverted bathtub.

Am I leaving the best till last? Could be. Because perched on the edge of the "pool" in water up to his pubic hair, directly across from two grungy cameramen who were half-asleep and waiting for something to happen, was none other than Rod Peter's new discovery, Solvig Hansen, otherwise known as Johnny O'Toole, buck-naked and blonde as God. He looked supremely bored. His body, I must say, lived up to its advance publicity. Every muscle was long and strong. This was no mere weight lifter. His proportions had the perfections of a Greek statue, and, like me, in the right light he looked like he'd been dipped in gold. But Mr. Hansen was, at least on the surface, not my cup of tea. Maybe I have an aversion to absolute physical perfection in men, or maybe I just wanted that Mexican skirt.

In any case, what I wanted didn't make any difference; Rod was not about to take no for an answer. He made the introduction with his black snake prominently on hand, or should I say "in hand," because he was holding it. Some people have no shame. I, at least, had my shoes on and was halfway into my angora sweater.

That was my first mistake. It's called the peek-a-boo routine—the unexpected glimpse of tit. It drives most men wild because it catches them off guard. Solvig's big lump of a penis, visible through the waves, began to straighten out and fly right. Metamorphosis. In no time, it was sticking straight up through the water like a periscope. Since he didn't know how to speak English very well yet, he figured his cock said it all. He was right. He just stood there grinning, with his arms folded across his sculptured blonde chest, staring at the plump nipples I couldn't quite hide. One of the grungy cameramen, fully alert by now, winked at me.

"Excuse me?" I said.

"I'll 'scuse the cooze when you play it where it lays," he quipped.

"What's that supposed to mean?" I said, putting on my dumb act.

The dumb act only served to rouse his Neanderthal tendencies. "Hey, baby, I've been waiting for two fuckin' hours for some action." Then, to Rod, "Hey, man, this chick's going to make you a million bucks!"

Rod said, "Hey, man, forget the million bucks, first she has to make a million fucks!"

By this time it was crystal clear to me that Manhattan's best-appointed British English gentleman had completely lost his Oxford accent, and his sense of humor had definitely lost its British wit. I wanted Angelo. But, of course, Angelo was out there tit-fucking Desiree Bernstein under an arc light, and Mr. Solvig O'Toole Hansen was talking to me, in broken English yet, like we'd had three kids and shared a life in Malibu. His dialogue was right out of a B movie, which was perfect for Studio B: "Diana, darlink, you haf look more beautyfull never. Vhere haf bin you? Come, Diana, take off your svimsuit. Come join me for the svim in the svimming pool. Diana, listen to Solvig; I am in luf vid your titties." Terrific. So terrific I needed a drink quick.

That was my second mistake. My first was agreeing to meet Solvig in the first place. Rod, ever the gracious host, had already anticipated my overpowering need to get drunk on the spot and had mixed me a vodka and tonic. Perfect. You see, there was a serving cart from Sears right there in SoHo's version of the good life. I felt like being a bitch, and I didn't open my mouth except to chug-a-lug the best vodka and tonic since my graduation from Beavertown Central.

I asked for another. Then something happened. Suddenly, I was inside a kaleidoscope, melting into a rainbow of blues and purples and lavenders, the air around me laden with the sound of violins, and Solvig, when I looked at him this time, was really gold, a cloud of gold, spun gold, and when he opened his mouth to speak, and his diamond teeth blazed in the white light, the sounds that emanated from his mouth were the sounds of the seraphim.

I wanted nothing more than to swim in the gold. And so I did. That much I remember. I remember embracing the god of the north. I was impaled on his cock. I was a human sacrifice. His cock ran through me like a sword of fire and ice; it reached straight to my heart and touched me there. I died in the arms of God. Amen.

Later, much later, from his hospital bed, Angelo told me what happened. He had finally ejaculated with Desiree Bernstein and was on his well-earned coffee break looking for me. The cameramen were out getting pizza. Then, Desiree had a mini-breakdown on the spot and needed him desperately to comfort her. It seems that Desiree, who was twenty-seven, had just been told that afternoon that she was adopted, and she didn't know why, but she was absolutely distraught. She begged Angelo to comfort her, adding that he could see me any time. Then, according to Angelo, he heard me screaming, which is something I have absolutely no recollection of. He says he rushed into Studio B to find kleig lights blazing and cameras whirring away. And where was I? According to Angelo, fucking Solvig like there was no tomorrow, laughing, chortling, gurgling, the broadest smile on my face, caressing his generous cock like it was a magic wand, cooing to him, "Johnny, you are my dearest source of infinite love; I will worship you in life and death."

Like I said, I don't remember any of the above-said activity, nor do I care to press charges in the matter, because what followed was far worse than merely being slipped a dose of LSD. Besides, because of what happened next, Muffie and Rod got their just deserts. They had to become permanent exiles in Brazil out of fear of the Mafia. Yes, I'm sorry to say the Venus Productions was blown up by a bomb. Those cameramen who went out for pizza had left their calling card behind. About a pound of what's called plastic. A massive explosion in Studio A. Clearly somebody did not want *Y'all Come* to hit the jack-off parlors of America.

Witnesses said it looked like the climax of a World War II movie; bits and pieces of timber, plaster, floorboards, linoleum, wiring, plumbing. Smoke and madness everywhere. Within minutes, apparently, the whole building was in flames, and from later reports, my beloved Angelo, unable to find me because of the acrid smoke and searing flames, was forced to jump naked out the fourth-story window. He broke both arms and legs. In the meantime, Muffie and Rod, both professional survivors and concerned about no one but themselves, grabbed their wallets and raincoats and slipped down the secret back staircase. It must have been secret. Nobody else knew anything about it. I was out on the fire escape with Solvig, both of us in our birthday suits, both, from all reports, screaming like Banshees at the top of our lungs, neither one of us able to make the rickety old fire escape descent.

And, believe it or not, there was more. The police photographer. He said later I was the most beautiful woman he'd ever photographed, on the job, that is. Later on, we became close and confidential friends, but that's another story. At the time, I wasn't aware that I was being photographed. The truth is, after I'd been slipped that mickey in the vodka and tonic, I don't remember one detail about what was probably the most exciting episode of my life up till then, although I do recall that the events that followed shortly thereafter were thrilling beyond belief. I guess the moral of the Studio B episode was, "Don't take a free drink of LSD from a naked film producer you've just had sex with unless you're ready to star in an X-rated film."

Chapter Five

The exact precinct house I was taken to in Manhattan shall have to remain nameless. What transpired there between me and the police was the most glorious testimony to participatory democracy that I have ever experienced, but I am afraid that the press and the Federal Bureau of Investigation, as functions of the Establishment, would fail to appreciate the true meaning of the phrase, "Power to the People," so I shall disguise the names of the "guilty."

The precinct house was a typical Manhattan bureaucratic-type building, fashioned during the late sixties, no doubt, out of poured concrete and cinderblocks, a bland-looking square structure which completely disguised the emotional possibilities within. And as I was to find out, there were possibilities galore.

As I entered the place, surrounded by two of New York's finest, I guess I must have looked like a hooker. Learning that I was caught out on that fire escape stark naked, the cops had brought me some clothes to wear. Oh, brother! The black patent leather shoes didn't fit; they were about two sizes too big, which made me look like a little girl in her mother's shoes. Then, there was an orange-red sweater dress, which was about two sizes too small and cut down to the navel. I was so embarrassed. But, as it turned out, there were compensations. I heard more than one devilish wolf whistle in the background, which I can only suppose was meant for me, especially since one burly cop hidden behind a filing cabinet kept shouting out, "Hey, big tits!" Not very subtle, but it sure as hell made me feel like some kind of sexy dame, just when I needed it, just when I was coming down off Rod Peter's "love potion."

At the front desk I was interrogated, that is to say, asked my name, address, and vital statistics. So what did I do? I burst into tears, saying, "I'm not what you think!" I heard the guy behind the filing cabinet guffawing.

The next thing I knew, I was being escorted upstairs to the Police Chief's office. The officer estcorting me was a muscular Hispanic type named Officer Sanchez. He looked like a Hispanic Elvis Presley. As he was escorting me, he kept putting his hand on my waist. He was breathing like he had asthma, and his hand kept slipping onto my ass, at which point he'd say, "Oh, excuse me," and I'd say, "Oh, that's alright," like nothing was happening. So what if he was deliberately touching me? I like to be touched, especially when I've just been through the kind of traumatic experience that would have sent most women to the nut house. Besides, I like my men to take risks with me, especially attractive men like Officer Sanchez.

When we reached the Chief of Police's office, the door was open and we walked in. The Chief of Police, whose name was O'Leary, was well suited to his name. He was leering. "How appropriate," I thought. If he hadn't looked so much like William Holden, my late mother's favorite movie star, I would have been insulted. He was a gorgeous specimen of the middle-aged American male, the perfect father-figure for a girl in need of paternal affection and advice. And like the perfect father, he got right down to business.

"That will be all, Sergeant Sanchez," he said. Sanchez looked at me and shrugged his shoulders as if to say, "What can I do?" There was a burning intensity in his black eyes, however, which clearly said, "You and I will see one another later."

I gave Sergeant Sanchez my best heartfelt "thank-you." After Officer Sanchez left, Captain O'Leary locked the door—double-locked it, in fact. I looked around. The office was something—fake wood walls, and a green shag carpet that looked like fake grass on the floor. O'Leary was no fake. Pure Americana. Six feet tall with a thatch of gray-brown hair. He had the creased skin of an outdoorsman who smoked too many Havana cigars and drank too much Johnny Walker Red for his own good. But he was one cop who hadn't put on weight. I had the feeling he went to the gym every day and worked out. As a matter of fact, his body didn't stop moving, and his voice—what an incredible voice! Gruff and gravelly, full of honey and grits, you just knew he ate pussy; his voice was full of it—it wasn't just saying what I wanted to hear. "So, young lady, you've just come to the city and already you're making dirty movies. My, my, my."

"Captain O'Leary," I began in humble protest, but he wouldn't let me finish.

"Young lady, how would you like to call your mother and tell her what you've been doing?"

I thought to myself, *If my mother were alive today and could get a load of you, she'd be on the next bus to New York.* "Captain O'Leary, I wasn't . . ."

"You wasn't what?" he growled. "We have pictures of you starkers on the fire escape at twelve o'clock high."

Something in me snapped. I decided I wasn't going to take any more shit from him. "So?" I said, bold as brass. "I was in a fire, an explosion is more like it, or hadn't you noticed? And while we're at it, what are you planning to do about the Mafia? They're the ones who did it."

Captain O'Leary didn't say anything. Ignoring what I'd just said, he showed me a just-developed color photograph of me on the fire escape outside the Venus Production Studios. I have to say my cunt looked pretty juicy. The afternoon fall sun caught the tips of the golden hairs on my blonde thatch. It was a blaze of glory. And because the police photographer was right underneath the fire escape and I'd just been impaled on one hell of a cock in Studio B, my labia, like the succulent edges of a raw oyster, ripe and juicy, were hanging out of me. Christ, that fucking picture could have won the Pulitzer Prize! (Excuse my gutter language. I get carried away by excellence.)

"Miss Hunt," Captain O'Leary continued in his fatherly way, which was beginning to carry overtones of lechery, "when I first saw that photograph ten minutes ago ... well, let's just say you could be in a lot of trouble. What do you have to say for yourself?"

"Captain O'Leary," I protested, "I originally went to that film studio to watch some friends of mine make an erotic film, which, as far as I know, is not against the law. The next thing you know, somebody, I'm not sure who, slipped me a mickey, and I had some guy's flagpole stuck up my cunt."

"His flagpole?" O'Leary asked, with a sly look on his face. "Please explain to me what a flagpole is, Miss Hunt."

"Captain," I repeated, "I was lying on top of some stud, this guy, you know, his erect, you know what I mean, his sexually aroused, you know, member stuck up my cunt and I was coming. I don't know why I was coming. He was this perfect Scandinavian specimen, all blonde and tanned, and his cock was in perfect proportion to me. I mean, I never met him, and there I was, against my will all juicy and sticky and coming. I mean if I was being raped, why was I so aroused?"

Captain O'Leary seemed to be fidgeting with something under his desk. I was so naive, I thought he must be taking notes or something. This man distracted me. His face looked so kind and weathered. "Go on," he said.

"About what?" I replied. I was completely distracted by his face.

But Captain O'Leary was so helpful. "How did you feel about fucking someone, I mean, having sex with someone you'd never met before?"

"Well, Captain," I began, "this guy was a real hunk, he was a stud, Captain, what was I supposed to do, he was some kind of Swedish athlete, fencing, I think, or wrestling, not exactly the type you'd throw out of bed on a rainy night, especially when your drink has been drugged and you don't know what you're doing in the first place."

Captain O'Leary looked at me for the longest time, like a lizard on the desert. He just didn't blink an eye. Finally, he spoke. "Miss Hunt, if you're willing to do me a big favor, I promise I won't press charges."

"What kind of a favor?" I said, then decided I wanted to get out of that police station as quickly as possible. "Sure. Anything, Captain."

With that, Captain O'Leary stood up to reveal an open fly. Sticking out of the open fly was a ramrod cock that would have looked great on a sixteen-year-old basketball player. I was absolutely astounded.

"Are you surprised?" he asked.

"I'm floored," I said.

"That's exactly what I had in mind," he said.

"What?" I said.

"The floor," he said. "Miss Hunt, I'm too old to play games. I want to fuck you. Please take off your clothes and make yourself comfortable. The best thing would be for you to lie down on my desk, if you don't mind."

"Captain O'Leary," I protested, "I have to tell you, I have no feelings for you. You're so unromantic." Of course I was lying, but I was really testing him. I don't make it with every man I feel attracted to. I also have to feel that I am desired, and at the moment, I wasn't sure.

"I know I look like a father-figure to you," he said, "but the truth is, I look like a father-figure to everyone. That seems to be the story of my life lately. I'm the guy everybody loves to hate, just because my hair is gray and I'm stooped in the shoulders."

This time he'd gone too far. He was being too hard on himself. I hated to see a sensitive man like Captain O'Leary, so close to the heartbeat of the city, begin to hate himself for growing old, when, in fact, there is nothing more attractive than an attractive older man who keeps in shape. I didn't know about the rest of him yet, but if his lean, tough, perfectly formed cock was any indication of his physical condition, stripped he must have looked like an Olympic gold medalist in the pole-vaulting division.

"You're very kind and understanding," he whispered gruffly, checking the double-lock on the door, removing his shirt, and dropping his pants.

My first impression: his body was a workingman's body, tough and sinewy from his neck muscles to his calves. His balls were enormous. I couldn't wait to hold them and squeeze out of them what I knew must be a flood of thick, sweet come. I admit it. I was turned on. I kicked off my shoes, wriggled out of my too-tight dress, and let it drop to the floor. At the sight of my naked body, his helmeted cock pulsated and turned beet-red. I have never seen a man react to my body so fast, so violently. From his wide-open, staring eyes, I could tell that Captain O'Leary was the original tits-and-ass man; the knob of his engorged cock changed from red to purple and almost doubled its size.

Who said there are no real men left in the world? Here was a father-figure with a gun in one hand and a cock in the other. What more could a young woman ask for? His husky body, milk-white and typically Irish in its square bulk, seemed to be molded out of the finest concrete. Even his stomach was hard, with no sign of flab.

His compliments were what I'd expect from a guy who's spent his life outdoors on the streets of New York: "Miss Hunt, get your ass on that desk." So direct and earthy and real. I couldn't understand how my older brother could have ever called policemen "pigs." Most women like myself, who can really appreciate a real man who lives by gut instinct, are not exactly turned on by anti-Establishment intellectual types who don't appreciate the value of a good cock.

Like I said before, all I wanted to do with Captain O'Leary was to milk his enormous testicles for every drop of come they were worth. So I disobeyed my master. I sank to my knees in front of him, my mouth a hair's-breadth away from his glans, just as his massive right hand came crashing into the side of my face.

"You slut, I'm going to tell you once more . . . and only once more! Get your fucking ass on that desk!"

I felt dazed. "Captain O'Leary," I whimpered, "please, I have to put my mouth on your fantastic cock! I have to have it, or I'm going to die! I don't want to live!" I could feel beads of cunt juice shimmering on my patch of honey-colored hair between my quivering thighs. Again, I felt the burning sensation of his open palm as he whacked my face. It had been so long since I had been the object of anyone's wrath, that intimate state between master and servant.

"Slut!" he screamed.

My tears ran hot onto my cheeks, and I began to sob. This was what he wanted. To see me vulnerable. That changed everything. He sank to his knees, clasped my buns with his big red hands, and, pressing against me, began to suck on my nipples. His own eyes were glistening.

79

"Please, Miss Hunt, my darling," he implored, "you have the most perfect cunt I've ever seen. Please, Miss Hunt, I'm no good, I don't deserve anybody, but please, please sit on my face, or else I'll have to whip you, and then arrest you."

I was just as bad, just as irrational. I couldn't believe my behavior. I mean, I'd never been into bondage or flagellation, and I certainly never went out on dates with men as complex and fascinating as Captain O'Leary. I found myself screaming, "My pussy is hot for your tongue! I want you to stick your whole face, especially your tongue, inside my cunt. Go ahead, Captain. I want to rub your cock inside my mouth, I want to rub your cock all over me!"

In a frenzy we stretched each other out on the green shag carpet. He lay on his back, his thick white rod sticking up, while I lay on top of him, sixty-nine style. Like a starving madman, he pulled my cunt on top of his face, his huge, thick muscular tongue dove through my fuck-flesh, into my deep, juicy cooze. Captain O'Leary was in animal ectasy, his strong hands fondling my ass cheeks, his broad tongue reaming my asshole. Occasionally, he'd reach down and fondle my breasts, fumbling for my stiff nipples, which had been gloriously aroused and which were awaiting the master's touch.

"Jesus Christ, I've never seen such a pair of knockers," he said. O'Leary ate me out with ooohs and aaahs like a five-year-old boy who'd been handed a whole chocolate cake just for himself. I slid my cunt-lips over his mouth as his teeth, tongue, and lips alternately caressed, sucked, and nibbled my pleasure bud.

But the real pleasure was all mine at my end of the playing field. My hands were free to hold his heavy testicles and massage them gently and steadily as I lowered my moist mouth on top of his throbbing jism stick. With a certain amount of patient stretching, I managed to wedge the scarlet head of his majestic sceptre into my mouth, where I rolled my cannibalistic tongue around the rim of his jawbreaker; gradually, by relaxing my throat muscles I got a large portion of O'Leary's cock into the hot meat of my mouth and throat. With savage slurping, he forcibly pulled my streaming cunt deeper and deeper into his face; by this time his nose and mouth were buried inside me, the bridge of his nose massaging my clitoris nonstop. His hot tongue felt like it was everywhere inside me, and I began to heave with tremendous orgasms. I tried to stop myself from coming so fast. I knew that if I held myself back, before long I'd have a mouth dripping with honeyed sperm, so I couldn't wait to bring him off. I could feel the nerves in his stalwart cock respond to my practiced, snakelike tongue. His balls grew larger and larger as zero point approached. My pelvis began to thrash in orgasm. I felt like I was balancing on a tightrope. O'Leary's hands grew frenetic and uncontrolled. He, too, began to thrash and moan. His glans had swollen so large I thought it would break my front teeth. He began to grunt like a pig; he lost muscular control of his mouth; his tongue and lips felt like warm mud. Then, his shaft became more swollen still and I knew his time had come.

Yes, the volcano broke. An eruption of liquid warmth filled my mouth to overflowing, as I milked his testicles. Or tried to. I, too, had lost control. O'Leary's lips and nose, as they thrashed in orgasm, gave my clitoris a going-over that triggered me so violently I lost track of time and place. My mouth sagged involuntarily to keep from choking as the come dripped over my teeth and lips onto the shaft of his cock. Warmth and tingling traveled into every crevice of my grateful flesh, as wave after wave of pleasure carried me high above earth. For the moment, at least, I had found the man of my dreams. For the moment I had no doubt that I was desired. I was at peace with Law and Order, with "pigs," even with me. I decided right then and there that if I ever had kids, especially girls, I would teach them that policemen can be the best friends they have ever known.

The day was far from over. After we fucked, O'Leary pressed a buzzer and told me to go clean myself up in the adjoining bathroom. When I had finished my "toilette" and reentered O'Leary's bureaucratic den, there was Chinese take-out food on his desk. O'Leary was dressed. He presented me with a dress he must have lifted from a dead hooker, a red-sequined shift with a slit up the left leg, the whole outfit much too tight—maybe that's what he wanted. There was also a London Fog raincoat that looked brand-new.

So far so good, but it wasn't enough. I figured I gave at the office, as they say. "So where are the shoes?" I demanded to know.

"Shoes?" he said.

"Captain, O'Leary," I began, "I'd love to lie on my back all day and fuck you blind, but..."

"Oh, shoes!" he exclaimed, suddenly realizing with force of revelation that a girl needs to take a walk around the block every couple of days. "Don't worry. We'll get you your shoes."

"One more thing," I added. "When are you going to let me go home?"

"Soon. Today. As soon as possible. I don't know. You're not completely processed yet. In the meantime, have some Chinese."

I was starving. One container was crammed full of my favorite: moo-shu pork with rice flour pancakes. I rolled up a sizeable portion of the delectable meat and vegetable mixture into one of the scrumptuous pancakes, creating something that looked like a very thick, long, white egg role. "This is your cock, Captain," I said to O'Leary. "And now I'm going to eat it." And so I did, taking it one inch at a time, only to burst out laughing at my own insanity. O'Leary was just as bad. The other dish was tofu, or bean curd, with lobster claws, a blend of soft pink and white lobster flesh steaming in a clear liquid.

"This is your cunt, madame," he said. "I'm going to slurp it up with loud obscene noises and then eat it." He was laughing. Soon, the spongy bean curd began to disappear between his smacking lips, the sauce dripping from his fleshy lips, staining his pants. We were both filthy dirty and having a wonderful time. Ordering Chinese can be fun if you know what to order.

Like I said, there was an Episode Two here. My time in court was not ended. I have had to completely change the names of the guilty parties, because there are too many public interest groups who would be only too happy to label me a professional slut, especially now that I am perceived to be a woman of great wealth and international glamor. Worse, the cops in question would get fired and there would be a whole spate of newspaper articles decrying American decadence. I look at what happened another way. I'm glad to know there are still men left in the so-called civilized world who know what a real woman is.

There was a knock on the door. O'Leary bellowed, "Who the hell is it?"

It was my Latin Elvis, Sergeant Sanchez. "I've got Kopecky and Cooke with me," he bellowed through the door.

O'Leary was visibly upset. "You can't come in now," he yelled back. "It's after six o'clock. I'm closed for the day."

"We're the night shift, O'Leary," Sanchez bellowed back. "Remember?"

O'Leary looked at me with the expression of a wounded puppy. The original hangdog. "You must understand," he said, "I have gambling debts from the precinct poker games. They've come to collect."

"Do you want me to leave?" I asked.

"No, that's just the point," he said. "They don't want money. They want you."

"Now, hold on here," I protested. "Just wait one cotton-pickin' minute. What are my rights?"

The guys outside were not about to wait for O'Leary and me to finish our conversation. "O'Leary, do you want us to break down the fuckin' door?"

"Just a minute, guys," O'Leary bellowed back. Then, he looked at me with his most fatherly expression, and spoke in his kindliest tones. "Miss Hunt, my only concern is for your reputation."

"What reputation?" I asked.

"Listen to me," he pleaded, "this whole case could get blown out of proportion."

"What whole case?" I joked.

"The only hole I know about has been blown all day and it's still as tight as a teen-ager's twat."

"Miss Hunt," he insisted, "don't you see I'm trying to protect you? If you accommodate every cop in this station house, you could be branded forever as one step above a slut."

"That's only because I'm a woman," I replied, trying to be as casual as possible. As much as I creamed over O'Leary, I sure as hell wouldn't throw Sanchez out of bed on a rainy night. O'Leary was obviously jealous. He didn't want to share me with anyone. Unfortunately, I am a total feminist, and if I'm going to be gang-banged, I'll be the one to decide who, what, when, and where. At the moment, I was curious to see what was on the other side of the garden gate.

"No, no, no," O'Leary continued, "you're a gorgeous dame; you've got a body that doesn't quit. As a matter of fact, those guys will break down the door in a couple of minutes. You have two choices. You can either follow me down the fire escape, except that there's no fire escape, or you can pretend you're unconscious, and I'll call for a doctor."

"Captain O'Leary," I said, not about to be intimidated by a man old enough to be my father, "I always make the best of any situation, and furthermore, like I always say, it helps to know a few extra cops!"

The truth is, I was scared shitless, but I wasn't about to let a jealous lover see me shaking in my boots, so I played it cool.

As it turned out, I didn't have to. One of the waiting policemen knew how to pick a lock with the best of 'em. The door opened nice as can be. They stood there, the three of them, Boy, was I surprised! Sergeant Sanchez I've already described: my Spanish Elvis with blazing black eyes that threatened to burn a hole right through the center of my forehead, and sensual lips that had pussy written all over them. But the big surprise was my traffic cop from the morning, the one I'd left with a hard-on in SoHo. He was back and he still had the hard-on. He must have seen the pictures of me on the balcony.

I was so happy and excited to see him I leapt into his waiting arms, exclaiming, "It's you! God, the last time I saw you, there was that terrible crash and I had your come dripping down my legs, my bush was soaked, I mean . . ." I stopped short. He was laughing. I knew I must have sounded like a real dumb bunny. A real bird-brain. I realized my only way to salvage my dignity was to imitate a European intellectual-type you know what I mean, a more serious kind of woman; so I gave him a soul kiss, sucking his lips, tasting his tongue, passing my vulva against his hard-on. Serious. No talking. I was the aggressor and I didn't say a word. Then, I rubbed up and down against the big gun imprisoned in his crotch. What was I supposed to do, shake his hand and say, "Nice to see you?" Officer Hunko, I mean

85

Kopecky, was an attractive man. No, Kopecky was a hunk and I was in heaven.

Unfortunately, O'Leary was no longer the jealous lover. Nothing so delicate. Nothing so sensitive. Our father-figure was now about to direct traffic. He wedged himself between me and my Slavic salvation, and said, "Just a minute, boys, the line forms at the rear."

"Whose rear?" Sanchez asked, tongue in cheek, adding, most unnecessarily "Hey O'Leary, I thought the only cock you allow up your ass is the Commissioner's!"

O'Leary's eyes were as red as my labia. "Sanchez, you want to get busted?"

"No, baby, I want to get fucked!" Sanchez teased, unbuttoning his shirt to reveal a massive chest black with thick curls. "Guess what, O'Leary, you owe me two thousand dollars from poker, you owe Kopecky eight hundred, you owe Cooke seven-fifty. How you want to pay up, baby? 'Cause I got friends to collect from you and your wife if you don't know how to be nice to inferior officers. I mean, I ain't asking you to suck my delicious delicatessen double-sized cock, now am I?" And with that he kissed O'Leary full on the lips, just like those gorgeous actors in The Godfather did when one of them was about to kill another.

O'Leary paled; he was as white as his ass. "Okay, Sanchez, you win."

Sanchez smirked, "O'Leary, baby, I been winning all year, that's what I been trying to tell you." With that he took off his shirt. He had black hair all over his back, too. He looked like a proud black sheep. His nipples were pink and almost swollen, and his aureoles were as big as half-dollars. I could feel my vagina begin to tingle with excitement and my blood thud like it always thuds, out of fear, when I'm about to fuck someone for the first time. Somewhere, down deep in my gut, no matter how many men I've fucked, I guess I'm always afraid of being rejected.

I forgot to mention the third cop, Officer Cooke, who looked about twenty-one. I was so grateful to finally meet someone closer to my own age, with my same coloring, the same gold skin, the same honey-colored hair, the same sapphire-blue eyes. We could have been related, we were so much alike. To hell with incest, I wanted to fuck his brains out. I wanted to fuck all their brains out. I'm so sick of gray-faced guys in gray suits, with pasty faces and pot bellies, that when I meet a real workingman who's got red blood in his veins and a cock between his legs that rises up to meet me, I can't contain myself. I know that as sure as Jesus came to earth to proclaim the Gospel, I'm here to fuck my brains out. At the moment, I felt like a kid in a candy store.

I lost all reason, all sense of perspective. Like a fool, I found myself blurting out, "My mother always taught me that policemen are my best friends!"

O'Leary said, "These guys are more than your best friends; they're in love with you!"

I must have sounded about twelve. "I love men who are in love with me!" I cried, sitting on the edge of the desk, thrusting my red-sequined pelvis in the direction of Officer Sanchez. His eyes were dark and smokey, the lids half closed. He looked right through me. He saw the sweet little girl, he saw the shy young woman, he saw the incorrigible tramp; in a word, he saw all of me and I loved his total honesty.

And his ability to give commands. Sanchez was a born leader. He said, "Take it off."

"I've been waiting for your invitation," I replied, pulling my dress off in one swoop. I gloried in my full ripe breasts that hang without sagging. I guess the guys got the message that I wanted to be touched. And stroked. And sucked. And pinched. And fucked. Not necessarily in that order. When it comes to sex, I take it any way it comes: boiled, baked, fried, or raw.

Well, before you could flic your Bic or suck my clit,

those guys had their uniforms off, and "Never-Say-Die" O'Leary, clothes removed, stood there with his night stick in hand, giving orders to the troops.

"Get in line, boys, or you'll get it in the butt," he said as he whacked my look-alike, Officer Cooke, whose name, I discovered, was Dennis, across the middle of his taut and muscular ass. With that, O'Leary's other "night stick" seemed to grow about two inches. Interesting what a little power can do for a man's virility.

In the meantime, my Latin from Manhattan, Officer Sanchez, bent down to bury his hot and heavy lips in the petals of my glorious cunt, but O'Leary whacked him across the butt.

"Hold it, spic," he said, "who says you're first?"

"Hey, you red-nosed mick," Sanchez answered. "what about the money you owe us?"

"Yeah?" said O'Leary, "and what about my cousin the Commissioner? Wait 'til he hears what you've been doing up in the South Bronx."

Sanchez went blank. The color drained from his face. He said, "Oh." Then he went over to his rumpled pants and took out a little brown paper bag. It was White Lady. Coke. Cocaine, for the uninitiated. I'd only had it once in Beavertown. Not bad, even if it is too expensive and illegal, and ultimately a destructive influence in the time-honored pursuit of life, liberty, etc.

O'Leary took out a china plate and a single-edged razor from his bottom desk drawer; with the razor he divided the coke into lines on the plate and passed it around. Like a protective father, he showed me how to snort it up my nostrils, and I pretended I'd never had it before.

Needless to say, it was the best cocaine I'd ever had. The effects were dazzling. I was transported into the temple of the gods. The four men in my life were golden statues vibrating with music, their eyes blazing like liquid diamonds, their flesh melon-ripe, begging to be mouthed, eaten, and devoured. There I was, up in the clouds, melting into a rainbow, face to face with four rampant rods that glowed golden, magic wands ready to invade my private property.

O'Leary raised his night stick again and said, "Okay, boys, get in line."

Sanchez had had enough. He grabbed the night stick out of O'Leary's hands and bopped him on the noggin. Whack! O'Leary was in a momentary daze. In that moment, Sanchez grabbed me by the waist with his two powerful hands, turned me around and entered my purring pussy from the rear. By this time I was well lubricated and ready to roll (as well as suck, pump, jerk, and shimmy). God, Sanchez felt great! I reached down to feel his rock-hard shaft like the devil's own prod tearing me in half with pleasure, his steel-hard balls rubbing against the bridge between my cunt and my anal track. "Fuck me!" I ordered him, as his tough fingers twisted and pinched my nipples and his black-fleeced chest stroked every nerve ending on my back. "Fuck me!" I screamed again.

This time, my words seemed to have a listener. He rode me like a bucking bronco, his rough hands squeezing and fondling my flesh in handfuls. His cock felt red-hot inside me; my vagina was at the boiling point; I felt like we were going to burst into flames. His hands were spastic, grabbing my cunt-lips like a sandwich with his cock the meat, his mouth slobbering and sucking on the back of my neck. I began to pitch and heave, as he screamed, "Fuck! Fuck! Fuck!"

Mind you, the other two warriors in blue were not about to wait in line for us to finish fucking. My traffic cop, Hunko Kopecky, stood up and encircled the two of us with his massive coal-miner's arms, embracing us with deep emotion, rubbing his right hand down Sanchez's broad back and ass and his left hand down mine, until finally both hands were working together at the point of genital entry, kneading Sanchez's balls, stimulating his undershaft, tickling and massaging my clitoris, finger-fucking the two of us.

"Christ!" Kopecky exclaimed, "it's the best of both worlds!"

I was concerned about young Officer Cooke. Where could I fit him in? For that matter, where could I put Kopecky? And what about O'Leary once he fully revived? I shouldn't have concerned myself. The boys were wonderful. They had their own system. They took care of everything. Sanchez brought me down gently to the thickly carpeted floor. Then, Kopecky sixty-nined it, his thick Polish sausage of a cock in my salivating mouth, his mouth and tongue like warm lotion spreading onto my cunt and Sanchez's invading cock, touching all the sensitive points, stimulating us as it reassured us that we were not alone .

Officer Cooke by now had his golden cock in my hair and was fucking me there. He told me later that my hair was like warm honey to him; he just couldn't help himself, it was the next best thing to my bush, and my bush was totally occupied. I loved having my hair fucked, if for no other reason than I loved the fact it turned him on. But everyone didn't agree, and what happened next almost ended in tragedy.

O'Leary, fully revived from his impromptu smack on the head, took one look around, observed the practically pornographic proceedings, saw that I was more than occupied, saw Cooke's situation with my hair, and misunderstood. Worse, he tried to be fatherly. He said to Cooke, "Don't worry, boy, I'll take care of you," and right then and there went down on him, lifting his prick out of the nest of my hair, and popping it into his mouth with a ravenous hunger. For one brief shining moment, Officer Cooke cradled O'Leary's head tenderly and guided him up and down on his big, golden cylinder until, with a start, he realized he wasn't getting full, emotional satisfaction. Then, I guess he must have realized where he was and what he was doing, and something must have snapped inside him. He began to smash Captain O'Leary in the head with his fists, shouting, "Cocksucker!" "Cocksucker!"

Personally, I didn't care. As far as I was concerned, O'Leary had been one terrific fuck, and I knew that he was probably just turned on by beautiful young golden-skinned, honey-haired people of either sex, like me and Officer Cooke. It wasn't his fault we were both so yummy. Besides, I knew that sooner or later Cooke and I would end up, well, cooking together. The truth is, the sight of two men making it, like anything sexual, only makes the world a safer place for extramarital sex between men and women, which for the most part still has a bad rep. My philosophy is, anything goes—why not?—but O'Leary and Cooke were slugging it out, both men with full erections, their balls swinging in their hairy sacs, with me viewing this heavyweight fight through the spread-apart legs of Officer Kopecky.

He and Sanchez had not stopped fucking me for a minute. They knew a good thing when they had it. Both of their swollen pricks were about to burst their hot seed into my velvet openings. My mouth was making slurping sounds in response to Kopecky's cock, which seemed to grow bigger and bigger. Then, almost without warning, the dam burst. I pitched and heaved as the two men inside me ejaculated at once, their orgasms seizing and releasing me, come spilling out over the raw, pink flesh of my cunt, over my porcelain white teeth, down between the gorge that separates my breasts until it met the sperm that had leaked out of my vaginal paradise.

That's when I knew something was wrong. I had not come. Not one tiny orgasm. For a moment I found myself in a state of sheer panic. Was I frigid? Was I a closet lesbian? Had I allowed myself to be turned into a fucking machine? What could the matter be? I wanted

91

to throw myself out the window, I felt so dead and useless. Then, it hit me. I knew. Under ordinary circumstances, I could have spent two weeks holed up with any one of these guys. They were all raunchy and terrific: O'Leary, so pure and fatherly in his desires, Sanchez the great Latin hunk, one-hundred-percent man, Kopecky, crazy to the death about every inch of my golden skin. But on this particular day I knew that none of them mattered. Not really. I wanted Officer Cooke. I lusted for his soul. He was part of me, and I of him. I knew it the minute I saw him. He was my spiritual twin. Oh sure, maybe if we got to know each other we'd find out we had different politics and different tastes in music, food, and summer sports; maybe he'd turn out to be a fucked-up slob, but that was the beauty of the moment: all we had to go on was the ecstatic fact that we were turned on by each other's magnificent bodies. There was passion here. How often does that happen with any two people, ever?

Thank God both of my studs came just at the moment I was getting ready to say, "Excuse me, boys." Like I said, there were thick globs of come running down my cunt, matting my bush. And at the other end was too much come for me to swallow. Kopecky had ejaculated in my mouth with such violence I thought his raw, vibrating pork prod would dislocate my jaw, but I held on with my strong cheek and mouth muscles, and I survived. His vanilla sperm was running out over my lips and down my chin. I realized I needed that sperm as a lubricant for Mr. Cooke before it dried, so I quickly unharnessed both magnificent members, kissed them both, one after the other, on their ultra-sensitive glans, and stopped the fight between O'Leary and Cooke.

I was absolutely furious with O'Leary. "You had yours, O'Leary," I shouted. "Why don't you give the kid a chance?"

O'Leary looked stricken. "I thought everybody liked a little head. What's wrong with that?"

"Cock-sucking fag!" Cooke shouted back. He looked like such an adorable little boy; hurt, vulnerable, in the throes of puberty, I wanted to reassure him as fast as possible. Fighting took too much energy, and besides, my sperm lubricant was drying fast.

"No, no, no," I implored Officer Cooke. "O'Leary's no fag. He's a great... a great... a great policeman! And a terrific fuck! Can you blame any man or woman who'd want to put their hungry mouth all over your gorgeous bod? Don't you know you're a fuckin' god?"

His eyes softened, and finally, for the first time, he looked straight into my eyes. I thought my knees would buckle, and I'd fall on the floor. I gathered up all the still-wet sperm I could, most of it still inside my mouth and cunt, and I lavished it on Cooke's chiseled erection. He looked like a Greek statue of a warrior, except those ancient statues never dared to have a full-scale erection.

As for myself, here was a first. I was beyond mere sex. I just wanted to hold him, to embrace him, to place as much of my skin next to his as possible, to melt into him, to merge the two sides of our twin selves into one splendid, magnificent whole, no pun intended. I stood on my tiptoes, spread my legs a little, and lowered myself onto his sculptured erection, or should I say, "perfection"?

For the first time that day I felt like a truly happy human being. Officer Cooke was so happy, too. Let's face it, I did a lot more for his warrior's ego than Captain O'Leary, who complimented him, but could never complete him.

"Who are you?" whispered my guardian angel, my bronzed and glowing seraphim.

"Don't talk," I pleaded. I didn't want to know anything about him; it might have spoiled the perfection of the moment. I guided him to the floor, where we lay on our sides, oblivious to the others, fondling each other's necks and arms, stroking our cheeks and noses, while Sanchez and Kopecky dozed on their backs.

Cooke finally spoke. "I don't want to ejaculate," he said, "because when I do, it will be over. I'll never see you again."

"Oh, we'll meet again," I said casually, knowing in my heart it wasn't true.

"No," he said. "I can only fuck a fantasy. You see, I've got a wife and four kids, and when I find out who you are, and what you like for breakfast, and what you do for a living, and who your boss is, then you'd become a person, and I'd have to get serious and join the real-life twentieth century, and the dream would be over."

I started to cry. "We're the same person!" I exclaimed. "When I see someone as perfect as you, I don't want to know who you are. You shouldn't have told me about your wife. Already I'm feeling guilty. Oh please, Officer Cooke, let's fuck our brains out and hope we're dead when it's over with."

And so we fucked our brains out and the statues came alive. The warrior and the fantasy. I watched the well-practiced muscles of my cooze holding him hard, sucking his stout pole, feeling to my bones the bridge of flesh that joined us, and the life-giving energies flowing through it. This was more than cock and cunt. He could have been a woman for all I cared. He was like no one I'd ever met. There was an energy between us, instant, automatic, electric, psychic, that made me feel I was truly part of the whole human race. We were two in one flesh. There was nothing to think about. It just was. And so we rode, skin to skin, our inner arms pressed together, our hands clasped, our nipples joined like electrodes, our navels sucking out the space between them, our thighs melting into one tremendous bond of flesh and blood and bone. Did we come? I guess we did.

I don't remember. I was lost in him. What made him so special, I don't know. I never plan these things. I don't go after people. They just come to me, like all good things.

And all good things also come to an end. The door that was supposedly locked opened suddenly, and there stood a man of about forty-five in a gray business suit, a bowler hat, an umbrella, a briefcase, and a watch fob. O'Leary gasped. Sanchez and Kopecky woke up with a start and stared in disbelief. Cooke slowly came out of his ecstasy.

The man in the bowler hat clearly did not look pleased. He reached into his gray flannel jacket, pulled out a small service revolver, and waved it at us. "Get on the floor. All of you. On your backs. On your backs. Get in a line. Get in a line." We did as ordered.

O'Leary blurted out, "Commissioner Cahill, I can explain!"

"Shut up, O'Leary!" said the man in the bowler hat. "I should have you fired. I should have you all fired. Not only that, I should release this information to the press." We were all lying on the floor on our backs, as ordered, except that O'Leary was unable to keep his big mouth shut. "Commissioner, what do you want?" he kept asking. And the Commissioner kept telling him to shut up.

Then, an amazing thing happened. First, Commissioner Cahill checked to see that the door was locked. Then, he calmly took off his bowler hat, put down his briefcase and his umbrella, and took off his clothes, all of them. He was a little man, no more than five feet four, with a tough, wiry body that looked like he worked out at the gym every day. He still had his revolver in hand when he had finished undressing. And no erection whatsoever.

Was he going to massacre us? Such things were not impossible or unknown. I still can't believe what happened. Commissioner Cahill walked over to us, took his cock in his hand, and released a stream of pale gold champagne, back and forth, over all of us. Steamy, hot piss. He flooded all of us. His flow was like that of a horse, strong, steady, gushing out at a rapid rate like a fire extinguisher. And he was laughing! I tried to look up to get a clearer view of what the man was doing and got a gusher right in my face!

When he had finished urinating he was still laughing. Then, he ordered everyone up. "Up, up!" he cried. Then, he lay down on the floor on the wet carpet. "Now you piss on me," he ordered, still waving the gun. Since all the men had recently ejaculated, they were all ready to piss, and frankly, couldn't wait to get back at Commissioner Cahill. Needless to say, I felt the same way.

"Wait!" the Commissioner cried. Then he ordered me to stand over his face and to direct my stream into his mouth. "Do as I say," the Commissiioner ordered, "or I'll have you all thrown into jail, and don't think I won't."

Again, Captain O'Leary was the loud-mouth. "But you . . ." he started to say.

Cahill was indignant. "But I what? No one would believe you if you told them about all this pissing business. Besides, I'm having your carpet replaced tomorrow, so shut up and don't worry about it."

So, as ordered, we began to piss, and the Commissioner started gurgling with glee. I shot a stream of glittering piss, aiming for his open mouth. The men spewed forth their fountains of frothy amber liquid. Cahill slurped up as much of my sparkling ginger ale as he could while he slathered the foamy streams from the guys all over his body like it was the finest coconut oil. We stood watching in fascination while he grew an erection that got so red and stiff it threatened to pop out of its jacket of flesh. He used the urine to lubricate his prick. With one hand he massaged his balls and the base of his cock; with his other hand he stroked his plum-colored glans with the inside of his palm, around and around, working toward orgasm.

He didn't have long to wait. Within seconds, a jet column of white liquid spurted straight into the air, arced, and came down on his face, lacquering his lips with melted pearls. He gobbled the stuff up like it was going out of style. And then, he lay there like an infant, happy and at peace. Finally, he spoke. "I'm going to make sure you guys get bonuses. You're really great under fire." Then he looked at me and it finally dawned on him I wasn't one of the guys. His come-covered face grew beet-red. "Are you a cop?" he asked meekly.

O'Leary butted in. "No, sir, she was arrested this afternoon for public nudity. . . ."

I couldn't believe it! O'Leary, who had been such a fantastic lay when I needed his warmth and attention, was now ready to sell me down the river! The Commisssioner had more sense. He could tell by looking at that row of tired and worn-out penises that I had done my civic duty. He said, "Case dismissed, O'Leary." Then, looking at me with the most soulful blue eyes, he said, "You can go home, young lady, provided you're dressed."

"But sir . . ." O'Leary objected.

The Commissioner was adamant. "Did you hear what I said, O'Leary?"

"Yessir," said O'Leary.

"There's a shower in your bathroom, isn't there, O'Leary?"

"Yessir."

"Alright, one at a time, go wash yourselves off. Little lady, you be first," the Commissioner said.

"Thank you for everything," I replied, kissing him on the top of his head.

"You're welcome," he said, just as polite as could be. "There's no sense in acting like animals, men. That's what the criminal underclasses in this city are looking for us to do," he continued. "Officer Sanchez, enough of this; there's a lady present."

"Enough of what, sir?" Sanchez replied.

"Cover yourself," Cahill remonstrated.

"Yessir," said Sanchez and the other two one-time sexual gods who had now been brought back down to earth.

"Like I say, O'Leary," the Commissioner continued, reaching for his shorts out of modesty, "I'll have your carpet replaced. If anyone asks you how it got so dirty, tell them a couple of prisoners staged a demonstration."

"Yessir," O'Leary dutifully replied.

Throughout all this, I never looked back at my glorious Officer Cooke. I guess he was but a moment out of time, as they say. A wonderful dream. But when it's over you can't go back to the dream again. It was magnificent. But it was over. The dream. Cooke. Kopecky. Even O'Leary. Yes, Sanchez. After all, how could I carry on an affair with four wonderful studs at a station house? The time had come to wake up. The time had come to get on with the rest of my life.

Chapter Six

I left the station house wih a clean record, a sore cunt, and an invitation to come back any time I felt a craving for "New York's finest." Before I departed, wearing the red-sequined "hooker's" dress with the slit up the leg that I had grown so fond of, plus a practically brand-new pair of black patent leather pumps they'd taken off a dead drag queen, Commissioner Cahill informed me that Muffie Free and Rod Peters had been spotted on their way to Rio. They were apparently terrified of the mob. The Commissioner predicted they'd be gone for a year. He also told me that my beloved Angelo O'Shaughnessy was laid up in traction at St. Vincent's Hospital with a couple of broken arms and legs following his jump from the Venus Production Studios. Commissioner Cahill was such a perfect gentleman; once I'd finished pissing on his face and he'd successfully jerked off, he never mentioned it again. We could have been a couple of nuns discussing the decline in religious observance. What class!

After kissing all the cops good-bye, I hitched a ride with Commissioner Cahill to Sheridan Square in the West Village, the nearest drop-off point to Muffie's apartment. I didn't want any of my many admirers, or, for that matter, informants of either the cops or the mob, to know where I was staying. I mean, with all those books on the Kennedy assassination, who can trust anybody, right?

But I was too late. By the time I'd schlepped to Muffie's address on Chambers Street, another little bomb had exploded. There were five fire trucks in front of what used to be Muffie's townhouse apartment. Black smoke rose hundreds of feet into the clear, blue October sky. I knew at once my toothpaste and lingerie were gone forever. But I have never been one to dwell on tragedy. Life is for living, even when you're twenty-two and don't know any foreign languages.

Thank God I was stacked and enjoyed the company of strangers. Thank God I knew that sex was a gift from God I know He wants us to pass on to others. At that tragic, smoke-filled moment, I resolved to get on with the next chapter of my life. The only thing I had going for me was Angelo. I had to find him and talk to him. St. Vincent's Hospital was only a few blocks away.

Fifteen minutes later, I was standing by his bedside in tears. Both of my beloved Angelo's legs and arms were in separate casts. He was in traction. Both his head and his torso, godlike and magnificent, were in perfect shape, thank God. "I tried to jump," he explained.

"But from the fourth story?" I said. I told him that Rod and Muffie were in South America, and that according to Commissioner Cahill, the Cafone Family of New Jersey wanted total control of the sex industry.

Thereupon followed an overlapping conversation of two people talking at each other, neither one listening. He was clearly upset by my incursion into the world of pornography and couldn't accept the fact that I had been conned into it.

"Diana, listen to me. Just because you've got a great little cunt doesn't mean you have to put in on the open market."

I tried to explain to him what had happened. "Angelo, it wasn't my fault. That blonde Swedish stud gave me a drink with some drug in it."

Angelo didn't buy any of it.

"Angelo, it's true," I insisted. "One minute I was politely saying hello, the next I was fucking on camera, and what's worse—Oh, Angelo, it was wonderful. I was impaled on a shaft of light and when I looked into his eyes, it was like looking through a telescope at the Milky Way. I was on a voyage to outer space, and every cell of my body was having an orgasm. Oh, Angelo, forgive me, sometimes I'm so weak."

"You're not weak," he said, "you were drugged."

"Oh, Angelo," I blurted out, "I just want to be a model. I don't know where to go next."

"First thing," he said, just make sure you don't have porn film footage of you lying around, because I've got news for you, kid. In this tight-assed Establishment world of ours, there's a double standard. If you get known as a porn star, drugged or not, the Moral Majority types will make sure that you're permanently kept out of television and movies."

That's when it hit me like a thunderbolt— the irony of our conversation. "But *you're* a porn star," I blurted out.

"And I'm going to stay a porn star forever, I'm afraid. Oh, Diana, I want so much more for you."

Angelo, my angel. Here he was in so much pain and thinking only of me. I kissed the dear man gently on all four casts, as silly as that may sound. I just pretended they where four big white erections. Yes, for the moment I forgot about my self-centered young being and the boring fact that I was homeless and penniless in New York City, a trivial matter compared with the plight of poor Angelo. Here he was, a porn star, against his will now immobilized in a dark, semi-private room for as long as six weeks. I knew I had to cheer him up the best way I knew how. With Tender Loving Care, the best healing force in the whole wide world.

I pulled the curtains around the bed and ran my fingers through the thick matted hair on his broad chest. I drank in his kisses. The tears of gratitude in his soulful eyes glittered like precious diamonds.

"Diana, Diana, you're the only one who cares for me."

"Oh, Angelo, I do care for you, more than you could possibly know. I'm so sorry about what happened. I'll do do whatever I can for you."

"Don't stop," he begged. "Please continue what you started. I'm sorry I can't reciprocate very well. As you can see, my arms are broken."

"Is your cock broken, too?" I asked teasingly.

"I'm not sure. You'll have to investigate," he responded.

I investigated, as he had suggested. My goodness, his cock was as hard as a rock, and the head was as purple as a ripe plum ready to burst through its skin. I lowered my moist warm lips and tongue onto his glans, coating it with glistening saliva, which caused him to sigh a little. When I looked up he was actually smiling. That's when I knew I was on the right track—at which point we were rudely interrupted by a very well-padded nurse with a clipboard.

"What's going on here?" she asked sternly, adding—unnecessarily, I thought—"What do you think you're ing, young lady?"

I was so embarrassed, I stood there dumbfounded. She looked like a disapproving nun. Beavertown had been full of them; I knew that look well. Her eyes were as ice-blue as the iceberg that sank the *Titanic*. What could I say? "Let me see that," she said, meaning my friend Mr. O'Shaughnessy's rampant, oversized cock.

"What?" I said, playing dumb, hoping she'd crawl back into her cave.

"That!" she said, pointing at Angelo's cock for added emphasis.

"It's nothing," I said.

"Thanks a lot," responded Angelo. The ice-blue nurse looked at me sternly. "What were you doing with that?"

I thought to myself, what the hell, the worst that could happen to me is end up in another sexy precinct house. So I answered her straight on. "I was giving him head," I said.

"You cheap little slut," she said, looking at me with dagger eyes. "You foul-mouthed little whore."

"You really have a mouth yourself," I said. I wasn't going to take any shit from her. "Damn right," she answered, referring to her mouth. Then, she did what I have since learned all competitive people do; they stop talking and act. Boy, did she act! She brushed me aside like a piece of trash, took Angelo's thick staff of life in her hand, and began to flick the head of his penis with the tip of her well practiced tongue, occasionally rimming it around its swollen edge. Then, unbelievably, considering her profession, or maybe I misjudged her actual profession, she somehow, without

102

saying a word, hoisted herself onto the bed, and, without touching any of his casts, lowered herself onto him in a sixty-nine position, with her pelvis on top of his face.

"Diana, forgive me, I can't help it! She's delicious!" Angelo wailed.

"Pull down my panties," the woman ordered.

"Are you talking to me?" I said, being just as snotty as I could manage.

"Who do you think I'm talking to, you dumb little cunt?" she said.

I was beginning to be very confused; the nun had disappeared, and in her place was a full-fledged Nazi. But I did as she had ordered. And I was glad I did. From behind, and what a behind, milk-glass cheeks with pale blue veins, her velvet cunt hung down. And I mean hung, its open pink gash framed by a lion's mane of thick blonde fur. It was so big I wanted to grab it in both hands and help Angelo tongue her. On the other hand, I felt cheated that this mean-sounding nurse had appropriated for herself the one sexual act I know how to do especially well, which is give great head. The entire Beavertown football team never complained once for three years running, and now here was this, this nurse showing me how to flic Angelo's Bic.

I had to admit that Miss Sourpuss was more accomplished than I was; it must have been her medical training. She knew how to stimulate the delicate ridge of flesh on the underside of the cock; she knew the right pressure points around the thick veins that entwined around it; she knew how to maintain and release pressure at the base of the muscular root where it joined the torso trunk. Ignoramus that I was, I lusted for Angelo, who was breathing more deeply than I could remember. I lusted and I was insanely jealous. But I had a strategy figured out; I decided that she couldn't deep-throat him and suck his balls at the same time. I went for the balls, those choice nuts nestled in their ample sac between the tops of Angelo's pink, golden-haired thighs. I lifted them gently and eased them as deftly as I could into my salivating mouth. Both wouldn't fit at once, so I decided to fondle one and suck the other, while I stroked the little bridge of flesh between his testicles and his anus with the top of my fingernail. Angelo, much to my satisfaction and delight, wafted into a different place altogether from than the harsh reality of the hospital room. He oohed and aahed, shivered and moaned, and then began to shudder. I took both succulent testicles in my eager hands and gently squeezed them, as the nasty nurse kept greedily gliding her fat lips and overachieving tongue over his plump and swollen member. Finally, the dam burst, and he shot such a huge load of honeyed sperm into Florence Nightingale's mouth that some of it went down the wrong pipe and she started gagging, and had to get off Angelo as quickly as possible and run to the ladies' room with her pink panties down around her ankles, while I stood there more than a little amused.

"Who was that?" I asked Angelo.

"Don't look a gift horse in the mouth," he answered cryptically.

"What about looking in her cunt?" I teased.

"I didn't look in her cunt," he said. "I was blinded by her cunt. My face was buried in her cunt. I had my tongue wrapped around her clit and my lower lip wedged about three inches into her private game preserve. And I've got news for you—it was raining sweet nectar on the wild animals."

So it was. Angelo's handsome face was glistening from her abundant cunt-juices. It annoyed me that he could excite a relative stranger more than me. Then I had to remind myself that I had known him less than twenty-four hours. But what good did that do? I knew I was already in love with him. I was raging jealous that my beloved cab driver with the copper-haired chest had inspired such a hatchet-faced nurse to such absolute bravado. Worse, she had brought him off without once smiling or giving her name. In a word, I felt like a total outsider to the man I loved most in the world. But, typically, I pretended not to care about his stickily gleaming face as I hungrily lapped up the last delicious drops of come on his relaxed cock.

Then, something even more terrible than the nurse happened. This new episode was to be my worst trial yet. As I was happily cleaning off Angelo's cock with my tongue, a doctor entered our little makeshift tent—another stranger, this one no taller than Napoleon. He introduced himself as Dr. Osgood. He had an efficient manner and a clipped "old money" voice with just the hint of a stammer. His face was lean and perfectly chiseled, with taut hollow cheeks as tight as a drum, and sunken blue eyes with hooded lids. His fingers were chiseled, too, each one long, sensitive, and perfectly formed, no doubt ideal for probing problem spots.

Dr. Osgood. Scrubbed and chiseled. And miniature. I wondered if his cock were miniature, too, and how it would feel to fuck him.

"Yes, Doctor," said Angelo, breaking the spell.

"Just checking your casts," said Dr. Osgood.

"Casts?" replied Angelo. In that case, you must meet my landing lady, Diana Hunt, a young model who's just arrived in New York."

With that, Dr. Osgood looked at me like we were in the middle of having sex. I resented that. I mean, enough is enough. I don't get intimate with every man I meet. Dr. Osgood's green eyes were full of wit and malice. I could see he was a complete egomaniac. He was also completely in charge of the situation, any situation.

"Young woman, I came here because there's a case of East Indian flu galloping through these hallowed halls. Your gentleman friend is clearly incapacitated already and will be given the flu shots as a matter of course. As for you, I've got to examine you before you will be allowed to leave the premises. Please take off your dress immediately, so I can begin the examination."

"What?" I gasped. But because this man had made me so nervous, my brain and fingers were not in syncopation and I had already begun to undress before I realized I was not in full agreement with such a plan.

"Oh my God! What a pair!" exclaimed Dr. Osgood. I could only assume he was referring to my generous and well-defined breasts, which were in full view now that my red-sequined dress was accidentally on the floor. "My God, what nipples!" he said, stroking them. "They're so soft and full, like little nose cones stuck onto the end of those bouyant breasts. Excuse me, I have to check your mammary tissue to make sure you don't have the plague as well." And with that, the good doctor was sucking feverishly on my tits.

He was so cultured-looking I could feel myself beginning to lubricate from the sheer intensity of this man. Then he came up for air. "Turn around," he ordered. I did as I was told, not wishing to collapse from a rare disease at my young and tender age. Then, suddenly, those chiseled fingers were kneading my breasts, and I felt his hot breath on the back of my neck. "Have I got the East Indian flu?" I gasped.

"I don't know yet; your breasts seem to be free of it, but I'm not absolutely certain yet."

"When will you be certain?" I asked.

"Please take off your panties," he said. "I have to examine your lower extremities."

Again, I did as ordered. When I turned around to lay my panties on the back of the chair, I had quite a surprise waiting for me. Dr. Osgood was standing there, shirt unbuttoned, and pants down. He was suffering not so much from the East Indian flu as from extreme sexual excitement. His normal-sized and perfectly formed penis was standing rigid, like an eighteen-year-old boy's, against the steely muscles of his torso. His nipples, tiny

106

and taut, like two small erasers, held strange sexual excitement.

Maybe good things do come in small packages, after all. This little man's will to power was stronger than any man's I had met so far. It made him extremely sexy. I have discovered that no matter how well-endowed a man is with cock, muscles, and brains, no man is really sexy until he is consumed with desire for an individual woman. This is why men are generally sexier than horses, who are afflicted with mere sexual appetite and who have never known desire.

Needless to say, standing there with my luxurious coral cunt-lips hanging out of the front of me, crowned with my honey-gold bush, I knew I was one terrific handful, mouthful, you name it, of prime fuck-flesh, and I was having a tremendous conflict. "Angelo," I cried out. "I love you so much. What am I to do, let this man rape me?"

"He won't rape you," Angelo said, looking so kindly and benevolent, "he just wants to examine you."

"Oh, Angelo," I cried, "please hold my hand."

"Turn around and face him," ordered Dr. Osgood in his most masterful and masculine tones. Again, I did as I was told. Again, the tough, chiseled, muscular fingers rubbing against my breasts, stroking my nipples, against my will making me grow hot and excited, especially as I looked at my cherubic tough guy, Angelo. Again, the hunger of the doctor's hot breath on my neck. I could feel my cunt beginning to grow warm from all the attention. Dr. Osgood, whoever he was, certainly had what is known as the classic bedside manner.

"Oh, Angelo," I cried again, "I'm so afraid."

"Don't worry, he's just examining you, I think." Then he grew alarmed. "Hey, Doc, you *are* just examining her, aren't you?"

Dr. Osgood's response was to lay his palm on Angelo's forehead, as if feeling for his temperature. "You're much

107

too hot," he decided. Within thirty seconds, he'd extracted a little white pill from his medical bag and made Angelo swallow it.

In the wink of an eye, Angelo was asleep. "Why did you do that?" I protested.

"Too much excitement for a man in his condition; it's wearing him out," said Dr. Osgood. "But don't worry," he continued, "he'll be awake again in a few minutes."

The next thing I knew, Dr. Osgood's right hand was between my legs, exploring my cunt, playfully squeezing it, kneading it, stroking my bush. "I can't stand it! I can't stand it!" he cried huskily.

"What's wrong?" I squealed, fearful that he had uncovered some grave disease.

"It's you. It's you," he answered, his hands wet from my cunt-juice. My furrows, my petals were soft and glossy—oh God, I couldn't help myself. He was so forceful. "What's wrong with me," I implored him. What he was doing hardly seemed like a medical examination. As a matter of fact, his behavior seemed all too familiar. "Dr. Osgood," I finally begged, "just what do you think you're doing?"

"There's something wrong," he said curtly. "I've got to go in."

"Go in?" I said, almost in a state of shock.

"Yes," he said, "I've got to do an exploratory."

"An exploratory what?" I gasped.

"An exploratory exploration, what else?" he explained, almost.

"Dr. Osgood," I said, in tears, "you're not making any sense. Don't you want to examine me further?"

His tone was cold. "What do you think I've been doing?"

"Doctor," I said, "I'm getting nervous. What are your intentions? Are you going to operate on me or what?"

"Or what," he replied. And with that remark, he entered me without warning, from behind, sexually, genitally.

He was cold and brutal, without foreplay, without tenderness. He just shoved his glistening tool into me. It might as well have been a screwdriver or a straight razor. I felt his invading presence in every pore of my being. He was overpowering, a barbaric intruder, a conquering Ghengis Khan. He had no sensitivity of any kind. I could feel his driving intent to dominate as he cleaved into my vaginal depths.

I kept telling myself I was not about to surrender to any man but my beloved Angelo, now fast asleep, but deep down, that was a lie. Deep down, I knew this mad physician, all muscle and grit, could not help himself, so great was my allure. It was without doubt a very sexy situation.

"Dr. Osgood," I screamed out of desperation, "have I got the flu?"

"I don't know," he answered, riding into me, rocking me, pumping me, feverish and obsessed, until finally his reserve broke down and he began to grunt, "Cunt, cunt, cunt, Christ! what a cunt!"

"Dr. Osgood," I sputtered, "tell me if I'm being raped?"

He didn't answer me. He had both hands full, cradling my pussy bush, his thumb on my clitoris. He was holding the whole machinery, my cunt, his cock, massaging them from the outside, finger-fucking me whenever he could find an opening. Within minutes, I felt him begin to swell and I knew he was about to come, which he did, like a machine gun, the white bullets shattering upon impact, dripping through my bush and down my legs.

At last, Dr. Osgood spoke up. Again, not a shred of warmth or humanity, but intensely sexy, the way a Nazi U-Boat commander is sexy. "Young lady," he said, "clean yourself up."

"Doctor," I pleaded wih him for the last time, "please tell me, have I got the East Indian flu?"

"No no," he said, "you're as healthy as a horse. Your breasts are in perfect condition and your genitalia work perfectly. In short, you're a fine patient. Thank you very much for your cooperation."

I was so relieved I burst into tears and hugged him like a long-lost relative. "Oh, Dr. Osgood," I sobbed, "I've been so confused since I arrived in New York. Nothing is quite what I expected."

He kissed me tenderly on the forehead, but pulled away from my embrace. "You're a very nice girl," he said, "very nice."

I couldn't stop sobbing. "Oh, Doctor," I cried, "don't you have anyone who understands you? Don't you have someone to talk to? I can feel your broken heart."

Oops. Wrong move. I saw the man flinch. I had clearly overstepped my bounds. Without saying a word, without looking at me, Dr. Osgood put his shirt and pants back on. He readjusted his tie, found his shoes, and grabbed his coat. Then, without turning around, he walked out of the room.

I looked at Angelo, who was just coming out of a deep sleep induced by Dr. Osgood's medicine. "Oh, Angelo, I cried, "I know what Dr. Osgood's problem is ..."

"Who?" said the groggy Angelo.

"Dr. Osgood," I explained. "He's short and he thinks I'd reject him. If men like that only knew what a turn-on their bruised egos are."

"Where am I?" said Angelo, not understanding a word I'd said.

"Angelo, Angelo, I'm so glad you're back. Never mind. It's not important."

"What's not important, you gorgeous thing?" he said.

"Bruised egos," I replied.

"Is my ego bruised, you sensational fuck?" he said, just as sweet as can be.

"You?" I laughed. "Your soul is bruised, just like me. Down deep we know we're both idiots. Kids, but idiots just the same. We're both such gorgeous specimens, so oversexed, it's ridiculous. But you know something,

110

Angelo, when push comes to shove, there's something called the human heart, and I guess I'm stuck with one. How about you?"

"Come here," he said, and I obeyed. He kissed me on the top of my nose. "I adore you," he said.

"Angelo, I'm going to get a job, any job, as a waitress, at P.J. Clarke's or someplace snazzy, until I can figure out how to break into modeling, okay?"

"Okay," he said.

I didn't want to tell him about the explosion at Muffie's apartment; he had enough to worry about. "Angelo, I don't have to stay at your place or anyone else's. I've got to find a place of my own, at least for now. As much as I love you, Angelo, I know I've got to travel my own road, at least for a while. I know I've got some kind of destiny that has to do with my career. I don't know what it is, yet, but I've got to find out. Okay?"

"Okay," he said.

"I'll come visit you every day, Angelo," I said.

"You can come any time you want," he said, looking at my thick blonde bush of pussy hair.

"I'll give you the attention you need, Angelo," I said.

"You give great attention, pussy-face."

"Meeow," I purred, and for the next hour made Angelo O'Shaughnessy a happier man than he had been the hour before. Like I always say, it's important to visit the sick.

Chapter Seven

When I emerged from the hospital after my mission of mercy, there it was again, that same black limousine as big as a hearse, that had been parked outside the Venus Production Studios just before the Big Bang. My heart, to put it plainly, thudded like a foul ball in a Yankees game. Was my beloved Angelo on the mob's hit list? Was the underground planning to blow up St. Vincent's Hospital? Was nothing sacred?

Quickly, I opened my shoulder bag to ferret out my dark glasses, so that I could, if possible, escape unnoticed quickly, although I was understandably terrified that my super-tight red-sequined shift with the slit up the leg would give me away.

It did. What followed was worse than a mugging. From out of the cavernous hearselike limousine with its dark windows emerged three burly bully-boys in dark suits and dark glasses, who grabbed me and whisked me into the back seat of the car, muttering, "Keep calm, we're not going to hurt you," "Easy now," and, "Christ, Louie, what a pair!"

"Who are you?" I demanded to know, as one of them, an Arabic-looking gentleman, smelling of cigar smoke, garlic, and first-class Scotch, planted his hard muscular mouth on mine and drank in kisses like he was dying of thirst. This, while the limousine bolted, lurched, and took off for parts unknown. Another thug, the one called

112

"Louie" shouted at my Arab, "Hey, Frankie, get off her! The Boss don't allow that!"

Frankie had no choice; he had angry hands pulling him off me, and I could feel a gun holster on somebody's chest.

Frankie sneered, "I ain't doing nothing." He sounded like a hood in an old Humphrey Bogart film.

The first one, Louie, was not satisfied. "The Boss says keep your hands off her, keep your mouth off her, and keep your cock in your underpants, understand? You wanna end up fucking fish in the bottom of the Hudson?"

With that, my Arabian stud with the Hoboken accent went into a sulk and remained that way for the rest of the trip. As for myself, after I'd wet my pants thinking I was going to be gang-raped or at least shot in the head, I summoned the courage to open my mouth. "What do you gentlemen want me to do?" I asked. Naturally, things being the way they are today, from the Holocaust to prison torture in South America, I had fantasies of being forced to go down on all three men in some deserted swamp and then being released naked in the streets of New York where I'd cause commotion and crisis and probably end up on David Susskind's talk show. I wasn't worried, not really. Men generally adored me, and I generally adored men. I mean, what else is there?

But these guys were playing it close to the vest. Their silence was deafening. They were clearly working for somebody else, "the Boss," whoever he was.

I couldn't see where we were going. The car windows were so dark, and, of course, I was sitting in the middle of the back seat. At one point, I sensed, correctly as it later turned out, that we were crossing the George Washington Bridge and were heading west into New Jersey. After a while, my panic subsided, I felt less confused, and began to look around the interior of the limousine. The back seat area was huge. As I later found out, the back seat itself was a convertible queen-size double bed. There was a fully stocked bar built into the back of the front seat. There was a small refrigerator stocked with the finest French wine, mixers, and all sorts of antipastos, from fava beans vinaigrette to stuffed artichoke hearts. There was a medium-sized television set, and a white telephone with a twenty-two-carat gold dial. I wondered how far I'd get if I tried to dial the police. Good old Arabian Frankie with the hot and torrid mouth slapped my hand down as I reached for the dial.

With that, I was beginning to be terrified. Kidnapping, I decided, is no joke. "Where are you taking me?" I finally blurted out.

"The Boss wants to see you," said Louie, right out of the side of his mouth, just like in the movies. Tough talk. But I knew the rock-bottom truth. Their Boss wanted me, and they hated me because they couldn't have me. I hoped against hope that the Boss was Chairman of the Board of General Motors, but I knew better. In any case, I decided to make the best of a bad situation and find the good in it for me. There had to be good in it for me. If not, I'd make it up.

With the orange sun slipping down into the deep purple sky of an October evening, we drove past what seemed to be tall wrought-iron gates manned by a swarthy gatekeeper in a tight brass-buttoned uniform up a winding drive flanked by parallel rows of ancient oak trees to the cobblestone courtyard of the biggest mansion I'd ever seen. It was something out of *Columbo*, a French chateau in the middle of New Jersey. Wow. The Humphrey Bogart hoods guarded me like an American hostage in Iran, but really, how much resistance was a girl like me ready to give them? I was hungry, had no money, and no place to go, no place to rest my weary blonde head. I sincerely hoped that the

Boss, wherever he was, had a well-stocked kitchen and a big warm bed. I was ready to treat my kidnapping as an adventure, provided somebody fed me and tucked me in.

But if I expected to be immediately introduced to the mysterious Lord of the Manor or given a private guided tour of the house and grounds, I was mistaken. Obviously, the "Boss" had other things in mind. I was led up the back staircase, which wound several stories upward through a stone tower to what must have been a servant's room under the eaves of the top floor of the mansion. The freshly painted pink and white room had recently been redecorated to appeal to a little girl's feminine fancy with tiny-flowered prints everywhere: pink rosebuds on the wallpaper, flounce pillows with white ruffles on the bed, and window seats under the three dormer windows. The wall-to-wall carpeting was rosebud pink, too, and most of the furniture had been painted an eggshell white. Getting back to reality, the goon squad hastily deposited me in this paradise for a suburban princess, then beat a hasty retreat to the back stairs, locking and bolting the back door of the room behind them.

As tired as I was, I was determined not to panic. I systematically began exploring every nook and cranny of my pretty little prison. I knew that sooner or later, the powers that had brought me there would make themselves known; I was curious to know the taste and sensibilities of my captors. Imagine my utter surprise when, quite by accident, I discovered what I had thought was a closet door, was an entrance to a spacious ultramodern dressing room with full-mirrored walls, which in turn led to a white marble bathroom, which I could see was equipped with a sunken marble tub. On the table in the dressing room was a perfumed envelope with one word written on it in pink: "Diana."

Quickly tearing it open, I read its dear contents: "My

115

goddess, my love: I hope everything fits. I will send for you later. P.S. Maria will give you your bath. Your greatest love, Lucchio."

My poorly educated mind was understandably reeling. Who was this daring and impetuous prince of the New Jersey suburbs? What Lothario was so enamored of a nobody like me that he would go to the trouble of kidnapping me, in other words, breaking the law and risking years in prison all because of an intense passion for some young woman he has never met? And people have dared to suggest there are no more heroes! And the wardrobe! Talk about being promised a rose garden! I opened the sliding doors of a closet that ran half the length of a good-sized suburban living room to discover three sizes of every particular item, obviously just in case my benefactor had erred on my exact size. Designer labels. Blouses. Skirts. Suits. All from Saks Fifth Avenue and Yves St. Laurent. There were cocktail dresses, evening gowns, underwear, rainwear, sportswear, shoes for every social activity imaginable. I had never seen such clothes, even on the richest women in Beavertown who went to New York twice a year for their wardrobe. What brilliance! What organization! What expense! And all for me!

The dressing table's many drawers and compartments held hundreds of dollars worth of consmetics, lipsticks and blushes in every imaginable shade from Desert Rose to Chinese Red to Heather Mauve. The shelves of the closets were stacked with thousands upon thousands of dollars of the world's most expensive perfumes, most of which I had only seen ads for in my old dog-eared *Vogues* and *Harper's Bazaars*, which I had stolen from my family dentist's waiting room.

While I was smelling Chanel No. 5 for the very first time, I heard the sound of a key in a lock outside in the bedroom.

When I turned around to investigate, there she was. Maria. Maria who was supposed to give me a bath.

Lucchio's Maria. My Maria in the maid's uniform, the gray silk dress with the white starched collar, with the little white apron and the little white ruffles. Maria. French, of course. No more than five feet tall, her sleek black hair cut short and urchinlike, her large expressive eyes like black coals ready to ignite, her tiny hands quicksilver in their fast, precise movements, her breasts larger than one would expect in such a tiny, perfectly formed specimen. She stood there, quiet and pensive, as I unashamedly drank her in, unable to fight my overpowering fantasies, one of which was that her pubic hair was as black and thick and shining as the hair on her head.

Another fantasy was a question: were her nipples as dark as cinnamon or were they pale like milk-fed veal? What was her ass like? Was it tiny, a cheek for each hand, or was her ass broad and generous, big enough to bury my face in? Her gray silk skirt covered too much flesh; it was too full, entirely too chaste. Something would have to be done.

Then, she spoke. Her voice was extraordinary, husky and feathery at the same time, like a little girl with a cold. I could not control the chill of sheer excitement that slashed through my gut like ice-water. I could not suppress the feelings of fear that gripped me: would this black-eyed angel reject me if I dared make a pass? Worse, would she imagine I was some kind of pervert from New York and run downstairs in disgust and loathing? As I said, she had spoken to me, but, shame, shame, I was so caught up in the mere sound of her voice that I did not hear her words. I had no choice but to beg her to repeat herself.

"I hope you won't be offended," I heard myself saying, "but could you please repeat what you just said?" Was this love at first sight or what? I wasn't like my Rio-bound Muffie Free. I had never really been into women, not really, but this little third-floor maid, whatever, whoever, she was, this delectable tidbit, I wanted her, and my desires, upon first sight, were already out of control.

Maria smiled a knowing smile, as if she'd run into women like me before. I was mortified. I wanted her to think I was unusual, but there was no way. I was clearly just another libido out of control. "How this poor thing must suffer from the likes of me," I thought, and imagine, her only possible crime was having a pussy ripe with succulent juices, mysterious in its perfect plumpness, its perfumed sensuality, its . . . but, wait, I had never seen her pussy! I had seen nothing but a gray silk skirt!

I was so ashamed, I wanted to bolt past her and hide myself under the bed where no one could see the lust in my eyes. But, no, it was worse than lust; surely I must be going mad! The blood drained from my face. I was caught, and we both knew it.

But she, ever the savior, and so unutterably dear, saved my life. Maria. She took responsibility for the situation with such straightforward courage my knees buckled, and I began to weep out of gratitude. She said simply, without blinking, without wavering, "Now I have to give you your bath. Take off your clothes, go into the bathroom, and get into the sunken tub."

The sunken tub? Was it filled? I turned around to look, and, to my amazement, saw that the white marble tub, surrounded on three sides by potted orchids and begonias, was three-quarters full. When I tested the temperature of the water with my forefinger, I found it was very warm, but not a bit hot.

Maria repeated her command. "Take off your clothes." Then, she paused, as if she were hesitating about something, then she whispered my name, "Diana," in her sexy French accent.

I was overwhelmed. I wanted to immediately contact God, if that were possible, to tell Him I had surrendered my immortal soul to His most perfect creature. And so

118

I did. Surrender, that is. I took off my clothes, slipping
out of my red-sequined dress and black patent-leather
shoes, terrified she would think my breasts were too
big and too unmanageable, or that my ass rode too
high, or that my bush was too thick, and that the lips
of my outer labia were too visible when I walked. I
sometimes feel that I'm entirely too sexual, and that the
more finely chiseled types of both sexes take one look at
me and turn away the way an ordinary person might
find a filet mignon slathered with oysters and heaped
with caviar and mushrooms too much of a good thing.

Maria seemed not to notice. She just stared ahead.
She was so magnificently well-bred, obviously a perfect
lady. I felt so gross, so indelicate, that if I had followed
my own instincts, I would have jumped out the window.
Fortunately, it was locked.

But there was no time to think about being in prison.
Maria issued her next order. "Get into the tub." Again,
the unexpected hesitation and the whispering of my
name. "Diana."

Not wishing to cause her the slightest displeasure
whatsoever, I got into the sunken tub, as ordered, knowing that when I stepped down into the tub, she would
be able to see my snatch from behind—if she looked. I
said a silent prayer her eyesight was twenty-twenty. But
when I actually lifted my leg to take the first step into
the tropical water, I had a sudden attack of that disease
known as Middle Class—I realized that my gold-furred,
crimson-tinged gash might possibly be construed as in-
decent by such a perfectly behaved and well-brought-up
young Frenchwoman. But I had no choice. After all, she
was backed up by guns. As I stepped down into the tub,
I felt the kiss of the surrounding air on the tips of my
pubic hairs. I deliberately and perversely held my leg
up for the briefest moment, as if in some mysterious way
my cunt-lips could whisper, "I love you," across the cold
white tiles of the bathroom.

But for the moment, at least, there was no response. I sank down into the warm-as-toast water of the tub and turned around so that Maria could see my young and delicious breasts bobbing in front of me. I mean, I hate to brag, but I decided that if there was even an outside chance that this angel of mercy could possibly respond to a terrific pair of tits, I was going to make sure she was given the chance. We looked at each other across the water. Nothing. I figured that she was strictly into men and the missionary position, that the only person she really wanted was a dentist in the suburbs, a station wagon, and two point five kids. Somehow, imperceptibly, I was beginning to hate the woman.

But Christmas came in October. I guess I'm in better shape than I thought, and, thank God, some people find me absolutely irresistible. Maria stood there with an almost blank expression. Then, without saying a single word, she started taking off her clothes. First, her starched white apron came off. Then, her dress. She pulled it right off, right up over her head. It lay in a gray heap at her feet. Then, she bent down and took off her dear old-fashioned white, lace-up shoes. So pure. So virginal. And then the camisole, the white cotton slip. She stood there in front of me in her bra and panties, both so clinging, both so fragile, I could see the shadow and the suggestion of raw, naked flesh lurking dangerously under them. I decided she must be deliberately torturing me. Yes, I could see the procedure. She would stand there in front of me, tormenting me with her silence, mocking me with her near-nakedness until I began to scream. I just knew it. I was in agony, wondering what she would do next. I could not contain myself. My hands were already deep inside my sweet aching cunt.

And she knew it, how could she not know it? Of course. A smile had begun to play around her lips. Why not? Who was I, after all, but some dumb kidnap victim whose only claim to fame was my natural blonde bush.

But after Christmas comes New Year's. It always happens that way, doesn't it? I decided there must be a God, after all; that my problem is I lack faith. Yes, delicious little Maria stepped out of her panties and took off her bra. And stood there. Facing me. Making my brain turn to mush. Her rounded, slightly overdone titties were so eatable, so suckable, so fuckable I was getting lightheaded. Her thatch was so absolutely sleek and thick and glossy and ... my God, I could not breathe.

And I could not stand up for lack of proper breath. I slipped and fell under the water and momentarily blacked out, only to revive with Maria the magnificent straddling the edge of the tub, holding me up under my armpits, my mouth pressed into her sweet pink and black pussy which smelled of cunt juice and Chanel No. 5—Christ leave it to the fuckin' French—while electrical charges generated by my heart were turning my brain into a tropical fish tank. I ate her out like it was my last meal before the electric chair. She tasted like raw oysters, No, to hell with it, she tasted like raw cunt, my favorite food after raw cock. Fresh, salty, and delicious.

Then, as my eyes were rolling back into my head, Maria lowered herself a little into the tub so that her big plump tits were suffocating me. And I was ready to die happy with those dark caramel nipples so chewy and delectable stuffed into my mouth. At this point, my reason snapped. I could no longer continue to act polite, to remain the perfect lady, and so, like some crazy small-town girl, I blurted out to her, "Maria, I love you; don't ever leave me!"

How could I say this? I didn't even know her last name! I had clearly taken leave of my senses. I was bonkers. The truth is, for the first time in my life I didn't care what people thought. I pulled her down into the tub with me, crying softly, "Maria, Maria," so that our cunts could make contact, touch each other, fondle each

121

other, our clitorises pressing together, stroking, touching, rubbing sweet flesh to sweet flesh, my ravenous mouth drinking in her mouth as she yielded easily to me, my teeth making deep indentations in her lip. I wanted so much to break the skin on her lower lip and drink her sweet, warm blood, just a little bit, just a taste, but I didn't have the nerve.

What a strange situation! I was the one who, by all rights, should have been terrified. I was the one who should have been upset and lonely. After all, I had been kidnapped, which is a Federal offense, and I had yet to meet my kidnapper. But imagine, my only concern of the moment was not myself, but my little Maria with the ruby-red lips and the pink diamond of a clitoris, which I stroked with my forefinger, allowing the rest of my hand to caress her pussy lips. She started moaning as the orgasms came, and finally, as the waves of pleasure hit full force, and her head was thrashing and her body convulsed from the incredible pleasure I was giving her, I felt deliciously evil for taking my pleasure from this once-sullen child who had seemed to be mocking me at first, but she had a kind of sado-masochistic revenge on me for breaking down her reserve: my own orgasms could not equal hers. I was too much in control for absolute physical release, but I experienced a mental pleasure that blasted my brain with light and joy.

"Suck me! Suck me!" she moaned as she kneaded her own tits, rolling her nipples between her thumb and middle fingers. I dove underwater, and like a predatory fish nibbled on the pink, raw flesh between her thighs, as her slippery little body shook with the spasms of orgasm after orgasm, and she bucked and splashed in response to my oral love-making.

I repeatedly submerged, ate her out, and then surfaced for air. Finally, tiring of playing deep-sea diver, I dragged her down into the watery depths of the white marble pool, where, magnetized by each other's flesh, we almost drowned in the intensity of our entanglement. Repeatedly, our tongues found their way into each other's mouths and cunts as naturally as if they had been born there.

Afterward, we hugged each other like little girls and climbed out of the sunken pool and dried each other with oversized bath towels from a specially heated linen closet. I was completely exhausted, but I found I could not stop kissing Maria. In the bedroom, there was a warming plate with a pitcher of hot eggnog generously laced with rum and a large bowl of warm rice pudding studded with raisins that had been soaked in sherry and smelling of nutmeg and imported cinnamon. Little Maria, ever concerned with my welfare, sensed how tired I was, and spoon-fed me with the sinfully rich food.

After gorging ourselves, Maria and I crawled into the soft clouds of the little girl's bed and fell asleep in each other's arms as the cold October sun sank into the oncoming dark.

When we awoke from our perfect nap later that evening, Maria was massaging me, and there was soft music in the room. "Maria, Maria," I whispered, "is everything alright?"

"*Oui*, madame," she said, "Monsieur told me to give you a bath, zen give you a massage, to give you zomething to eat, zen let you sleep until he zend zee gentlemen to come get you."

"Who is 'Monsieur'," I asked, hoping for the moment at least that the mysterious "Monsieur" would never make an appearance.

"Monsieur Cafone," she replied. "Lucchio Cafone."

The name meant nothing to me. But what did I know? The world outside of Beavertown was probably full of rugged, highly sexual, self-made men in magnificent mansions with henchmen wearing pin-stripe suits and revolvers.

"Hurry up," she said. "We must get you dressed for

Monsieur Cafone." Then, reaching onto the other side of the bed, she lifted up the dream dress she had picked out for me, a full-length sweater dress made out of soft, furry, white angora wool. The neck was open right down to the navel, where a single diamond clasp held it shut. It was a perfect fit. My breasts were exposed right to the edge of my aureoles; the garment hugged close to my round little tummy, and it fit my spectacularly tight little ass like a lover's kiss. The shoes, clear plastic pumps, fit just right. I felt like a concubine out of the Arabian Nights being prepared to meet my Lord and Master.

So far, so good. I must say that except for the fact that I had been forcibly carried across state lines and was now being held against my will, I had no real complaints. I figured I'd play "Monsieur" 's little game, and go along with whatever it was he was trying to accomplish. For all I knew, I might be on "Candid Camera." "I look magnificent, thank you," I said to Maria as she brushed my thick honey-blonde hair in front of the full-length mirror, "but don't I need underwear under this dress?"

"No, cherie," she sighed. "Where you go, you don't need underwear."

"Well, then," I said, trying to make the best of it, "give me a spray of Chanel No. 5."

Smiling wanly, Maria took an atomizer bottle of the fabled French perfume, lifted open the front of my white angora dress, and sprayed me on my glorious blonde fur. Then, she kissed me there. She seemed almost in tears.

"Maria, Maria," I said, "I must tell you a secret. I don't know where I am or who this Monsieur Cafone is, but I do know he wants me, and I have the greatest faith in my ability to make the best of a bad situation. Like they say in the self-help books. "When life hands you a lemon, make lemonade. Maria, Maria, don't be so sad; I have always been able to make lovers out of enemies, because I love people any way they come." I lifted her adorable chin up by my fingertips and looked straight into her eyes. The moment of truth had arrived. "Maria," I said, "I do love men very much."

She looked shocked. "You do? Men?"

"Oh, yes, my darling, it's true; men take my breath away, even more than women. You see, Maria, when a man desires me, that's when I'm really a woman. And when a really masculine man sinks his big hard cock into me and starts humping me and riding me like there was no tomorrow, that's when I feel like I've made contact with the gods. The only time. I can't help it, Maria. I like being a woman the way I've defined it for an hour or two every day. For me, being a woman is better than drugs. It's better than being rich. It's something very basic. If you've been born with a cunt, fuck it, Maria, it's really the only way to go. I mean, you've got to get *down*, Maria."

Poor Maria, that delectable piece of ass, that ripe little cherry, she looked so sensitive. That's what I loved about her, but that's what did her in, no doubt. She looked so lonely. She looked at me with tears in her eyes. I could see she'd been hurt deeply by men, no doubt by "Monsieur" himself. I decided right then and there that if Mr. Macho Monsieur had sex with me on his mind, I would proceed to have the greatest lay of my life as a way of making it up to my woebegone little Maria. I wasn't going to be anybody's victim. I was going to have one terrific fuck.

Chapter Eight

There was a knock at the door. "Zee gentlemen," otherwise known as the thugs, were back. This time they came through the "front" door, and I was immediately ushered out into dark-paneled hallways with flickering brass sconce lights. A narrow staircase led to something grander with balustrades and banisters that led downstairs to a large marble vestibule, two stories high, lit by a massive crystal chandelier. Tubs of evergreens—boxwoods, azaleas, laurel—flanked settees and love seats upholstered in bright, flowered silks, fresh yellows and whites and pinks.

Then, quickly, since I didn't have time to look around, another journey down yet another dark-paneled corridor to a room at the end of the hall. A new man in an expertly tailored three-piece pin-stripe tailored suit and a machine gun stood outside the door, guarding it.

Naturally, I couldn't wait to see the Boss, whoever he was. Frankie, my old Arabian friend with the great kissing mouth and the Hoboken accent, knocked three times, each knock sharp and distinct.

The door swung open as if by remote control. I couldn't believe my eyes. Sitting behind an impressive looking desk was "Lucky," the tall, lumbering cameraman, the incredibly built, Latin aristocrat cameraman from Venus Productions who had disappeared shortly before the explosion.

"Lucky!" I cried, "it's you!" I couldn't believe my good

fortune. That was it! The lucky charm he had given me, the four-leaf clover imbedded in the clear lucite disc—it had worked! Lucky sat behind what looked like a turn-of-the-century railroad president's desk, looking like a cross between Tyrone Power and Sylvester Stallone smoking a cigar and stripped to the waist—at least I could only assume he had pants on. The torso was not to be believed. An olive-skinned Greek god, his forearms wrapped in ropes of veins, his nipples sticking out like little fingertips waiting to be stroked and sucked, his hands like a surgeon's, long, strong, and tapering. Fantastic.

"Strip her," he ordered.

"Lucky, what are you doing?" I screamed, but he paid no attention to what I was saying. He clearly was more interested in the nonverbal aspects of my personality. Within minutes, the goon squad had cut, torn, or ripped off every thread of my magnificent angora dress. Even the clear lucite shoes disappeared. My nipples stood straight out, rigid with fear.

"Don't worry, Miss Hunt," Lucky said in a more soothing tone, "the boys aren't going to touch you. Are they, boys?"

The "boys" shook their heads. Frankie seemed to be smiling through his gritted teeth. I felt so apologetic. It wasn't their fault, and it really had nothing to do with me. It was my body. It got in the way every time. Frankly, my twenty-two-year-old equipment made an overpowering statement. Men were more than ready to kill for a taste. I had nothing to do with it. It just stood there in its magnificence. Sometimes my tits amazed even me, the way they came to a delicate point in mid-air without drooping or sagging like a billion-dollar suspension bridge. My ass was the same way. I loved to look at it in a full-length mirror and finger myself. Anybody else with such a fully rounded tight pair of buns would have worn full skirts to cover such an obvious piece of sexual

127

equipment. Not me. I wore it proudly. In tight skirts. Like I say, a black ass in white skin.

Lucky interrupted my self-flattering fantasy with the order, "Okay boys." A strange, nonspecific order. What could he possibly mean? As I found out, these guys spoke in code. At the sound of the master's voice, "the boys" dropped their pants and started jerking off in front of me. Lucky took out a large jar of Vaseline from the top drawer of his desk and tossed it to my favorite goon, Frankie. Frankie unscrewed the cap, took a glob of the stuff, and smeared it on his perfectly formed member. It wasn't a huge cock by any means, but every cock looks good to me if its attached to a man who desires me. What I liked about Frankie's cock was its nakedness, its vulnerability in contrast to his crude mouth. Given the man's overbearing personality, his cock seemed almost frail in its normal proportions.

What a turn-on! Frankie was really a person! I felt like he was revealing his soul to me. Funny how desperate sex-starved men jerk off. Frankie lay down on Lucky's Oriental rug staring at my bush, his free hand outstretched toward it, wanting desperately to touch my labia. The man was in torture. "Please, Boss, let me feel her, just for a minute. I promise you, no more than a minute!"

Lucky ignored his pleas. Frankie didn't persist. He knew what was allowed. He ran his hand back and forth over his well-greased pole until he began to moan. I had no idea the man was so sensitive.

Hood No. 2, Little Louie, didn't use grease. He used his own spit, and his eyes were closed as if he were in some private fantasy. Louie kept rubbing his spit over his glans like he was polishing an apple, and stroking his sizeable balls, which hung down like eggs in a soft, dark, down-covered sac.

The third hood, the nameless driver of the black limousine, was a skinny bald man of about forty who kept begging, "Please, Boss, let me eat her pussy. Please, there'll be plenty left over for you. I won't touch her, Boss, I'll just eat her. Please, Boss, I won't touch her."

"Shutup!" bellowed Lucky. The driver had an incredible cock, a cone-shaped organ that got bigger as it left its base. At its widest point, his glans must have measured three inches across. He had other strange and unusual talents, which, frankly made me jealous. He bent over and took his cock in his mouth, sucking himself off. He managed to stuff the glans and about half of his cock into his mouth.

Lucky's next order was to me. "Bend over, beautiful." I bent over willingly, knowing my golden bush looked spectacular from behind, and besides, he didn't tell me I couldn't peek around my own shoulder to see what was going to happen next. At first, he just looked at me with absolute longing, with the face of the Christ on a Byzantine icon, his eyes full of sadness and intensity. Again, I could not help but notice the man's chest, so tanned and muscular and tough I figured he'd done a lot of work outdoors chopping trees and hauling freight, the way the men do in Beavertown. This was no ordinary weight-lifter's body.

Then, without warning, the Boss stood up. What a surprise! He had been completely naked from the waist down all the time. He was rampant. He was engorged. He was hot. His cock, by far the biggest in the room, was tough, muscular, defiant—all nine or ten inches of it. I don't know why, but I always seem to attract big cocks, not that I am particularly attracted to big cocks, but big cocks seem to come my way, no pun intended. And let's face it, you can't fuck a five-year-old, no matter how adorable he is.

But the truth is, women like me need more than a big cock. We need more than flesh. We need to fall in love, if only for a moment, which is about the duration of my usual love affair. I'm just kidding. The truth is, for my

129

Big Romances, which can go on for days and days, I need some kind of emotional excuse to get hooked on a man, some reason to make me feel he's vulnerable, that he needs me. As far as Lucky Cafone was concerned, up till now, after having been kidnapped and ordered around like a slave girl, I was not about to fall in love with him—yes, love was definitely out of the question—until I saw his stump. When he walked around, or rather pulled himself around the side of the desk, I was shocked! He had no left leg below the knee! As I found out later, he'd swum into a boat propeller as a small boy, and after four unsuccessful operations, surgeons had to amputate. He'd grown up with prostheses, artificial legs, which had to be replaced with every inch he grew. He had never been able to participate in any team sport except water polo, where he wielded his stump as an effective club. And since most American boys had never heard of water polo, Lucky had grown up different, and mostly alone.

As shocked as I was, I was overwhelmed with pity and compassion and tenderness for him. In short, I was madly, hopelessly in love. After all, anybody can be a Mafia boss (I'll get into that later) with a ten-inch cock and a body that doesn't stop—but a stump! Christ! The pain in that poor boy's life! The agony of being different, of being deformed and mutilated!

I was petrified. I'd been condescending, or whatever the word is. I wasn't sure what to say to make him feel better, so I spoke from the heart. "Fuck me," I whispered. "Fuck me."

And he did, first pulling himself over with his great limping strides, then holding onto my firm hips for support, and then, oh! he lay on the Oriental carpet, his head under my kneeling pelvis, and he stared at my cunt like it was a religious shrine. Then he tongued me. I was so touched that he would think of me that way I began to cry. My God, the love in this world, when it

130

comes, comes with such surprise it takes my breath away. I screamed in ecstasy, doubling over from the shock waves of orgasm that exploded within me.

Then, Lucky pulled my cunt down into his face and my cunt-juices ran onto his tongue. He lapped them up with desire and gratitude, huskily whispering, "Yes! Yes! Yes!" between his sucking, slurping sounds. That's when the three thugs started to come, one after the other, Arabian Frankie shouting out unintelligible gutteral sounds as a thick globby stream of white come arced into the air in front of him. Little Louie made no sound at all. The semen gushed out onto his belly and chest in spurts, until his stomach glistened under the dim light of a reading lamp. As for the third one, the master of self-gratification with the spade-shaped cock, who could tell? His sperm trickled down the sides of his mouth, over his lower lip as he squeezed and massaged his balls and the root of his cock for every last ounce of pleasure.

I, on impulse, pulled myself back to kiss Lucky's stump, which I found as sexually stimulating as a cock of the same size. For me, that stump was the phallic symbol to end all phallic symbols.

But how could Lucky have known that? "No! You cunt!" he shouted, slapping my face hard. "Stay away from that! You do-gooder! You Christian freak!" And with that, he roughly held me by the waist, lifted me up off the floor, and forcibly entered me, immediately pounding away, up and down, up and down, a pile-driving piston.

What could I do but surrender to him completely? I I wanted him to fuck me raw, to fuck my fucking brains out. Until that moment, I had never believed in love at first sight, but now I realized it depends on what you see the first time you look. I saw a ruler from ancient Rome, the Nero who never had a chance, thanks to the Christians, who had lost sight of the mysteries of sex and violence.

Lucky kept pounding and pumping, one-legged warrior that he was. For ten minutes straight I sucked his hot iron pole with outer lips and inner lips, with all my inner muscles holding him tight. I bore down hard, so that the tip of my clitoris could become entangled in his pubic hairs as he moaned, "I want you! I want you!"

My orgasms came so fast and frequent I could no longer stand it. I shouted out, "I'm going to fall!"

Without uttering a word, he collapsed on top of me, falling with me, pulling me down. We were two high divers careening through space, Siamese twins connected by a bond of throbbing flesh.

And then a miracle happened. Lucky experienced his first wave of orgasm just as we hit the floor. The shock waves of pleasure and release ran like electricity through his body from the tips of his fingers right down through his mutilated leg. He lost all control. I could feel the hot come spurting into my guts. That triggered me; my whole being was drowned in a rush of tingling pleasure. I forgot where I was. My mind was bathed in a soft gold light. I lay on the silent bottom of an ocean of light. So relaxed. So quiet. So still. I was a little girl again.

Then the god on top of me spoke, and I was back in New Jersey again. "Get out of here!" He was talking to the goon squad. "No, not you." Yes, he wanted me to stay.

"Hey, Boss, you was terrific," said Little Louie.

"How would you know? I wasn't making it with you, was I?" Lucky said, grinning. Little Louie grinned back, then beat his hasty retreat, no doubt so that he could go back to his room and beat his meat. The rest of them followed. Lucky withdrew from me, hoisted himself up. then, using a blackthorn walking stick that was lying across his desk, hobbled over to the lighting panel and dimmed the lights in the room. The lights changed color, too; the room was bathed in dark rose hues, the most flattering color there is. He lit candles; the scene could not have been more romantic. His thick, resilient dong, still half-aroused, swung in front of him across his hard, chiseled thighs.

Then, still hobbling with his blackthorn stick, he opened an armoire and tossed me a blanket. Except it wasn't exactly a blanket, as I discovered to my utter surprise and delight. It was a full-length, black, emba mink coat. "This is for you, hot-lips," he said, "and don't ask me where I got it. The woods around here are full of mink."

I was overwhelmed by his generosity. The coat was a perfect fit. I had never felt so warm and so wanted in my entire life. The Mafia, I decided right then and there, must be absolutely wonderful people with a bad press. People are so jealous. I vowed to myself right then and there that I would do everything in my limited power to treat Lucky with the respect he deserved.

"What do you want to drink?" he asked, typically generous.

"I don't drink, the hard stuff, I mean," I said.

"Really?" he replied. "I'm the hard stuff. Someday I hope you'll try drinking me. You'll love it."

With that, I knelt down in front of him, and licked up the last drops of come that were dripping out of the end of his big white firehose. He was right. I loved it. Then, I kissed his nozzle head. Lucky was grinning, the teeth dazzling, the dimples right out of the movies. He handed me a glass of sherry. How did he know I liked sherry? Lucky was one of those guys who knew everything without asking. Such class.

Then, he kissed me, tenderly, like he loved me as deeply and as completely as if I'd borne him three kids and was responsible for his career success. Then, he talked about himself. "My name's Lucky Cafone. That's Sicilian for 'Gypsy.' My real name's Lucchio."

"Were you born in Italy?" I asked.

"No," he said. "My mother was. The rumors were she was the illegitimate daughter of the Duke of Windsor and an Italian princess. They were supposedly both under twenty the time it happened. She was adopted by the princess's aunt and uncle. The uncle was half-Sicilian, and when the Second World War broke out, the bombs started falling, the aunt and uncle got killed, and my mother, aged fourteen, ended up in her great-uncle's house in Palermo. He was a Capo. A Godfather. After the war, one thing followed another, deals were made, and my mother arrived in New Jersey a blushing bride. When I was born my mother claims she finally knew the meaning of true happiness, but after my boating accident and amputation, she turned on my father. He had too many girlfriends, I guess, and she decided to devote herself completely to me. Anyway, she left the Church, started consulting psychics, and eventually learned she herself had psychic powers."

"But where is your mother now?" I stammered. "Is she alive or dead?"

"Mama lives here with me. Be careful. If you run into her, she'll insist on reading the Tarot cards."

"I'd love to meet your mom," I said, thinking that whoever had raised this stud and decorated this shack must be one chic chick, as we say in Beavertown.

"Feel free to wander around our country seat," Lucchio said.

"The cunt in the country," I murmured under my breath.

"I heard you," Lucchio said, winking slying and grabbing a handful of pussy through my open mink coat.

What a doll! (Incidentally, after hearing his gorgeous Italian name, I resolved never to call him "Lucky" again.)

But there was still something I hadn't exactly figured out. "But wait a minute," I stammered. "If your mother is the illegitimate daughter of the Duke of Windsor . . .

134

then you're descended from Queen Victoria, because he was Queen Victoria's grandson or great-grandson ... and you're in the Mafia?"

"It's one and the same, we're just downstairs royalty," he whispered gently, and kissed me again. "You've got the greatest tits I've ever seen," he said as he pushed his face through my fabulous mink and nibbled on my breasts. Then, he eased me back and bent down to kiss my luxurious cunt. My God, was he a gentleman! Even the way he fucked—like a hardhat holding a jackhammer—offered no real clue to the man's essential gentleness.

I must say I was overwhelmed. No wonder so many middle-class American housewives want Italian studs in their beds. I must say that Hollywood had never prepared me for the beauty of a Mafia home or the sweet masculinity of its best men. I realize that only a few Italians are actually members of the Mafia, but there's always the mystery of who is and who isn't, isn't there? Outsiders never know for sure. And danger can be such an intoxicant. I was enraptured. I had completely forgotten my kidnapping. I lay on the antique Oriental carpet in that ten-thousand-dollar mink coat, sipping Harvey's Bristol Cream, allowing "the Boss," Lucchio, to kiss me, fondle me, nibble me.

Then, with a start, I realized I had not eaten all day. I told him so. "Darling, I'm starving."

He was shocked at his own insensitivity. He made a quick and magnanimous phone call to his housekeeper, Putana, and ordered me something in Italian. It sounded wonderful. We had just enough time to make love again, but first, Lucchio had another surprise for me. He wanted to talk about my career. He had a business proposition for me. Actually, it was more like a *fiat*, the command of a feudal lord. Since he had so much royal blood, I decided to indulge him a little.

"My splendid Diana," he said, holding me like a baby

in a great, out-sized red-leather wing chair and nibbling at my shoulder, "you are so voluptuous, I could make love to you all day and all night."

"You're not so bad yourself," I said, trying to sound sophisticated.

"No, you don't understand, Diana. I want to do something for your career," he said, sucking on my belly.

"What career?" I teased. After all, I was already twenty-two, and still a complete nobody.

"I'm going to make you the porn movie queen of all time," he said.

"But, but . . ." I stammered.

"But nothing," he said. "There's never been a superstar of porn. Before I'm through, you'll be bigger than Farrah Fawcett and Dolly Parton combined."

"But Lucchio, I tried and failed because I don't really want to make porn movies. I want to be a fashion model like Cheryl Tiegs, I . . ."

"Fuck fashion models! Fuck Cheryl Tiegs!" he bellowed. "I'll have America standing six deep in line to watch you give head. Face facts. You've got the sexiest body since Brigette Bardot."

"Thank you," I said, not knowing what to say next.

Fortunately, he hadn't finished. "Besides which, there's a gang war going on right now over who controls the sex industry. And that's exactly what it's going to be before long—an industry. It's already into the billions: books, magazines, mail-order sex aids, lingerie, birth control. But the pornographic films are still considered dirty little movies, because that's how they're filmed and presented. They *look* like dirty little movies. The truth is, I'm willing to remake *Gone With The Wind* and cast you as Scarlett O'Hara, the real Scarlett, the one who runs naked under her hoop skirts and fucks everything in sight, black and white, male and female. What do you say?"

"Lucchio. Lucchio, I'm so flattered," I stammered, "but I don't have that kind of emotional depth, to act, I mean.

136

I really just want to see my smiling all-American face in a magazine ad selling French perfume. Like Lauren Hutton for Revlon. And maybe then go into the movies and wear beautiful designer clothes. Don't you know successful models can make a million dollars a year these days?"

Lucchio bent his beautiful, battered boxer's face and began to kiss and lick my cunt-lips. I was beginning to get confused. Truly confused. I was willing to dismiss the rumors that the Mafia was held together by machine guns in the night, but as for being a porn star, I had finally realized that for me there were boundaries. I could have all the sex I wanted with whoever I wanted twenty-four hours a day, but not on camera. In other words, I wasn't a fuckin' trained seal.

Shocked as I was to realize that I was, at heart, a bourgeois conservative type, I still felt that I had a right to those convictions. America, after all, was originally founded by people with strong convictions, wasn't it? I was proud to count myself among the stalwarts.

But for the moment, there were other considerations, especially Lucchio's bull head with its mass of black curls between my things, as I held onto him with both hands while the point of his tongue darted up into the little quivering sheath that enfolds my clitoral bud. Within minutes he had complete control of me. We made it again. Big. Imagine a battering ram pounding against the walls of a medieval stone castle. Make it the champagne country of France. The desirable prize. Just like me.

That's how I felt with Lucchio. Utterly romantic. Finally, I could resist no longer. The stone wall crumbled, and the castle surrendered, but the battering did not stop until every inner wall had collapsed and lay in ruins. The bull was king at last. His massive hands grasped my buttocks. His hot mouth seemed to be on the other side of my throat, his tongue fucking my heart out. I was possessed. My breath was on fire. You can't imagine what it's like to be wanted that much; the man's passion was his prayer to me, and, like God, I answered him, cooing, "Lucchio, Lucchio," while he rode me and I met him, my inner flesh fucking and sucking every ounce of hot cock-meat, his heavy balls thudding against me as he rode my loins.

We were in love with each other's bodies. My orgasms came from deep within, beginning with small rumbles, climaxing in hurricane waves that drowned me again and again, miraculously without killing me, as I kept coming up for air and diving back for more. There is nothing better in life, if you are a woman—I can only speak for my own sex—than to be desired. It is the ultimate luxury. In fact, my greatest desire is to be, well, *desired*, and Lucchio gave me what I wanted, like nobody has before or since.

When he climaxed, he did so with a cry edged with agony. We both understood: with orgasm there is a kind of death and separation. It is over. At least for now. He came in heavy spurts, shooting the blobs of semen straight into me. I begged him, "Lucchio, stay inside me."

He said, *"Exquisita"* and nibbled my lower lip. And then, without warning, he dropped the same old bomb again. "Diana," he implored me, "be America's porn queen for me. I'll make you a multimillionaire."

At that delicate moment in time, I felt totally defenseless, totally vulnerable. Like the dumb-cluck broads all the feminist writers of our magnificent century seem to hate and despise so much, I decided that I'd do anything for Lucchio, anything he wanted, as long as I could have him desire me at least once a day. "Alright," I finally said. "I'll do anything you want. I guess this is my destiny; I must have been born to be the porn queen of the Mafia."

We talked for almost an hour about the kind of movies Lucchio planned, films with wonderful background music and magnificent East Side townhouses. He wanted the look of luxury, and he also wanted blood and guts along with the sex. He talked about making a porno version of *The Godfather*, with me as the woman the heads of the different families will kill for. "Blood always looks scarier on naked bodies, and naked bodies look sexier covered with blood," he said. With his typical brilliance he explained to me how there will always be a big worldwide market for sex and violence, especially when they're combined. He fantasized about porn versions of *Hamlet*, *Othello*, *The Song of Bernadette*, and *The Three Musketeers*. I also found out that Lucchio was in the middle of a bloody feud between the Cafone family and the Del'Fresca family of Cherry Hill in South Jersey over territorial boundaries and distribution rights of the East Coast porn empire. He said a cousin of his had been murdered the week before with a poison dart at his daughter's debutante party, which is why he needed his round-the-clock bodyguards, Frankie, Little Louie, and the Driver. I felt so drained of energy after our conversation, I just wanted to gather my mink coat around me, schlep upstairs to bed, and take Lucchio with me, but he wanted to give me a tour of the palace first. And he wanted me to meet his sainted, psychic mother, Contessa Cafone.

There's nothing like a private midnight tour of an underworld *palazzo*. After a gourmet seduction dinner with my own Italian Heathcliff, served by a naked waitress with double-size labia, hot-pink in color and surrounded by jet-black hair that grew clear up to her navel—a person who almost cost me my relationship with Lucchio and he with mine, as we were both ready to jump on the girl, and she knew it. However, we decided to restrain ourselves until the next day. He said the girl, Putana, thought about nothing but sex, was like a crazed animal when approached sexually and was best left for a time when we both had more energy, namely the next day.

As for the villa, it was overwhelming in its splendor. Talk about winning through intimidation! Lucchio, by now walking normally enough with the aid of the prosthesis he usually wore, and wrapped in a full-length purple silk robe, led me from one spectacular room to the next. The all-white media room was right out of Milan. It was equipped with a word processor and a six-foot television screen. The kitchen seemed to be mostly mirrors, glass, and stainless steel. His private gymnasium looked like an ad for Jack LaLanne. The indoor swimming pool, by contrast, was out of the Renaissance, with its blaze of gold tiles. As for the private den, the library, the drawing room, the solarium, they successfully maintained the air of Old Money, East Coast, at that. The British Royal family would have felt right at home. All I could say by way of response was "Wow!", which made Lucchio laugh.

Then, suddenly, the thought struck me, where was his family? "Lucchio," I said, "I know your dear old mother lives here with you, and I don't mean to pry, but this is such a huge mansion, and so magnificent, do you live here alone?"

He looked at me with those sad, intense Mediterranean eyes. Pools of black sorrow. "*Cara mia,*" he said to me, his voice breaking, "my wife died in childbirth ten years ago. Her sister took the child to raise as her own. I live here just with my mother and the crazy guys you met earlier. And of course there are servants, Maria and Putana, to help me ease my loneliness."

Well, at that point, I wanted to round up Maria and Putana, tie them both to my bedpost, and go down on their indescribable pussy flesh. I almost passed out thinking about the possibilities in that house, aside from the furniture and the view of the good green hills of New Jersey, but I was not, after all, a lesbian by preference, and I was with the man of my dreams, who absolutely

140

desired me, so I decided to keep my wits about me and try and learn the art of politics.

"Your mother!" I cried, "Oh, Lucchio, is it too late to meet her? She must have long since retired for the night!"

"No, no," Lucchio said. "Mother's upstairs waiting to meet you. In your room on the third floor. You see, Diana dearest, Mother wants me to marry again, and there's something else . . ."

"Something else?" I replied, wondering what on earth he could possibly mean.

"You see," Lucchio said, "Mother's a psychic. Actually, she's a medium."

"Yes," I said, "I think you told me she reads Tarot cards."

"You're not afraid? "said Lucchio.

"Afraid of what?" I said.

"Of a psychic. Of someone who reads your future."

"My church," I explained, "the Tabernacle Witnesses, would never allow psychics or mediums or hypnotists. As a matter of fact, they didn't allow smoking, drinking, or dancing, either. Or fucking. So if you're asking me if I'm afraid, the only thing I'm really afraid of are the Tabernacle Witnesses. Where's Mama?"

Upstairs, in my third-floor room, that white and flowery playground for an unknown little girl, Contessa Cafone was sitting on the double bed. A sight to behold. What's called an Aristocratic Beauty. If she was sixty, she looked closer to thirty-five. She was wearing a silver turban, and her neck was wrapped in ropes of cultured pearls, which crowned her long brocaded cape. She extended a white-gloved hand, which flaunted out-size bejeweled rings on the outside of the glove. Her accent, partly Italian, was mostly upper-class British. Her eyes were emerald green lined in dark gray. She glittered like a temple cat out of Egyptian legend.

Who was this woman? Would we end up in bed together? I couldn't imagine her ever having sex with anyone. "Come in, my dear, come in," she intoned. "Lucchio, my darling, you may go downstairs and wait for me. This child you have brought me is tired. Very tired. See, her aura fades. I will be brief. Here, child, beautiful child, sit down on the bed, and I will contact my sources."

I did as told. Lucchio kissed me like a father kissing a child—on the forehead. Then, he whispered so she couldn't hear him, "Leave your door open, and your cunt, too. I will be back later." Then Lucchio left the room and descended into the dark.

On the bed, the Contessa had launched into her reading. "Now, child," she shid, "let me see what I pick up on you." She seemed to listen to voices from a place deep within her head. Then, she began to scribble what looked like precise letters, but which, upon closer examination, were indecipherable markings. Then she began to speak. "You've just been involved with an explosion of some kind."

"Yes," I replied.

"And the police took care of you—were they good to you?"

"Yes." I realized she could have gotten her information from Lucchio. "Will I be working in films?" I asked, absolutely suspicious of her motives and sources of information. I didn't want to shock her with the pornography plan, but still, I wondered if she already knew about it, and supported it.

Apparently not. "No, no, no," she answered. "You will have a job in the fashion world."

Hallelujah! "Contessa Cafone," I beamed, "that's what I came to New York for, to be a fashion model."

"No, no, no," she said again. "No, not exactly. I see you sewing."

"Sewing?"

"Yes," she said. "Do you sew?"

"Well, yes," I said. "I design and sew all my own underwear, and..."

"Yes, I see you sewing," she repeated. "Wait, I just remembered. Let me give you the name and address of a woman who sews. She has sewn for me. I think she sews for the important designers in New York. Tell her I sent you. She will help you." The Contessa took out a small alligator-covered address book and copied down a name for me on a card. It read "Lulu Touché."

"Anything else?" I said.

"Yes, I see you traveling all over the world."

"Doing what?" I said.

"My sources keep telling me that if you keep sewing, you will be richer and more famous than you ever dreamed."

"Sewing what?" I asked, "underwear?"

"Sewing whatever comes to mind. It's up to you. Wait. I see a dark-haired man. He is somebody very important. He will help you. Anything else?"

Again, I wondered about the motive behind the reading, so I came right out with it. "What about me and Lucchio?" I asked.

With this, she furrowed her brow, listened a bit, and then began to write in her precise little markings. Suddenly, her eyes opened wide; she had a look of horror on her face. "Oh my God! Oh my God!" she screamed. "I've got to find Lucchio. Something terrible could happen. *Bambina, cara mia*, you get into bed, and turn off all the lights and lock the door. Never mind about Lucchio. You take care of yourself. We will talk in the morning. Anything else you need is in the bathroom. Your nightgown is in the bathroom." And with that, with an undisguised look of horror on her face, she fled into the night.

I thought to myself, "My goodness, these Italians are emotional people," and decided to take a bath before retiring. As in the same Arabian Nights fantasy as before, the bath water had already been drawn. The temperature

of the water was perfect. I slipped out of my mink coat
and left it on the bed. Then, I slipped out of my shoes,
and within two minutes there I was, in that magnificent
marble bathroom with its gold fixtures, staring at myself
in the full-length mirror. I had forgotten how spectacularly beautiful I was. It amazed even me. How many
women are perfectly round and smooth without being
fat and lumpy? My hips and ass were all of a piece, and
what a piece! I could understand why men, and women,
too, were wild about me. My skin glowed like gold in
perfect complement to my thick, honey-colored bush. My
shoulder-length hair was thick and tawny like a lion's
mane. My lips were full and moist, my eyes large and
ice-blue. As warm as my skin was, my eyes seemed just
a little bit cold. You see, I was always Fire and Ice. I
had often been told that was the secret of my so-called
"spellbinding charm." Men could never take me for
granted. Even when I, for one, thought that I was absolutely, totally, in love, men could look into my eyes and
see my mind clicking away like a computer. At least
that's what I was often told.

My own response was more elemental. I could not take
my eyes off my reflection in the mirror. My breasts were
so full, they begged to be touched and stroked, my
nipples hungered to be sucked. Since there was no one
around, I decided to make love to myself. Like I aways
say, you take the cards life deals you, and you play your
hand. For the moment, in a strange house in a strange
town, I had only myself. I memorized my image in the
mirror, then climbed into the tub, which had easy access
to bath oils and perfumes.

It's amazing what a woman can do with one finger
and a little imagination. My cunt loved the oil massage.
You see, when I found myself in total control of my
sexual experience, something possible only in masturba-
tion, I felt completely relaxed. I could take more time
stroking my clitoris and indulging myself in my favorite

144

fantasy in which I was naked on a shipwrecked raft with a naked Arab prince, who spoke no English. My prince had eyes like burning black coals, a full black beard, and the dark body of a chesty, muscle-bound blacksmith. How my prince got to look like a blacksmith was part of the man's mystery and his fascination to me. My Arab was the ultimate chauvinist pig who wanted nothing more than to fuck me into oblivion until we were both finally eaten by killer sharks, who were probably jealous for all we knew. My Arab had no name; he didn't need one. He was the Total Male. Nothing gave him pleasure but a woman like me. If he had boys on the side, like Arabs supposedly do, I never knew anything about it. That was the advantage of not speaking Arabic and of being on a raft. There was nobody else. He was all mine. Sitting in that sunken marble tub, I felt so relaxed, with such a great handful of prime pussy, my orgasm was like an epileptic fit, total, far-reaching, blotting out any sense of time and space, except for one strange sound. My orgasm seemed to coincide with a far-away popping sound like champagne corks or firecrackers. I thought I heard yelling or screaming. I wondered if Lucchio was watching a movie in his media room, hoping his mother would retire for the night, so he could sneak back up-stairs without any motherly remarks from her in the morning. I decided to do him one better. I would get all dressed up, and then go downstairs, and surprise him.

I finally got out of my bath, dried myself with a thick turkish towel. Then, because there was a chill in the air, I donned my red silk nightgown, which looked more like a designer evening gown with its gold border. It even had a wrapper or outer coat with long full sleeves, and a high mandarin collar, which hooked together in front. To complete the picture, and because I could feel the nip in the fall air, I put my shoes back on, and then, hurrah, my brand-new mink coat. To my way of thinking, I

145

looked better than a high-fashion model on a Madison Avenue runway. To complete the picture of late-night glamor, I put a little blusher on my cheeks, then added some eyeliner. Then, I decided to casually saunter downstairs looking for Lucchio. I wanted to surprise him with my glamorous, voluptuous self, hoping he'd seduce me one more time before the night was out. He had such a wonderful cock, it deserved all the pussy it could get.

At the doorway to my room, I listened and didn't hear a sound. I walked down to the second floor. Not a peep. For a moment, I thought I heard sounds in my bedroom one floor above, almost as though the bodyguards had run up the backstairs, and broken into my bedroom looking for me.

I slipped into a dark, shadowy area until the sounds died down. After about three minutes, I heard a door slam below, probably in the kitchen. A car engine started up, revved its motors, then grew more and more distant. I wondered if Lucchio had gone out for a pizza. I walked around downstairs through the various rooms, hoping to surprise him. There was no one in the kitchen, no one in the drawing room, or the library, or the living room. The media room! Yes, I heard voices. Familiar voices. The door was open a crack. There was a movie on the screen. Now I understood why the voices were so familiar. It was Edward G. Robinson in the last scene of *Little Caesar*. He'd just been shot. Those must have been the popping noises I'd heard. Gunfire in the movie. Poor Edward G. He was the two-bit gangster Little Caesar calling out his dying words, "Mother of God, is this the end of Rico?"

So that was it. A movie. I pushed open the door and almost had a heart attack. On top of the shining white control panel, wrapped in each other's arms for a final embrace, were mother and son, Contessa Cafone and Lucchio, not so "Lucky" after all. Their heads and faces were smeared with sticky red blood. He had the back of his head blown away. She, with her sightless eyes wide

146

open, was staring into the dark, bloodied sockets of her only son's eyes. I kept saying to myself, "Get out of this place."

Good advice, Diana. I tiptoed through the kitchen and out the back door. Then, I remembered. Christ, I had no money. Can you imagine the terror of having to rifle a dead man's pockets? Thank God there was no blood on the pockets or the money. Three thousand dollars in cash. For once I believed in a God. God is good. Yes, ma'am. I knew for sure He, the good Savior of Mankind, intended me to stay in New York. For sure.

I was also thinking about lifting the Contessa's pearls, but I figured that was pushing my luck. And so, with new clothes and new money, I somehow got through what seemed like ten miles of suburban roads and streets until I reached the main drag of what turned out to be Morristown, New Jersey, where I called a cab, who for fifty dollars drove me to Manhattan, where for a hundred dollars more I checked into the Waldorf at two a.m., and, without taking off my clothes, fell into bed and cried myself to sleep. That night I dreamed of Muffie and Rod, and my beloved Angelo and the anonymous Swedish porn star and all the wonderful policemen, and Maria the maid, and, most of all, my poor Lucchio. I had met so many wonderful people.

As they say, "Lose a few, win a few." That night I slept deeply and well. I had been in New York a little less than a week. In the next few months, my life would change utterly, but not entirely in the direction I had planned. One thing was for sure. I was a long way from Beavertown.

PART II

Chapter Nine

The Waldorf! Manhattan's most legendary hotel, with its lobby a city block wide, its crystal chandeliers, its custom-made carpets, its marble pillars, its international clientele: the richest families of South America and Saudi Arabia, Scandinavian millionaires, German and Italian aristocracy, best-selling authors, movie stars past and present—everyone who's anyone wants a week at the Waldorf!

And the hookers who ply their ancient, tawdry trade both in the downstairs bar and the upstairs bedrooms are absolutely incredible. I couldn't get over the call girls. They looked so glamorous with their gold and diamond jewelry, their expensive furs, their expertly made-up faces, I thought for sure they were fashion models. As far as I could see, the only difference between the high-priced call girls and the upper-class wives is that the call girls are affectionate in public.

But all this is too deep for me; I'm not that complex. I'm just an old-fashioned American girl. I prefer a roll in the hay with the stud of my choice, no money attached. I don't have the stomach or the education to separate good honest sex from good honest emotion, otherwise known as the turn-on (or the hard-on). What happened to me in the Waldorf is all because some hotshot German millionaire thought that I was a hooker for rent, and I thought that just because he manufactured cameras he could get me a job in the fashion

151

world. But, thank God, by the time our short-lived "affair" was over, I had returned to my roots and regained my sense of direction, my old-fashioned values intact.

When I woke up late that first morning, I figured I had just enough money to last about a week at the Waldorf, after which I'd have to move in with some Pan Am stewardesses in Yorkville on the upper East Side, or rent a room at the YWCA. It must have been one o'clock in the afternoon when I finally straggled downstairs in my mink coat and gold-trimmed red pajamas to get a cup of coffee, after which I knew I'd have to buy a new supply of toilet articles and personal effects, everything from makeup to pantyhose.

The newspaper headlines in the Waldorf Coffee Shop were shattering: "Mafia Boss Slain!" "Mafia Massacre!" and "Mob Job!" I picked up the *News* and the *Post*. Gruesome photos of the blood-spattered Lucchio and his psychic mother, the Contessa. There was no mention of Putana, the cook, Maria, the upstairs maid, or of any third-floor mystery guest. As far as the police were concerned, the rival crime family, the Del'Frescas from Cherry Hill, was clearly to blame. There was no mention of theft or robbery, since the Cafone chateau was still full of its priceless Georgian silver and antique Chinese figures from the T'ang period, B.C. Estimated value: about 1.5 million.

With a sigh or relief, I decided I was scot-free, and, for the time being, at least, resolved to treat my New Jersey episode as a bad dream, a nightmare; otherwise they'd have to take me to the Bellevue observation ward. I decided to plunge into life whole hog, to make new friends and meet new people. In short, I resolved to learn to love again, a habit of mind that in future years would save me again and again when friends, lovers, and relatives of mine met their untimely deaths. As far as organized crime went, considering I'd been kidnapped and would have been raped had I resisted, I figured I'd paid my dues. In the meantime, I had several thousand dollars to help me launch my New York modeling career.

My face must have reflected my sudden upbeat change of mood. A lean, boyish-looking gentleman who turned out to be a German millionaire in his mid-forties said, "Good news?"

"Good as gold," I replied, noticing his custom-fitted pin-stripe gray banker's suit.

"Then, we'll have to celebrate," he announced.

"Celebrate?" I answered, playing dumb. The truth was that despite my best intentions, I was not ready to jump into bed with a perfect stranger so soon after my brush with tragedy and violence.

"My name is Jerry Ballzig," he said with almost no accent, extending his hand. "You'll have to let me take you to lunch?"

"Where? In a restaurant?" I said, refusing to take his hand, hoping he'd be completely turned off by such a dumb broad as myself.

His reply was more to the point. "Well, I don't usually eat lunch in bed. Unless you do. Do you?"

"Mister," I said, looking as unnaturally fierce as I could, "the truth is, I am in mourning for a friend who was killed yesterday. I . . ." But I couldn't go on. My tears started to flow. I had really deeply felt for poor Lucchio trapped by his aristocratic family in a life of organized crime and isolated wealth, not to mention his tragically missing foot. And imagine—his poor mother with all her unusual gifts marooned out there in that humongous villa with him.

I guess my expression must have changed. For a fleeting, and I repeat, fleeting moment, Mr. Ballzig's eyes seemed bluer and softer. He looked like a little boy lost. A tear rimmed his lower lid. I was absolutely devastated. This stranger really seemed to care. "Yes, I'll let you take me to lunch," I said, quietly.

We ate lunch at Sardi's, the theatrical restaurant on West 43rd Street across from the Shubert Theater where the legendary musical *A Chorus Line* was playing. The Italian waiters in their tuxedos were rakishly charming, and the food, if you got what you ordered, was wonderful. But the best part was the celebrities. Three of my favorite actors from *A Guiding Light* were there, and apparently Senator Edward Kennedy, that fabled stud from Massachusetts, had just left before we arrived. I was sorry I missed him; I have always been interested in politics and willing to learn more, if only someone would teach me.

In any case, I had chicken salad, all-white meat, and Mr. Ballzig, who I was beginning to call Jerry, had chicken salad, all-dark meat. "Do you always eat dark meat?" I said.

"I eat my meat any way it comes," he said.

"But it comes in white, too," I said.

"Then, give me a taste of your white meat," Jerry replied. "Then, you can taste mine. Who knows? We might end up eating each other's meat."

"Maybe that's what you intended in the first place," I commented.

The dessert conversation was even raunchier. "I'll bet you like cheesecake," I suggested.

He was much too fast on the pick-up. "Yes, I love cheesecake," he said, "because it's white, creamy, sweet, and delicious, but I like chocolate pudding, too."

"Chocolate pudding?" I replied, somewhat surprised.

"Yes, my dear; it's dark and sinful and much too sweet for the likes of me. So you, see, Ms. Diana Hunt with the white meat, you won't trap Jerry Ballzig into baring his soul."

"Then, why are you trying to trap me into baring my body?" I said, hoping he'd give me the right answer.

Apparently not. "You probably think I'm just another

obnoxious middle-aged businessman on the make," he said.

"Close," I replied.

"How close?" he asked, moving closer and putting his hand on my knee so he could continue his spiel. "The truth is, I'm riddled with guilt. I can give pleasure to a woman, but I'm too shy and guilt-ridden to take the initiative."

"What are you trying to tell me?" I cried. "That you've never had sex?"

"Well, not quite," he said. "The truth is, I can't penetrate a woman unless she begs me to. Otherwise, I feel like I'm abusing her in some way. I mean, with all the rape that's going on these days—have you read the rape statistics?—and wives being beaten—have you seen the television documentaries?—all the pain, I am so shocked and saddened, I want only to give a woman pleasure to make up for all the terrible things members of my own sex have done to them."

By now, his hand was on the inside of my upper thigh, on the skin itself. "That's what I get for wearing a mink coat with nothing underneath," I thought to myself.

Jerry had more to say. "In Germany, we are so far advanced, we know the meeting ground of pleasure and pain."

"Yes, I think I know that ground," I said. "As a matter of fact, I think I'm there right now."

"Then you must punish me for causing you pain," he replied.

I was aghast. "Jerry, you want me to punish you?"

"Yes," he practically chortled. "I have whips for you. Wonderful whips from the Black Forest, originally used on horses. And I have chains. You can beat me with the bare metal."

I looked at him blankly, in shock. He wouldn't quit.

155

"Diana, I cannot come, sexually I mean, unless I am beaten, and beaten hard."

In the meantime, I had noticed a shy hulk of a man sitting by himself at the next table. He had massive cheekbones and a granite chin, and he seemed downcast. I simply had to get to know him. I had to get him to laugh.

"Jerry," I said, "you do know I'm a transvestite?" His roaming hand snapped back to his lap so fast I thought he'd been bitten by a rattlesnake.

"You're kidding!" he exclaimed.

"Why would I kid?" I replied.

"But what about your breasts?" he said.

"What about them?" I said.

"They're magnificent."

"Silicone," I snapped.

"You're really not kidding?" he asked.

"Do you want to see my cock?" I said.

Jerry laid a hundred-dollar bill on the table. "This is for lunch," he announced.

"But Jerry, that's far too much."

"Keep the change. Buy yourself a doctor's appointment—at a psychiatrist's!" And with that, Herr Macho, Jerry Ballzig turned on his heels and fled, as they say, the premises.

The waiter, who looked like a brother of Marcello Mastroianni, sauntered over. "Will that be all, madame?"

"No," I said, "please ask that gentleman over there to please join me for a dinner drink."

The gentleman, the downcast one, of course, looked up. He'd heard my imperial decree. His eyes were enormous and sad-looking, like an August sky just before a storm.

"You look so sad," I said.

"I was listening to your conversation," he said, without changing his sad expression. My heart went out to him. What could possibly be wrong with him? "You're no guy," he said, finally.

"How do you know?" I said, playing dumb again.

"I know. You were just trying to get rid of him, weren't you? And if he was stupid enough to believe you, he's not good enough for you, is he?"

"You like to ask questions," I remarked.

"I like answers," he said.

I was beginning to wonder if this guy had any sense of humor, and where did I go from here? "Are you a professional football player?" I said, hoping to break through the gloom.

This guy wasn't about to lighten up. "What are you?" he spat out. "Some small-town chick who came here to become a movie star, and instead, all you've been doing is sleeping around, right?"

"Hey, mister!" I cried out, "that's not fair! I've been here less than a week. I came here to become a fashion model. I don't know nothing from nobody. I've been dragged into a pornographic film studio, been arrested for something I didn't do, been practically gang-banged by the police, and I've been kidnapped—all because I'm one terrific piece of ass!"

I never should have made the last statement. It was like waving a red flag in front of a bull.

"You think you're one terrific piece of ass?" he said. "Who says so?"

"Hey!" I said, "why don't we talk about you? And what would you like to drink? I'm having a Harvey's Bristol Cream myself."

"No," he persisted, "I want to know why you think you're a terrific piece of ass."

"Don't *you* think I'm a terrific piece of ass?" I said, not knowing what to say.

"I don't know," he answered. "I've never seen your ass."

"Look," I said, "I'm not trying to sound conceited, but when I think of my absolutely fantastic cunt and my knockers that don't know how to stop, I mean, if you were a man who liked a nice piece of ass, you'd know one when you saw one. Obviously, you're looking for something else, but I've got news for you, friend, you won't find what you're looking for down there in your navel."

With that, he took my hand and kissed it, then he put it under the table and placed it on his rock-hard erection. "I guess there's more down there than your navel," I admitted. "A lot more." With that, I reached down and felt for his balls. They felt so soft and full, nestled there, so different from the rest of him. I thought that maybe there was a chance for the two of us.

"What are you going to do about it?" he said.

"Do about what?" I said, absolutely distracted.

"My cock. What are you going to do about it? Do you think your ass is terrific enough for my terrific cock?"

"What do you think I am?" I exclaimed.

"I'll pay you anything you want. Anything. How about five hundred dollars?"

With that, I let go of his cock, grabbed the hundred dollars Jerry Ballzig had left on the table, told Daddy Gotrocks to pay the bill, and left Sardi's in tears, heading back for the East Side. I was ready to pack it in and take the bus back to Beavertown. I decided I could tell the folks back home I'd had a religious experience or something. I'd had enough of this crazy city and its crazy men. It was just too hard for a half-educated ex-waitress with no contacts.

Then, I remembered Lucchio's mother's predictions about how I'd be rich and famous in the fashion world, and I felt more depressed than ever. Down deep, I knew I was too short and too big-breasted to ever be a famous model. Not only that, my nose was first cousin to pug, and my cheekbones weren't nearly prominent enough.

158

The truth was, I looked like a well-stacked milkmaid. Admittedly, I had a great pair of legs and a stand-out ass. I thought maybe I could get a job modeling pantyhose, but face it, I wouldn't know where to start. I didn't even know one photographer, and my one big contact, Muffie, who I'd been completely dependent on, was in Brazil for an indefinite amount of time.

I was so desperate and full of pity I thought of suicide, but since I wasn't sure about life after death, I didn't want to risk it. Walking through Rockefeller Center watching the skaters in the rink, I tried to reconstruct my life, to list the positive attributes, the good things that I had to live for. At the top of the list was sex. There was no question that my cunt was a work of art. My clitoris, when aroused, was as big as my nipples, and the prepuce covering it was as delicate and lovely as the petal-flesh on an orchid. My vulva was plumper than most women's, and my bush was a thick golden nest.

Most importantly, I felt warm and comfortable around men. They knew it, and they responded to me. I hate to sound conceited, but let's face it, I was born to fuck.

The power of positive thinking was beginning to take effect. So what if I'd had a rotten day? So what if I'd met a couple of weirdos? I decided to learn my lesson right then and there, and resolved to appreciate the good guys, the ones who loved me for what I was and let it go at that, without trying to change me or control me.

Next on my list of good things was my talent for fashion. I had always loved to sew, and I particularly enjoyed designing sexy lingerie. I was already famous in Beavertown for my open crotch panties.

Then, it struck me! My trump card! My beloved Angelo! I'd been so dazed because of the events of the day before, and so full of self-pity, I'd completely forgotten my beloved boy lying in his hospital room at

159

St. Vincent's imprisoned in leg and arm casts, surrounded day and night by nymphomaniac nurses.

A half-hour later, after a cab ride with a fat man with a dyed black beard who couldn't speak English except to say, "You want to sleep with me?" I arrived at Angelo's bedside. Needless to say, he was not alone. I had to wait a full ten minutes while he was being "washed" by two teen-aged Candy-stripers. Then, I realized a strange thing was happening; I could hear their high-pitched giggles, but couldn't see any legs under the curtains around the bed. Apparently, they had to get into the bed with him to wash him properly. I decided to investigate. Sure enough, one American dream girl had her pink and white skirt hitched over her head, with her tasty little pussy smack in Angelo's slurping mouth, while the other one was taking full advantage of my favorite cock.

I was seized with a fit of jealousy. I guess I turned into a real bitch. "Allright, girlies," I said, trying to sound like somebody important, "get out of here before I call the cops and get you fired!"

Boy, were they fresh! The one with her mouth full of prime pork meat looked up and said, "You can't fire us; we're volunteers."

"Yeah, and I'm a vigilante," I replied. This was one orgy I didn't want to take part in. I wanted Angelo for myself. I grabbed for the black bush of the little slut with her easy virtue hanging wet and hot in Angelo's sucking mouth. I pulled hard.

"Ow!" she cried out. Then, before she could even notice what was happening, I quickly fingered her slippery cunt, probing for her clitoris with my practiced index fingers, using the rest of my fingers to stroke the quivering lining of her aroused cunt lips. Her clitoris was unusually large, a pink marble of flesh. When I touched it, it throbbed and glistened. I could hear her sudden gasps of pleasure when I touched her. "Slower," she begged, "we're just amateurs."

To put it bluntly, she noticed me. She started rocking back and forth on my fingers, then switched to pumping up and down on them. I let her have her fun. Why not? There is nothing more comforting in all of nature, especially to the woman herself, than the feel of an aroused vagina. The volunteer Candy-striper's hot juices were streaming down my hand. I could feel the convulsions of her orgasm rock her entire being, as she writhed, with an open moaning mouth.

Angelo lay there in total fascination. "What are you doing?" he asked, completely turned on by what he pretended not to understand.

"Eliminating the competition," I said, winking at him, and then kissing him square on the mouth. I knew he wanted desperately to finger my twat, but how could he, with both arms in stiff white casts? I quickly remembered there was a third party in our little group who was about to gobble up all the free whipped cream for herself at the opposite end of the fucking machine. So I said, "Just a minute girls, this is the twentieth century. We have to learn to share and share alike. Let me show you a trick. It's called the Volcano, and it's something we can all enjoy."

With that I got Pussy Lips, the volunteer who was pleasurably impaled on my fingers, to let go of me and turn around in the opposite directions so that she was now facing my beloved Angelo. Then, I wedged her streaming cunt right up against Angelo's majestic rod. The petals of her cunt were rich and red and ripe. Her pussy began to twitch the instant it touched that thick, white, blue-veined cock. I felt a familiar wetness spread throughout my cunt, hot and tingling and driving me crazy. There was so much pussy, so much cock, so many good-hearted people here, and I had so many conflicting

161

feelings about two of them, love-hate I think it's called, I wanted to take a dagger and carve out their hearts for me and Angelo to eat bloody raw while we fucked ourselves into oblivion. But I wanted to spend a day with each of the girls, too, my face wedged into their fuckflesh, coming up for air only when necessary. For the moment, I did the best I could with what I had; that other little volunteer cocksucker and I started licking Pussy Lip's cunt and Angelo's cock at the same time, slurping and sucking, using our hands whenever necessary, one side to a customer, greased with all the ooze we could get from our streaming cunts. We were competing; we were hungry, but there was too much for either of us to fully consume. We were both ecstatic, both sighing; obviously, deliciously erotic vibrations were traveling through both of us. Finally, though, I got selfish and wedged my aggressive little mouth over the super-ripe sugarplum on the end of Angelo's most prominent and most attractive muscle, just in time for his simmering volcano to explode in my mouth, like clotted cream.

I felt so full, so happy. It didn't bother me a bit that I had cleverly robbed the spotlight from the girls. They were stunned that I had taken Angelo from them right at the climax.

"Hey, what's the big deal?" the cocksucker said.

When I'd swallowed the last of my high-protein lunch, I said, "I'm sorry, I had to do something before my mink coat got wrecked."

Angelo, by this time, was in seventh heaven. "Diana, how can I ever thank you?" he whispered.

"You can help me get rid of the groupies," I said. "Hey, girls, you're great," I said, in frankly sarcastic tones, "why don't you go lock yourself in the supply closet and finish what you started?"

"Thanks a lot," said the little cocksucker volunteer. I could see she had mixed feelings about me. The other one, Miss Pussy Lips, was more grateful, as she should have been. After all, I'd probably given her her first multiple orgasm. She kissed me tenderly on the cheek and looked gratefully into my eyes. I never did find out her name, but I'll never forget her hot, ripe, red cunt either.

Finally, Angelo and I were alone together, facing each other, staring into each other's eyes. His eyes really were pools of filtered light, just like in the poetry our high school English teacher hated so much. Somehow, second-rate poetry has a simple, direct truth more exalted works sometimes miss. Angelo had blue eyes like the blue skies, and when I looked into them it was June Moon Spoon all the way. I felt so much love for him. He had to be the Love of My Life. Yes, I was sure he was. I knew we were meant for each other. All the cliches, and absolutely true.

My only question, a burning one, was did Angelo feel the same way about me? For the moment, I didn't want to know the answer. I was afraid he'd tell me he was in love with every woman in New York.

"Boy, have you changed," he said. "What's happened?"

"If you're referring to the new coat," I replied, "yes, it's real mink."

"That, too," he said, "but that's not what I meant, sugar-tits. You're tougher. You take change. You're a real winner. Something's happened. Tell me."

"I still love you, Angelo." I was hoping to steer the subject onto a different track.

"But where did you get the mink?" he said, "and where as you staying? I hear Muffie's apartment went up in smoke." He must have caught the grim expression on my face, because he knew it was time to lay off with the hard questions. "Hey, babe, it's great to see you!"

With that, I burst into sobbing, hot tears and collapsed on top of him. I told him about Lucchio Cafone kidnapping me and the subsequent massacre in New

163

Jersey. I told him how I got the mink, and how all I really wanted out of life now was to become a world-famous model with a devoted husband and kids, what was wrong with that, but I had no idea where to begin or how to begin. As far as I was concerned I looked like an overfed farm girl who'd gladly open her legs for every passing salesman.

"Don't worry about anything, babe," Angelo said. "I know that you'll be a success at whatever you put your mind to."

At that point, I switched to my prepared speech. "When you get better, Angelo, I thought that maybe we, you and I, could share an apartment in the Village; and don't worry, Angelo, I promise I wouldn't get in the way of your sex life, no matter what."

There it was. My brilliant idea. It was out. I waited for his reply with a sinking feeling in my stomach.

"You're terrific," he said.

"What do you think?" I said, as persistently as I could.

"About what?" he said.

"About our living together in the Village." Already, I knew my idea was in Big Trouble.

"Hey, babe, Diana delicious, I got something to tell you."

I figured. I could feel it coming and I didn't want to know.

"Diana babe, there's a woman in my life you don't know about. A woman I already live with. In the Village. I love her more than anyone I've ever known."

Like I said, I really didn't want to know. Anything.

But Angelo had to tell me. Everything. Shit. "Her professional name is Gloriana Bronx. It was a choice between that and Hot Lips O'Hara. Don't worry, her real name is Gloria Bronkowski, but she thought that sounded a little Midwestern. Gloriana Bronx is a great business name for a model, don't you think?"

So that was it. A model. Well, I thought to myself,

164

we've established that this gentleman likes models. Great. I tried to sound reasonable.

"What kind of a model is she?" I said, as coolly as I could.

"She's a fashion model for what's called a couturier house; that's where a great designer shows his original costumes for astronomical amounts of bread," Angelo explained.

"I know what a couturier house is," I said. But the truth was, I didn't. For someone who says she wanted to be a fashion model, I knew next to nothing. I was already in way over my head.

"The House of Adoro."

"What?" I said, half-listening, hoping against hope that Angelo had just said he adored me.

No way. "Adolfo Adoro is the world's most successful designer after Pierre Cardin."

"Right." I sounded so well-versed in the ways of the world. Ha! I wasn't even sure who Pierre Cardin was. I thought he only made perfume. The only designers I had ever heard of at that point were Halston, who designs for Liz Taylor and Liza Minnelli, and Bob Mackey, who designs for Cher and Carol Burnett, and who made the rounds of the television talk shows. I had always thought a designer gown meant a lot of sequins and a lot of leg.

"Gloriana's really Adoro's right hand," Angelo said.

"What does he do with his left hand?" I asked.

"As a matter of fact," Angelo informed me, "Adoro's had both hands up most of the well-trimmed pussies on both sides of the Atlantic."

I decided I really wasn't interested in Gloriana Bronx. I didn't care whose hand she was, or whose pussy she'd gotten into. As fate would have it, exactly then, Gloriana Bronx arrived for her daily bedside visit. I couldn't believe my eyes. If I felt like an overstacked milkmaid when I walked into St. Vincent's, looking at her now, I felt like a combination of town trollop and professional wet nurse. Christ, I felt like a sow. I really needed a few tits-and-ass men to cheer me on, but Angelo wasn't about to rip my clothes off and fuck me blind in front of the Great Love of His Life. Besides, he was out of commission. How convenient.

Back to Gloriana Bronx. Around thirty. Five feet ten. Built like a gazelle, a healthy one, with legs that zoomed all the way to her shoulders with nonexistent tits and minimal hips. So how come she was one of the sexiest women I'd ever seen? I knew the answer, but I wished I hadn't. Gloriana Bronx was a fucking animal. Everything about her was animal, from the way she moved to the way she smelled. And good ol' Gloriana was surer of her body than I was of mine. Because as hard as I tried, I could never get myself to come across with that special element of danger that only animals and the world's sexiest women seem to have. I guess my basic problem, as far as being a legendary beauty goes, is that I've never been that afraid of men and they've never been that afraid of me. Of course, when I began to mentally strip the great Gloriana, what I found, at least in my imagination, was lithe and sleek and warm. Her eyes, black as coal, were almond-shaped which made her look Oriental and mysterious. Her face had the perfect bones of someone who'd probably been on the covers of a hundred fashion magazines. I could see why she fascinated Angelo. She fascinated me, too—so much so I hated her on sight. In time, as it turned out, I came to love her. Yes, she became part of my life, because she helped guide me in my career and was ultimately responsible for my breakthrough in New York.

The day I first met her, however, I had no idea of our future relationship. And to the end of my days I will always believe that I, and not Gloriana Bronx, am Angelo O'Shaughnessy's greatest love. Not that Gloriana would ever be capable of admitting this. One thing was clear: the source of my greatest pleasure, Angelo, was also the source of my greatest frustration.

"This is Gloriana Bronx," Angelo said, introducing us.

All I said was, "I figured." What I really figured was that I was not hiding my hostility very well. Neither was Gloriana. She ignored me so that she could kiss Angelo passionately and obscenely. They were like two long-lost lovers. They made noises with their lips. They slurped. They gasped for air. She had her long-fingered hands all over his chest, grabbing his carpet of red-gold hair like she was falling from a height and needed something to hold onto. Since Angelo was in traction, with his limbs immobile, she was clearly victimizing him. Their passion was absolutely disgusting, and in bad taste, besides. They completely ignored me. I was never so embarrassed in my life. I have to admit that if I had not known how much he loved her, I would have jumped into the bed with them, but knowing what I knew, I realized that my great gift for sex would not make me more attractive to Angelo. He'd had me at my best, and still he loved this Gloriana person the most of anyone. At least, that's what he'd said.

Thank God for the humpy doctor who just happened by. He was one of New York's leading orthopedic surgeons, as I later found out. The dear man allowed me to graphically demonstrate to my beloved Angelo that I have many other fish to fry and certainly am in no way dependent on a stupid porn star with a limited future. The surgeon, Dr. Baker, seemed shocked to find Gloriana and Angelo going at it, which surprised me, considering she wasn't even on top of him. "This patient needs peace and quiet," Dr. Baker said.

"I know. I'm the piece," Gloriana remarked. "And she's the quiet," she added, nodding at me.

What a trashy remark! I didn't say a word. I just stood

167

there in my fabulous mink coat, sizing up Dr. Baker (that, too), trying to figure out what my next move would be.

"Doctor," I said, "I think you're one hunk of modern medicine. How sick do I have to be to get you?"

"Would you like me to examine you?" he replied.

"Are you the bone doctor?" I asked. "I think I'm missing a bone."

"Where are you missing a bone?" he said, with a gleam in his eye.

"Right between my legs."

"That's what I thought," he said. "There's just a hole there where a bone should be, isn't that right?"

"I think so, Doctor," I said, "but I'm not absolutely sure. I think you'll have to examine me." And with that, I opened my fabulous mink coat and unsnapped my red, gold-trimmed kimono. There I was. Exposed. Vulnerable. My juicy nipples stared at him like two wide-open eyes. I guess Dr. Baker didn't see too many women patients who looked like me. I began to fondle my breasts, drawing circles around my aureoles, pinching my nipples. Then I let my kimono drop to the floor in a red and gold heap at my feet.

The man instantly grabbed his crotch like he'd just been shot in the groin. All I heard was a muffled "Oh Christ!"

"But Doctor, I want you to see my hole," I said, just as nice as I could be. With one hand cupped under my bushy vulva and with the other running a finger up and down through my slippery ruby slit, I said, "See. There it is. I just know I'm missing a bone."

I kept waiting for Angelo to become absolutely furious and dismiss Dr. Baker, but he and his Gloriana were kissing again, making more obscene noises than ever. In short, they ignored me completely, and I found that I was the one who was furious. "To hell with them," I said to myself, "I intend to have a terrific time."

Dr. Baker had opened his shirt to reveal a swimmer's chest. Then, he dropped his pants to reveal his "bone." An impressive bone it was, with a lot of red meat and a purplish head shaped like a large mushroom cap. "Is this the bone you're looking for?" he asked.

"I think we'd just about fit," I said in a loud voice, "but I'm not sure. We better measure to make sure."

This man was obviously such a brilliant doctor that he had little available time for foreplay. He was all work. He pressed his cock head against my labia. "This will only hurt a little bit," he promised. I doubted it.

In a flash, his broad cock head parted my fat pussy lips as he penetrated me. I wasn't completely ready for him. As a matter of fact, I was pretty dry. "I love a dry cunt," he whispered, nibbling at my ear and blowing into it. He started grinding away. Really grinding.

"I feel pain!" I cried out.

"Good!" he answered. "That's why you need a doctor!" Then, savagely, with no finesse, no gentleness, no technique except brute force, he bore down on me with sheer physical mass. I felt like a locomotive was boring into me. It was, nonetheless, a highly sexual experience. After a few minutes, the man's force was something my body naturally responded to. I rose to the challenge. I grew wet. I felt my cunt-lips finally grab hold of his strong cylindrical cock, hug it, and suck it, even though my mind was on Angelo, who didn't say a word.

By now, Dr. Baker was crying, "I love you! I love you!" and I was moaning, "Yes! Yes!" even though half of my brain was pretending I was fucking Angelo. I grabbed the back of Dr. Baker's iron-hard legs and squeezed his large, strong ass as he sucked on the sides of my neck. He thrust deeply into me as we collapsed together onto the floor, entangled with each other. I finally let go of his body, as he kept battering me with his big piece of meat. My head thrashed back and forth, as I cried out, "Fuck me! Fuck me! Ram it into me! Tear

169

me apart! Oh baby! Oh baby! Give me all of your bone! Your bone! Give me all of your bone!" Oh Christ! I was filled up with heat; his cock swelled so big inside me, I felt like it was reaching up to my throat to choke me.

Then, the Big Event. The orgasm. The monsoon. He pulled out his big bone and rained come all over my stomach, my tits, my nipples. There was a small pool of it in my navel. My bush was come-soaked, its golden hairs glistening like a Christmas tree. I lubricated myself all over and massaged his balls with it. He looked at me dreamily through half-closed eyes, smiled a half-smile, withdrew his "bone," buttoned up his clothes, and said, "I hope I was of some help."

"You're a wonderful doctor," I said, soaked to the skin in my own perspiration. "I feel better already."

"Here, take my card," he said, dressing himself. "I hope that if you ever have that trouble again, you'll come visit me." Then, before I had a chance to answer or even tell him my name, he left through the same opening he'd entered.

Angelo was so wonderful, I guess. No mention of my present feelings of longing for him. But the whole time I'd been "occupied" with Dr. Baker, Gloriana and he had been discussing my career. That's funny. I thought they'd been making out. But as it so happened, Gloriana considered herself a perfect lady and never fucked in public.

"Gloriana and I have been discussing your career," Angelo said. "She'd like to meet with you as soon as possible and suggest some photographers and agents for you to meet. How would you like that?"

What could I say? Obviously, when it came to the fashion world, I could only fake it so much longer. I had a lot to learn. Gloriana was clearly a woman of the world. I was just a sexpot from Beavertown, Pennsylvania, where, as a matter of fact, the last real beaver had left fifty years before. Yes, as much as I hated to admit it, I knew instinctively that Gloriana and I would become close friends and that neither one of us would get the man we wanted. For me, that man was Angelo. For her, it was someone else, a someone who would fall in love with me and shape my destiny. His name was Adolfo Adoro.

In time I would meet him, but not yet. Not yet.

Gloriana and I decided to have dinner together to discuss my "career." She kissed my beloved Angelo on his lips. Then, she walked out. I followed her, but not before I kissed him, too. On his big, thick cock, which responded and began to grow larger. That's how I left my beloved Angelo that day, with no hands to jerk himself off and not a Candy-striper in sight. In a word, unfulfilled. Yes, there were ways of dealing with my beloved Angelo.

Chapter Ten

It was dusk on Park Avenue. The glass skyscrapers twinkled like Christmas trees. The working-class throngs thinned out. Couples dressed for the evening began to appear; tall lean figures with thick hair and long, lean legs, the men in pin-stripe navy blues, the women in black sheath cocktail dresses. I had invited Gloriana Bronx to be my guest for dinner at McMullen's Restaurant on Third Avenue. I had overheard businessmen talking about it in the Waldorf lobby. It was supposed to be the epitome of Manhattan of the eighties with its vigorous executives of both sexes, its political chatter, its occasional celebrities like Princess Grace and Ali Mac-Graw, and, better yet, the owner was rumored to be a successful model. I figured that for once I'd be in the right company.

We were early, so we had no trouble finding a small table between a bare brick wall and a potted palm. Our conversation, as they say, began in earnest. Gloriana couldn't stand my guts and said so. "Darling Diana, I hate to sound negative, but you'll never make it in New York, as a model, that is."

"Why not?" I replied, trying not to sound too defensive. "Men find me very attractive."

"Don't get me wrong," Gloriana continued. "As a whore you'd be terrific."

"I don't have to be a whore," I said coolly, "I get all the sex I want for nothing."

"Let's get serious, Diana, I'm talking business, career, dollars and cents. Your face and body suggest an over-sexed milkmaid on a Wisconsin dairy farm who lifts her skirts for every traveling salesman with a hard-on. Face facts. No American housewife would buy toilet paper or even a box of soap from you."

I was furious, even though she was verbalizing my worst fears and I had often come to the very same conclusions myself. "Gloriana," I said, "are you suggesting that I'm some kind of an easy lay?"

"I'll do you one better," she said. "You're what's used to be called the town switchboard."

"Then, I'll be a movie star," I said. "I'll be another Marilyn Monroe. She was the town switchboard, too."

"My dear Diana," Gloriana sputtered in her nasty-nice intonation, "a pushover like you never becomes a movie star. Marilyn Monroe was driven by demons; she transformed herself from a drab nobody into something larger than life. Look at you, darling, you're not driven, you're not hungry—even if you were starving to death you wouldn't be hungry. You've got this disgustingly healthy look to you. It will never sell."

"Maybe you're right, Gloriana," I said, "but I want to try. And I want you to help me."

"Why should I help you?" she snapped, nibbling furiously on a mussel vinaigrette.

I played it cool. "And Angelo wants you to help me, too," I added.

"Angelo!" she hissed. "What is this Angelo business? He doesn't owe you a goddamn thing, and as far as I know, he only met you last week!"

I was desperate. "Please! Gloriana! I'm not asking you for a job. I only want to know where to get an agent and a good photographer. Nothing more."

"Oh," she said. The mussels and half a bottle of wine seemed to be working more magic than I ever could. After a while Gloriana calmed down. She decided it wouldn't be worth fighting Angelo on this. Yes, she knew of a top-flight modeling agency. As a matter of fact, she knew the directors personally; they were a husband and wife team, Mary and Barry Chrysler. The Chrysler agency, as it so happened, had about half the world's best models in its stable. She promised to give them a call "sometime during the next week," she wasn't sure which day, she was very busy, and she'd get back to me.

As Fate would have it, the very people she was talking about, the Chryslers themselves, were sitting on the other side of the room. And guess who was with them? No, it couldn't be! Yes, it was! No, it wasn't! Yes, it was! Her Serene Highness, Princess Grace of Monaco. Grace was wearing the "layered look": beige coordinates, a cardigan over a turtle neck with a pleated skirt, and simple gold jewelry. She looked a ravishing thirty-five, a generation younger than her newspaper photographs.

I thought Miss Gloriana Bronkowski Bronx was going

173

to pee in her purple ultrasuede pants. "It's the Chryslers!" she screeched, "and Grace Kelly's with them, I mean Princess Grace. Oh my God! She comes to Adoro's all the time. I better go say 'hello'."

"You better bring me with you," I suggested.

With that, Gloriana went into a state of shock. "You? You and Princess Grace? Who are *you*?"

"They're looking our way, dear Gloriana. Mr. Chrysler is very attracted to me. He's staring at me, Gloriana, me, not you, and if you go over there and leave me here, they will all assume that I'm your lesbian lover and you're too embarrassed to introduce me." Gloriana got my point.

I was introduced as "My cousin who wants to be a model, and I'm trying to talk her out of it, I mean, look at her, Mary, too short and no bones, right?"

Princess Grace saved my life. "When I was a model," she said, "they told me I was too tall and too blonde. You must find your own style."

"Oh, Your Majesty," I blurted out, "I want to be just like you!"

"Gracie, isn't she a stitch!" said Mary Chrysler.

Barry, on the other hand, was a little more serious about my possibilities. I noticed he was giving me the old once-over, looking me up and down, mentally stripping me of every stitch. With his brawny, football player's build and his thatch of thick brown hair cut in a preppie collegiate style, he looked young enough to be Mary's oldest son. And humpy. I figured he was my best bet. For everything. I wanted more than anything to take Barry Chrysler and the blonde princess back with me to the Waldorf and leave Mary Chrysler with Gloriana to pick apart this year's Rich and Famous.

Barry said, or rather, announced, "I say we interview Diana Hunt. Frankly, I'd buy anything she was selling."

Mary looked at him. "I'll bet you would dear, but I say she's not selling anything; she's giving it away!"

"Oh, Barry's just attracted to beautiful women, aren't you Barry?" said Princess Grace, taking in both Barry and me with her dazzling smile. She seemed to be hinting at some hidden meaning known only to her and to Barry, which surprised me, because I had always thought that she probably had never had sex. My sister, who preferred Liz Taylor, always said Princess Grace's children were born from artificial insemination just like the calves on my grandfather's farm. Little did I suspect that even, as I stood there before this perfect lady and one-time Oscar winner, that before two years were out, I would be an honored guest at her palace in Monaco (when the Prince was away on safari, unfortunately). Even though I was never to have sexual adventures in Monaco worth telling about, at least not until the people in question are dead, I have always credited my extraordinary rise in the fashion world to the kindness of Princess Grace.

"Mary, this girl is lovely," said the Princess. "She exemplifies America at its best: young, healthy, and wide-eyed. She has an abundance about her, don't you think?"

"An abundance?" Gloriana interjected. "What you really mean is, she's got big boobs, and if you'll pardon my French, I've been trying to explain to my cousin Diana here that housewives are too insecure to buy from girls with big boobs."

Princess Grace did not look pleased. "Well, I'm a housewife," she said, "and I'd buy from this girl. Mary, if you don't sign her, I'll get the Jacques Tunisia Agency to sign her. He owes me."

"Okay, I'll see you tomorrow morning." It was Barry. He handed me his business card. It said, "The Chrysler Agency. The Lever Building." He told me to be there at nine o'clock sharp. I said absolutely yes.

"But Barry, darling, tomorrow's Sunday," Mary said.

"All the better," replied Barry. "I can give her my total attention, then go home and go to bed."

175

"In a state of total collapse, no doubt," said Mary, hinting that Barry was as good as he looked. But, of course, I played dumb, hoping to get out of McMullen's alive and then some.

"Come join us," said Barry to his wife with the wrinkled face.

"Darling, as you well know, I rarely come anymore," said Mrs. Chrysler.

"Well, you're invited anyway," replied Barry, looking deeply into his Bloody Mary.

Gloriana ignored all of this bitchy husband and wife talk by speaking sweetly to Princess Grace. They seemed to be blowing smoke into each other's faces. I, feeling that I was definitely too young for this august group of celebrities, thanked everyone, especially Princess Grace, went back to my table, paid the check, and walked back to the Waldorf with stars in my eyes.

The next morning. Sunday. Nine a.m. sharp. The Lever Building. Barry Chrysler was waiting for me in the Chrysler Agency's reception room. He was wearing an alligator shirt that was much too short. His midriff was showing. Pure muscle. Not an ounce of flab. He greeted me with a heavy kiss on the lips. "Hello, gorgeous," he said.

Maybe I was. I was also being a little outrageous, deliberately. Under my ever-present mink, I was wearing a black see-through dress with no underwear. The dress was made out of the same material as black see-through stockings. I believe the word is "sheer." I was sheer. Even *I* was a little turned on by the sight of my ripe breasts bobbing up and down under my dress as I moved. In Beavertown, I would have been called a cheap-looking show-off. But my body looked like a million dollars. And the mink was real. *And* I needed to attract the attention of the right person. Otherwise, I was as good as dead. "Do you think I'd make a good model." I asked.

"I'd have to see how you photograph," he said. "Don't

worry, I've got a dark room in my office. We can do this quickly."

"Do what quickly?" I asked, doing my dumb act.

"Fuck," he said, adding quickly, "I'm just kidding. No, but seriously, I have to take some pictures of you."

I was a little bit distracted by the muscles in the man's stomach. In my fantasy, I kept seeing them rippling as he fucked me. I saw the broad muscles of his back contract and expand as he thrust a long, stiff cock between the petals of my cunt and thrust deeply and passionately, pounding like a piston with an insistent beat over and over again in my wildly throbbing pussy. I had to check myself. I had come to the Chrysler Agency for a job. I had to pay the rent. This man's wife was the head of the agency. What was I thinking of?

"First, let me see you walk across the room." What? Who was speaking? Where was I? Christ, I could feel the man's cock inside me, and he was standing ten feet away from me, fully dressed, except for that tantalizing patch of hairy, muscular stomach.

"First, let me see you walk across the room."

Yes, it was Barry speaking. The hunk.

"Oh, yes," I said, trying desperately not to look in his eyes, not to look at his body. I was in a panic. I didn't know where to look.

"Do you mind taking your mink coat off?" he said.

The coat was off before he finished the sentence. I felt absolutely naked, and his eyes were glued to my tits. "Where can I lay the coat?" I asked, trying to sound as cool as possible.

"You can lay it anywhere you want to lay it," he said.

When I bent over to lay the coat on a chair in the reception room, I could feel my boobs swing away from my body. I knew they were outlined against the beige wall behind me. I knew my nipples were visibly erect, and I knew without looking that Mr. Chrysler had an uncomfortable bulge in his crotch which was begging for release. But I continued to play it cool. I was determined to separate my private life and my professional life. I wanted a career. I wanted a job. I could have any man I wanted. Fuck it, the truth was, this man was driving me crazy. He was a Wasp. He was my father. I wanted him.

"That's an interesting dress you're wearing," he said, referring to my see-through black chemise.

"This is a very expensive outfit," I said, lying through my teeth.

He cut me off. "I've got to find something that shows off your figure when you walk."

"Shows off my figure?" I said.

"Yes," he replied, "I really can't get a good sense of your figure with that loose black dress, as interesting as it is."

So that was it. We were both lying. We were both playing games. I wondered how much longer I could hold on. My crotch was already full of heat and tingling and fear and exhilaration. I wanted to embrace him and grind my juice-laden pussy into his bulge until he came in his pants so that Frigid Mary would see them and go beserk. "Stop. Stop, Diana," I kept telling myself. "Your passion is getting out of hand."

That's right. It got completely out of hand. I wanted my Daddy's mouth on my tits. I wanted his strong hands pinching my ass, kneading it, caressing it. "As a matter of fact, to answer your question, Mr. Chrysler," I said, still cool, but breaking out into a sweat, "I've got some new underwear in my puss, I mean my purse, and it looks just like a bathing suit." With that, I opened my little black velvet evening purse and removed the miniscule panties I had planted there, and I stepped into them. Then, I slipped out of my sheer black dress. To put it bluntly, I had plain forgotten two important things. One, I wasn't wearing a bra. It's something I

178

normally never think about, as I walk around naked in my room all the time. That's innocent enough. The second thing I'd forgotten was far more serious. The panties I'd put in my purse were different from the ones I thought. They were open-crotch panties trimmed in crimson ribbon. I had made them myself as a turn-on for Angelo, and the truth is, I'd forgotten about the open crotch. I was never so embarrassed in my life. My fuck-flesh was hanging out in front, the lower part of my labia drooping out like two coral lips in my thick nest of golden hair.

Barry Chrysler hooted.

"What's wrong?" I said.

"I don't believe it! I don't believe it!" he shouted, jubilant and exultant. He started snapping pictures like someone possessed. "Diana, Diana, do me a favor, here, sit in the desk chair here. That's right. Put your feet on the floor. That's right. Sit with authority. Right. Legs apart. Right. Good. Wonderful posture, Diana. Good. Let's hear it for women executives. Great." He was just like the father I had always wanted. Firm. Enthusiastic. Supportive. I felt so protected, so cared for, so desired. I wanted to whisper, "Thank you, Daddy," but I didn't dare.

Then, the worst happened. There was a draft from somewhere. I felt cold air on my juicy, hot labia. I looked down to see what was the matter, and there it was, my cunt exposed. I was mortified. I gasped, "Oh no!" and covered myself with my hands. Then, worse, I began to cry."

"What's wrong?" asked Barry in the most kindly, solicitous tones imaginable.

"Only that I've ruined everything!" I sobbed. "I didn't realize those were my open-crotch panties. I saved those for my boyfriend, but he doesn't love me, and now look at me, in the reception room of one of the world's biggest

179

modeling agencies looking like some kind of cheap tramp, posing for nude photos." I was sobbing so much I couldn't get my breath.

"I think you're one of the kindest, sweetest little girls I've ever known. I'm sorry. I just got carried away when I saw those dear, sweet little nipples of yours. I'm sorry, baby, I got carried away, I couldn't help myself. Please, little baby girl, forgive your papa." And with that he kissed me on my breasts so tenderly and rubbed his open mouth and his nose and his cheeks over and over in the space between my breasts.

"Daddy, Daddy," I said. "Please love me. I'll be a good little girl." And with that I unbuttoned his tight jeans and unzipped him to allow his sweet cock to breath. Christ, he was hung! I lifted his dork with both hands out of his imprisoning underpants. I could feel the intense heat in that big piece of meat, and I could smell the mingling of so many delicious masculine smells, sperm and piss and sweat and leftover deodorant. It was wrapped in veins. What a wonderful Daddy. "Oh, Daddy," I cried in my little-girl voice. I opened my mouth as wide as I could and took the head of that momma between my hot lips and pressed against it, while "Daddy" fondled my breasts with his strong hands. I worked my mouth over the broad cock as I squeezed its base, and worked the thick, loose flesh back and forth over the hard, blood-engorged inner core. I could feel the tip of his glans pounding away at the back of my throat. I felt so useful, helping my Daddy get off. I knew Mommy Mary would never help him like this. She was mean and nasty. She didn't know Daddy was a real man. She didn't know what a real man was, she was so used to second-rate imitations in the modeling business. She couldn't appreciate the meaning of a thick, red-hot cock.

"Baby, baby, I don't want to hurt you. But please suck on Daddy's putz. Poor Daddy's putz."

180

"Tool! Fuck! Come! Cock! Suck! Fuck!" I shouted out. "See, Daddy, I'm a bad girl! I used bad words!" I shouted right in his face, with tears in my eyes. Then, I resumed my cock-sucking, guilty that I had spoken so boldly, and loving my guilt, loving the sickening feeling in the pit of my stomach that Daddy would have to take care of, Daddy would have to make all better.

God, was I sick, and I loved it! So did he. His hand went to my cunt. What a hand! He was so kind, so careful, so loving. He explored me with those wise, all-knowing fingers. I could taste the thick liquor that was oozing from the end of his rampant cock. He pushed me down onto the thick, soft carpet and spun around into the sixty-nine position. "Oh, Daddy," I cried out. I felt his tongue in me. It was an animal tongue, a lion's tongue, soft and ragged at the same time, dragging electric sensations across the center of my soul. What a fucking good father I had, what a daddy, what a man! What a lucky little girl! We both oohed and aahed as we settled into the warm pleasure of having our mouths crammed full of such desirable family flesh. Our make-believe incest bordered on insanity, which made it fantastic sex. We responded to each other's slightest movements like tango dancers; when he moved, I followed, and when I moved, he was right there, close to me, his warm breath like a spring wind in the flower garden of my rosy-petaled cunt.

"Baby, forgive me, but Daddy has to fuck you. I have to do it, baby, I just can't pass up the mouthfuls of your tit, the mouthfuls of your sweet cunt, baby, oh baby, I was born to get inside you and tell you what a fucking sweet little girl you are." Then, the huge weight of him was on top of me, the fullback on the playing field.

I instinctively wrapped my legs around his waist and then rubbed them back and forth over the strong muscles of his ass.

"Come to Papa. Come to Papa."

I took his dork in both hands and lifted it into me. Christ, it was heavy. It was like a low-slung pipe hinged onto him between his legs. A hot water pipe. A hot come pipe. I pushed the full face of my furry pussy against him as he pushed into me, separating my rosy lips of flesh.

He came almost immediately. "Aaagh!" he moaned, as he shot his load of ambrosia, his body quivering, his head thrashing. I came at the same time. I shrieked and wailed and grunted. My flesh was burning, my mind was blurred. I was in heaven. It was better than drugs.

Daddy obviously felt the same way as he shot his precious fluid into the hidden recesses of my flesh. He collapsed on me, utterly exposed and vulnerable, my little boy. "Daddy. Daddy," I cried, "I've always wanted you."

We were glued together in heat and ectasy. "I've always wanted you too," he said. "You're the best little girl I've ever had. You're so sweet. You're so clean, so honest. Oh Christ, baby!" And he began to cry, sobbing softly.

"Don't cry, Daddy, don't cry. You're a wonderful, strong man. You're my big boy. You're my wonderful big boy."

Mary Chrysler, that bitch on wheels, had been hiding in the half-open coat closet the whole time. With tape recorder and camera. In case she ever wanted a divorce, she later explained.

"She's fired," ordered Bloody Mary.

"But she's never been hired," answered Barry, suddenly subservient and scrambling for his clothes, his big dork shrinking before my very eyes. "I was just interviewing her."

"So I see," answered Mary, not so much in the tones of a woman scorned, as a woman who had never been desired, because she had never wanted to be desired in the first place.

Well, my fantasy trip was over. It was back to earth and confrontation with the Wicked Witch of the West. "You certainly are one mean lady," I said, and I wasn't about to stop there. "If you can't make your husband feel like a man, what's wrong with someone else giving it a try?"

"I can't deal with this," shrieked Mary. "Please leave the premises immediately!" And then, as if she'd suddenly been inspired, she did a complete about-face. "I've got it! I've got it!" she squealed.

"What is it?" asked the shamefaced Barry.

"What is it?" chimed in yours truly.

Mary was triumphant. She turned on her husband like a matador in the bull ring. "You want that tramp to be a big-time model? You want to launch her career? You want her to be given a chance to get her name in the papers?" Then, without waiting for his reply or mine, she turned to me. "Okay, girlie, you've got yourself a job. Barry, the Putangi!"

"The what? The who?" said I.

"Who, pray tell, dear wife, are the Putangi?" said Barry. "They sound like an African tribe."

"Precisely!" said Mary, who then proceeded to explain the situation. Neither Barry nor I knew exactly what she was talking about, but she was seized with her idea. "A very famous department store has been trying to do a special fashion spread to advertise their new line of sportswear," Mary explained, her eyes glazed over. They want to use the Putangi tribe of southeastern Africa as the backdrop for the spread. Wait! I know what you're thinking—that black Americans would be offended and outraged at their ethnic cousins being used for a fashion spread, but the Putangi are more than simply black. They are quite simply the most exotic tribe in Africa. They are descended from the Vikings,

183

the Masai, and the Bedouins. They are the most striking-looking people in the world. They've got shaven heads, emerald-green eyes, and skin that ranges from *café au lait* to Swiss chocolate. They're tall and athletic and brilliant dancers. So far, my problem with getting models for this job is that sexually, the Putangi are off the wall. The women are like animals in heat every day of the year. Most of them have clitorises two and three inches long. The men are reportedly hung like horses and fuck everything in sight, including their own children, who have to be sent to separate villages to avoid the consequences of incest. I can't get one model in our stable to agree to go. The truth is, there's been a rumor going around the modeling agencies that the Putangi, when they catch sight of a Western woman, fuck her to death, or almost. We did have one girl who couldn't wait to go, but she was a certified nymphomaniac and had a nervous breakdown just thinking about the assignment. She's in Bellevue doing nicely. They say she should be out in another six months. So what do you say, Miss Diana Hunt? Are you interested in modeling with my agency?"

Ha! I wasn't about to let that cunt Mary Chrysler scare me off with these fairy tales about exotic heathen, so I let her have it right between the eyes. "Absolutely. I'd love to go!"

Mary looked maliciously pleased. "Well, then, my dear, just as soon as we get you a passport, which unfortunately may take weeks..."

"I've got one!" I shouted. It had always been my fantasy that one day my most interesting lover would say to me, "Hey! Let's got to Paris for the weekend!" and where would I be then if I didn't have a passport?

Mary gave the orders. "Barry, darling, tell our photographer Jake Turnby we've got the girl. Then, tell the fagola Mr. Max Blacker to call the store, dig the rags out of the closet; and what else—you book the flight."

184

Amazing. She was so ⌐ _____ ⌐ moment, she forgot completely _____ ried woman would have been ti____ her life. I have since come to admire the stee_ ___ successful women like Mary Chrysler, but I don't envy her that quality. I have always enjoyed the drama of my emotional crises. I have cherished the hysterical moments of my love affairs as much as the calm quiet of them, too. I allow the people around me to be exactly the same. Maybe that is why people love to work for me, and why I have traveled all over the world visiting my friends. My trip to the Putangi was actually my first trip abroad. I was determined that no matter how pathologically sexual these exotic people were, I would find something to enjoy and someone to be fond of. As it turned out, I had one of the great adventures of my life and ended up costing the Chrysler Agency a million-dollar account. But Mary Chrysler couldn't say she didn't ask for it. She thought she was sending me to Africa to be gang-banged and left for dead. That showed how much she knew about sex. Or men. Or me.

Chapter Eleven

Two days later, I was sitting on TWA Flight 761 to Nairobi, which was the closest airport to the Putangi. I was wedged, by design, I'm sure, between Max Blacker, who was sporting a white silk tank-top jumpsuit with a black silk shirt underneath, and our photographer, Jake Turnby, with his overgrown toupee, coral-colored che-

... to the navel with his matted gray chest and about five hundred dollars worth of gold chains on open display. I was wearing a brand-new London Fog raincoat, underneath which I had on a white pleated cotton-polyester sun dress with a halter top and no brassiere.

I had to keep looking down at my breasts, because that's where Jake Turnby kept looking. I was afraid my nipples were visible. They weren't. For once, I thought, I was playing it safe.

I'd had a couple of brandies, however, and somewhere over the Azores, I must have fallen asleep. I had told the Joy Boys to wake me up the minute they spotted the West Coast of Africa, ancestral home of some of the sexiest men in America. Instead, I awoke with a start about half an hour later. Jake Turnby had one hand cupped around my left breast, which he was kissing like there was no tomorrow, and a finger inside my one and only cunt, which, to my horror, was lubricated and in good working order.

I guess I'd been dreaming of my beloved Angelo. But how was Jake Turnby to know that? The man was such an egomaniac, he probably thought he had power over my dreams. I didn't know what to do. Jake was obviously a sexually active man, or he wouldn't have exposed his chest, not to mention his putting his finger in my cunt. I really did not want to insult his masculinity, and needless to say, I really needed the job experience. There was another ugly truth: since we left JFK Airport I had had my eyes on the pilot, a Captain Harper, a real hunk, about six feet five with the body of a collegiate wrestler; in other words, stocky without being fat.

I had assumed that Captain Harper was too busy flying the airplane to pay any attention to me. As my friend Fate would have it, Captain Harper had noticed me. Not only that, just as I was waking up with Jake Turnby's finger up my cunt, a sexy little red-headed stewardess with pointed nineteen-fifties' tits brought me a note from the pilot in question. The note said, "Come up to the cockpit and I'll show you something about flying. Captain Harper."

Jake, who had been reading the note over my shoulder, didn't know what to say or do, so he stuck another finger up my cunt, hoping I'd beg him to stick his cock in, too. But I was one step ahead of him, and I had something better in mind. I said, "Thank you, Jake, that feels wonderful," as if he were scratching my back, and added, "I'll have to get back to you later; I've got to go see the Captain." With that, I took Jake's fingers out of my cunt, kissed his hand tenderly, and put it back in his lap.

Jack began to beg, "Oh please! Oh please!" Within the space of ten seconds I excused myself, climbed over Jack's knees, kissed him on the forehead, and was halfway up the aisle to my Captain, my new idol, my possible infatuation. I was already in torment because I could not remember what he looked like, and I hated myself for that.

When I opened the door to his cabin, his "cockpit," there were two of them! Two brawny head-turners. Two square-jawed, red-faced, gray-eyed, hard-drinking soldiers of fortune. "Who is the Captain?" I asked with a frog in my throat.

"That would be me, you gorgeous piece of pussy meat," said the gravelly voiced man on the right. He certainly didn't waste time with formalities, and his opening remark was only the beginning. "I really want to get it on with you," he continued in his noticeable Texas accent. "If I'm offending you, you can always go back to your seat and I won't bother you again."

By this time, I was standing behind his chair, unbuttoning his shirt from behind, my hands diving onto his massive wrestler's chest, smooth and strong and muscular with large, pale aureoles as big as half-dollars,

187

so he must have realized I wasn't about to go back to my seat, at least not yet. I noticed a sizeable bulge beginning to grow between his legs. So far, so good.

"What do I do?" I said, doing my dumb act.

"You don't have to do nothing," he said, getting up from his seat.

"But what about flying the plane?" I said.

"That's what the copilot's all about. Turn around, Chester, and watch the road!" And with that, this aggressive daredevil of the skies unzipped his fly and struggled to work his jockey briefs down and around his erection.

Sensing his difficulty, I offered to help. "We don't have much time," he said, "otherwise I would have taken everything off, little lady."

I managed to release his masculine root; his cock was big and fat and as pale pink as his aureole. Glistening drops of pure oil were already dripping from its tiny open mouth.

"Hey, Romeo and Juliet," the copilot cracked, "hurry up and get your rocks off; it's thunder and lightning up ahead!"

I quickly glanced out the tiny front window and saw deep purple clouds. There was thunder and the crack of lightning everywhere. Captain Harper acted as though he had five minutes left to live. He pulled down my panties, and with his two practiced hands, he gripped my buttocks and then cleaved into me. Like a dive bomber cutting through clouds. Like an ocean liner dividing the waves. Like Moses parting the Red Sea. I was parted. I was divided. I was cut through.

Wow! I was completely unprepared for the raw power of his cock. I'm so used to a man's hot breath on my cunt, his tongue searching through my rose-petaled lips for my precious clitoris. In other words, a gentleman. This man, this warrior, was more like a Samurai.

What happened next was probably the most unusual,

188

the most unplanned, the most spontaneous sexual thrill of my young life. Just as Captain Hunter was driving in more forcefully, pumping away in my delta of pussy flesh, and I was spreading myself as wide as possible to admit him as deeply as I could, just as the helmet of his big member touched bottom inside me, just as he was getting maximum pleasure out of plowing in and out of me, and I was screaming above the roar of the motors, "I love you! I love you! I want to fly forever and never touch ground!" and he was yelling, "I'm going to bomb you with come!" we ran smack into high-voltage thunder and lightning, so powerful in its primal force that when it struck the plane again and again, the copilot lost control. The plane pitched, turned over, swooped, dove, seemingly headed straight into a bloody, blazing crash in the icy Atlantic.

Captain Harper, with the supreme ego of a war hero, thought it was him and me. So, as the passengers in the cabin shrieked and screamed, and the half-conscious copilot went limp from terror, Captain Harper thrust his member even deeper into my suction cup, and I, like a fool, dug my fingernails deeper into his back as we rode to victory, with him shouting, "Right on! Hallelujah!" and "Baby, you did it! You did it for me!"

As he neared climax and his mighty staff grew turgid, he groaned with animal lust, then cried out in a hoarse voice, "Yes! Yes! Yes!"

I was white with fright, unable to breathe; I felt like I was falling down an elevator shaft, which was closer to the truth than I dared imagine; like a little girl, I thought the air giving way and the free-fall of my heart was all due to my magnificent stud of the hour, Captain Harper. I had the muscles of his hard ass in my hands, as I pushed my cunt-meat hard, hard against the trunk of his battering ram, crying my favorite poetry, "Fuck me! Fuck me! Fuck me!"

Time stopped, gravity went dead, and I began to

disappear out of sexual heat. Flesh burned away into the vapors. Diana Hunt became part of the clouds. Pure perversion, dangerous to my self-image, perilous to my psycho-sexual identity, and an absolute thrill! I was pushing hard against the limits of pleasure, letting my body flaunt my mind, letting the devil in me tell my angel self to go to hell—the flesh was about to rise from the dead. My labia went from baby pink to scarlet, my vaginal temperature rose, my glands let loose with that salty, viscuous stuff sexual men love to smear on their tongues and mouths.

Suddenly, my heart leapt! It became more than sex; now I was emotionally involved. I *wanted* this hunk, this macho pilot straight out of American myth. I wanted all of my internal, vaginal muscles to hug and suck every little ounce of his thick, driving tool as my way of thanking him for picking me out of the crowd. For the next five minutes, as the aircraft pitched and dove and flipped on its backside and plummeted to the death depths below, I took all of him. Our bushes ground against each other, his balls thudded softly against my inner thighs, the hairs of his scrotum tickling me and arousing me, as the plane kept losing altitude.

We came together in fast, violent bursts of release. I grabbed his heavy swinging balls and held them in ecstasy as one surging climax after another shook me and released me. Then, overwhelmed, I let go of everything. I could not hold on any longer.

Nor could my Captain. He fell into me, a dead weight, his river of sperm exploding inside me like a small grenade. "Oh, Diana, Diana, puss meat, pussy meat," he cooed, lapsing into silence and peace.

Then, abruptly, with a shock, he realized Something Was Wrong. We were heading straight into the Atlantic Ocean, and a quick watery grave! He screamed, "Oh my God!" got up straightaway, and grabbed the controls with just inches to spare. By the time the aircraft righted itself, it had already contacted the top of an ocean swell. The impact resulted in a skidding splash that felt like the bottom of the airplane was being ripped off. Obviously, the two of us had come just in time, sexually speaking, that is. Within minutes, we were in the air again, and all was well.

The poor copilot, however, was about to throw up, and when I went back into the body of the plane, what a sight it was! Aside from the gallons upon gallons of bodily excretions that were dripping from the ceilings and walls of the plane, the passengers were in various stages of hysteria, screaming, weeping, and/or just plain rigidity, otherwise known as catatonia. My two co-workers from the Chrysler Agency, Max Blacker and Jake Turnby, had passed out cold. I felt distressed at having been the cause of so much pain and suffering, but I judged it singularly unwise to apologize, as I didn't want the pants sued off me. Besides, the passengers in distress were free to suck and fuck, which is the only real comfort we humans have in times of stress. Like I always say, if people can't take advantage of each other's genitals, then what's the point of anything?

Chapter Twelve

"The African Episode," as I like to call it, is what got me blackballed by all the modeling agencies in New York. The truth is, if I had not been blackballed, I would never have arrived at my present success, which I shall talk about in due time.

In any case, "The African Episode" was responsible for a series of vicious rumors about little old me, which, thank God, cannot be substantiated by photographs or documents, since the rumors happen to be true. The plain, unvarnished truth in this case is so outrageous that no person of brains, breeding, taste, or sanity would believe a word of it. Hence, my reputation is not only safe, the mere existence of the rumors makes me look more interesting than I really am. In reality, of course, I am far more interesting than I really am, in my official, public, business image, that is. I am a woman; what more has to be said by way of explanation?

The Putangi, like I said, have a curious history. A tribe of green-eyed, red-haired Bedouins, who were almost half-Viking by ancestry, thanks to the Crusades and invading Norsemen, traveled to Africa in the fifteenth century looking for the lost city of Sheba, where they claimed they would discover the tomb of their fabled ancestor, the Queen of Sheba. Instead, they found an offshoot tribe of Masai, the super-tall, black herdsmen, who subsist on cattle blood and milk. Within days of the two tribes meeting each other, they had literally fallen in love and were fucking each other's brains out to the point where the physically weaker members of both tribes died from diseases brought on by their lowered resistance. The people who survived decided to make sex their god, since only sex, it seemed, was capable of breaking down the barriers between people caused by religion, race, and nationality.

In time, a distinct new tribe appeared with the best features of Masai, Vikings, and Bedouins, a tall, stocky people, who called themselves the Putangi, or "Children of Love." They boasted coppery skin, light eyes that ranged from gray to yellow, and most notably, outsized genitals. Many of the women were said to have clitorises two inches long, and fuck-flesh so abundant that when they squeezed their vulvas together with both hands, their outer cunt-lips and exposed inner labia looked like a huge tropical flower. The only instrument who could do justice to an aroused vagina was another woman's vagina, since there was too much exposed flesh and too many lips for a cock to be able to handle. The Putangi men supposedly had the largest male genitals in the world—so large, in fact, that they wore penis sheaths strapped to their thighs in two places. Many of the women did not have mouths or cunts deep enough or large enough to contain the aroused penises, so bisexuality was as rampant among the men as it was among the women. Moreover, as the story went, many, many Putangi, including the king himself, were true hermaphrodies, with the genitals of both sexes, and could thus perform both as a man and a woman within the same love-making session. So, as rumors of these extraordinary human specimens spread throughout the so-called civilized world, it seems that one of America's most famous department stores, no names mentioned, decided that the ideal way to sell their new sporting equipment and casual clothing would be to use the Putangi as a backdrop—as a prop, in other words—making sure to keep their genitalia out of reach of the camera, although we were explicitly told by Mary Chrysler not to worry if a few genitals were inadvertently photographed, as the New York office could always air-brush them off or stencil in the word "censored" on top of them.

Cute. As I said, according to Mary herself, no self-respecting model in the wilds wanted to get fucked by anyone but the cameraman or the director, but I think the truth is, the job had just come up, it wasn't paying all that much, and Mary figured she'd offer me my big chance. At the very least, my adventures in Africa would furnish her with a great excuse to write to her friend, Princess Grace.

As for myself and the Putangi, I was always up for sex, why not? Let's not be hypocritical; sex is a wonderful way to meet new people. Seriously. All the game-playing that goes into conventional courtship just isn't worth it, particularly in view of the fact that if you get married or try to set up house, you can be stuck with that one person for a very long time, both in and out of the law courts. And once that other person knows you're stuck with them, they start doing numbers on your head, such as sulking in a corner or forgetting your birthday or being two hours late for your mother's funeral. The ultimate revenge is having sex with somebody else, so I figure why not start with the ultimate?

The Putangi village, one hundred fifty miles west of Nairobi, is situated on the northern edge of the two-hundred mile-long Lake Shebathor, named after the legendary Queen of Sheba, and the Viking god of thunder, Thor. The houses resemble Irish farm cottages, whitewashed stone rectangles with thatched roofs. Like the Masai, the Putangi people keep herds of cattle. Like the Vikings, they fish and build impressive boats, with which they trade cowhides and pottery with other villages on the shores of the lake. Except for their penis sheaths, which they wear only outside their village, and the loincloths which the women wear when they are menstruating or pregnant, the Putangi walk around stark naked, proudly displaying their anatomical gifts.

I couldn't believe the hermaphrodites! Some of the most beautiful, full-breasted, gorgeous women I'd ever seen had cocks instead of cunts, and some of them, on the other hand, had vaginas, as well. Some strong, muscular men also had vaginas under their cocks. Since the Putangi of both sexes shaved all of their body hair, it was not hard to see their large, well-defined genitalia. In the United States, it is rare to see the inside flesh of a woman's cunt, even in a shower room, but with the Putangi, all the cunt-lips and much of the cunt's inner flesh was visible and hung down between their legs, sweet and meaty and reddish, large folds of fuck-flesh ready to stiffen with blood and suck onto an interested cock. Even their clitorises were visible, even in repose.

Jake Turnby and Max Blacker were going crazy. All Max really wanted, by his own admission, was a big cock to suck on, and Jake, poor Jake, claimed if she wasn't a blonde, forget it, he had no desire for anything else. According to him, the assorted Putangi cooze left Jake Turnby as cold as a witch's tit. In other words, the madman still wanted me. Apparently, he thought our little safari "shoot" could cover for a handful of ass and a mouthful of tit, all mine. Either way, he wanted to get laid.

Our first conversation was in the local guest hut where we were staying. I was given a loft all to myself. Jake decided it was big enough for two or three. "Jake, dear," I said, "you know, Africa is wide open, sexually speaking."

"So why are you a closed book, sexually speaking?" he said.

"Oh, no, Jake," I protested, "I'm an open book, and you must take a page from it. My book is entitled, *Free Love is a Two-Way Street*."

"I see," he said, not seeing anything, and carefully plotting his next move. "First a book, now a street. Diana, you're mixing your metaphors, and all I want to mix is you and me."

"Jake," I said, "right now all I can think of are the Putangi gentlemen who escorted me here. They were absolutely lovely. They wanted to fuck me immediately. I invited them back after dinner, after I have had a chance to take off my clothes and anoint my aching body, and if you can't take advantage of the Putangi women in the same way, I don't want to discuss this further."

195

Jake was furious. "If you get yourself all tired out tonight, you're going to look like shit for our shoot tomorrow."

"Don't worry, Jake, dear," I replied. "A mouthful of come always puts me right to sleep. I'm sure I'll be fine."

In the meantime, Max was laying out the clothing for the next day's shoot. I had planned to take a shower, but then I discovered that the only water in town was at the community bathhouse. Oh well, then, I really had no choice but to pay a visit to the community bathhouse, to wash out my undies, and take a nice cool bath before dinner. And since everyone in town was completely naked, I'd be completely naked, too. Why not?

So, with tits bouncing and my comparatively generous cunt lips visible from behind and rubbing provocatively against each other, I guided myself down the rickety wooden ladder which served as the stairway to the loft.

Watching me climb down, Jake almost went beserk. He pulled out his cock and started whacking off. "Diana, you can't do this to me!" he pleaded. "It isn't fair! You're being unnaturally cruel!"

"Please, Jake," I said, as calmly as I could, "I've got to go take a bath. I know I sound like a cunt, but you're being a pest. You're my photographer, and that's all!"

Apparently, that was not to be all. Jake felt it necessary to issue a warning. "If I'm a pest, Diana," he intoned, "just remember that pests can sting and bite."

I should have paid attention to his warning. When I walked out onto the village street on my way to the bathhouse in that late afternoon, so hot and steamy, I must have evoked in the Putangi males a vision of some ancient Viking ancestor, because I really did cause a riot. These males, as I said, were as muscular and as well-formed as Greek statues—coppery, glistening muscles, flaring nostrils, hooded, gray Viking eyes, full Negro lips, with cocks like fire hoses hanging down in front of them. When they caught sight of me, gold and pink and white, they became immediately aroused, and they began to follow me in small groups. All told, there must have been twenty or more.

And the women! The same look as the men with huge pendular breasts, dark coffee-colored nipples and aureoles, shaved pussies, huge vulvas, the cunt-lips hanging down between their legs, and the clitorises sticking out like little boy's cocks. When they saw me, those same clitorises began to stiffen, and they grabbed their cunts, as was their custom, as if they were bouquets of flowers. There was that much developed flesh where most American women have only a hole or a slit or a crimson gash.

So the women followed me, too. And also the hermaphrodites, whom I've already described. When I finally arrived at the bathhouse, I threw my wash in the corner and jumped into the water. At that point, there were perhaps three people, a youth and two older women, stroking each other as they washed. As you can see, there was no division between male and female in this bathhouse.

When the crowd arrived, it was as if every sexual fantasy I'd ever entertained was there in front of me. Human gods. The best of all races. The one who finally spoke up, spoke English. As I stood in waist-deep water by the edge of the community pool, he approached me, holding onto his humongous erection in his left hand. At first I thought it was some kind of a club. But no, it was Desire in the form of a cock.

His speech was brief, and it touched my heart. No, that's a lie. It pierced me to the core of my being, my very soul. His speech was the most beautiful oratory I have ever heard. It was short. It was to the point. It bespoke an eloquence this planet has not seen since the days of the ancient Greeks. What he said was this: "Diana Hunt, American, we, the Putangi, make you the

197

Goddess of Love. We wish to pay homage to your immortal flesh. We wish to worship you."

In my entire life, no one had ever said such beautiful words to me. I was half in tears. They were so sincere, and the man's erection looked so hot, so hot, what could I say to them but, "I accept your honor, because of my great respect for your wonderful culture. Yes, you may pay me all the homage you desire."

Immediately, the two largest women straddled the edge of the pool, facing me, one at each hand. Then, each of them took one of my hands and placed first the right, and then the left, as if it were a religious ritual, into her sweet pussy meat. Christ, my hands were buried in rose petals, in raw oysters, in raw cunt, all the beauty and the bounty of the earth!

I almost lost my mind, and they knew it! They howled with delight. The man who had spoken to me beckoned the most muscular and the best endowed of the young men. He came forward. He was about eighteen. I could scarcely contain myself. He was the color of gold, his muscles were like carved marble, his cock, the largest I had ever seen, was foaming at the end; I was afraid he'd come too soon. He also straddled the edge of the pool, his erection, the size of a baby's arm, staring me in the face. His tight, muscled body rippled every time he breathed. I started to reach out with both hands to hold onto his cock, but the women wanted my hands on their cunts, to bless them, I guess. I didn't mind. After all, I was a goddess, and I was finger-fucking them royally, and they were in ecstasy.

The young stud god lowered himself into the pool, swam between my legs, the muscles on his back creasing my labia as he passed underneath me. I shuddered with absolute pleasure from the depths of my cunt. Then he stood up behind me and mounted me from behind, spreading my legs apart as far as he could. I don't know how he was able to drive the length of it into me; the

198

water must have helped. I felt like I was being split apart by a red-hot poker.

The Putangi on the edge of the pool—there must have been about fifty of them—were beating drums and chanting, "Go! Go! Go!" The golden stud's tight masculine tits and solid chest rubbed hard against my back as he drove his way home.

The ritual was only beginning. Two of the most voluptuous women who have ever lived got into the water, and each positioned herself on one side of me, and then, without warning, started rubbing the inside of their cunts up and down on the outside of my upper thighs while they incessantly and hungrily kissed me and ate me out on the neck and on the cheeks and face, and with their hands joined the stud god in rubbing my breasts. They seemed to know where each nerve ending was, where the blood was marshalled, where the soft spots were.

From out of nowhere there was an underwater face, first staring up at me like a prehistoric monster, then sucking and licking on my clitoris, and with his practiced hands massaging and stroking the balls and cock of the stud god at the very place he was joined to me. I felt filled up and cheated at the same time. I wanted those golden girls one by one. I wanted to suck on their big stiff clits and then run those miniature pricks along the edges of my labia. Mostly I wanted to let go completely and rub my blood-filled cunt in and around the folds, flesh-petals, and crevices of their fantastic vaginas. I craved to touch their inner thighs, using my pussy as a mouth that sucks and caresses the warm, breathing, golden flesh of the world's most erotic women.

I was enveloped in sex. And so were the Putangi. The particular crowbar that cleaved into my cunt could pump away all day without coming, and the face licking my clitoris underwater must have been part fish or had constant replacements, because he never came up for

199

air. My entire body shook with waves of pleasure released by the energy of passion in my decidedly passionate cunt. I liked being a goddess. I liked the Putangi even more.

Then, the worst happened. The Joy Boys, Max and Jake, came into the bathhouse to take pictures of the world's greatest fucking machine. The Putangi knew what going on, and they were not about to be exploited like performing seals. My English-speaking admirer gave the signal. In a flash, a squad of the Putangi youth patrol smashed Jake's cameras, all four of them, threw the film into the community bath, and then gave orders for Max and Jake to be delivered, buck-naked, at the Nairobi Airport.

I found out later that they'd been arrested in Nairobi the very minute they were dropped off. The Putangi, dressed in Western garb for the occasion, had told the police that Max and Jake were perverts who came to Africa looking for cocks to suck. Neither one, of course, had his passport, money, or tickets home. It took two days for them to clear things at the American consulate in Kenya. And when they got back to New York, they started rumors that I was an insatiable nymphomaniac with a hatred for my own countrymen, the American people.

When the truth finally became unravelled, it turned out that we had been allowed into the Putangi village on the one condition that no pictures be taken of them engaging in sex, because they knew, and quite rightly so, that the "world," Moslem, Jewish, and Christian, would condemn them for it. Jake had promised he wouldn't. What he was being punished for, in essence, was his lying to their king.

As for myself, I spent an entire week among the Putangi fucking all comers, no pun intended.

When I was ready to go home, I took a couple of the best dresses Max had left behind in his hasty departure, together with their wallets, which I returned to them. I, of course, already had been paid my advance fee, plus passage home. It wasn't my fault that Jake Turnby and Max Blacker knew nothing of business etiquette or international relations; it wasn't my fault that they knew nothing of the real power of sex.

The Putangi taught me more than I ever hoped to learn about being a guest in somebody's house. I learned a great deal about entertaining. I learned a great deal about dealing with people from a different culture. The key is, "Look for the positive energies and go with them." This small wisdom is, perhaps, a clue as to why, today, I am a favorite everywhere.

Chapter Thirteen

A week later, I was back in New York with just enough money for a week's lodgings at the Y. I felt that, all things considered, what I had just experienced with the Putangi was far more interesting than those American Ph.D. women who go to Africa to search for fossils and observe the behavioral patterns of apes. The only television show I'd seen on the Putangi was on "In Search of ..." with Leonard Nimoy from "Star Trek" as host. This was called "In Search Of the Crusades" and showed some of the astronomical equipment, primitive telescopes, and the like that the Putangi had inherited from certain Viking crusader ancestors. In the show, the tribespeople were dressed in togas; no sexual behavior was shown.

So that was it. Nobody in New York, and certainly

nobody in greater America, wanted to see an oversexed, multiracial people who fuck and suck their way to Nirvana in mass orgies, even though our ancestors did just that in their harvest rituals and in the sexual sidelines related to war.

I called the Donohue show; I figured I had a controversial story to tell. They wanted to know the name of my book and how many pictures I had. The David Susskind show said they'd get back to me, and didn't. Finally, I called Barry Chrysler. The first two times, as his secretary was supposedly switching me onto him, the line went dead. Finally he answered. His voice was cold. "What do you want?" he said.

"Barry," I blurted, "Max and Jake wrecked everything; it wasn't me."

"I heard you started a riot," he said.

I countered with, "All Jake wanted to do was get into my pants."

"Why didn't you let him, Diana?"

"What do you think I am!" I screamed.

"I don't know," Barry screamed back, "what do you think you are?"

Then, before I could discuss my belief about free love, he went on to accuse me of costing the Chrysler Agency a million-dollar account because I was the all-time slut of the Western world, and furthermore, Jake Turnby and Max Blacker were two of the greatest guys who had never given anyone an ounce of trouble. They were a great team, a great photographer and a greater wardrobe man. Furthermore, Jake was a devout Buddhist and Max was not only a practicing Catholic, he was a daily communicant, who was so conscientious about everything that he'd had two complete nervous breakdowns.

In the case of the Putangi, in other words, it was crystal clear who the troublemaker was. Furthermore,

202

my newly acquired reputation as an account wrecker was all over town. Nobody in New York would hire me as a model, and if they did, Barry's beloved spouse Mary would make a couple of phone calls to make sure they changed their minds. He hung up with a bang, just as I shouted, "Don't worry, Barry Chrysler, some day you'll come begging at my feet, some day you'll beg my forgiveness with tears in your eyes!" But it was too late. I was talking to myself.

It was the low point of my life. I was devastated. I didn't know who to call. Muffie and Rod were still in Brazil. Angelo and Gloriana, I discovered by visiting the hospital and asking a few questions, were at some resort in Arizona or New Mexico—no name given, the nurses weren't even sure which state—where he could rest and get some sun for at least a month, until his casts came off.

I went back to the Y, removed all my makeup, put my hair in braids, and got into a pair of Levi's and a faded blue sweatshirt. I was thereby taking myself out of the sexual sweepstakes for the time being, at least. I looked about twelve years old. I had no idea of how I was going to survive much longer in New York. I sat on my cot in my plain beige room at the Y and thought and thought and thought. Then, I read the Help Wanted in the *New York Times*. I read and read and read. My typing speed was fifteen words per minute. Not nearly enough. I couldn't manage shorthand. My ability to take dictation was nil.

I decided to walk over to St. Patrick's and light a candle. I am not a religious person, having been raised in a fundamentalist sect, but I have always believed in lighting candles in a church. And so I did. St. Patrick's! That indescribable New York landmark! What an experience! It was just like being in Europe, where I had always hoped to go someday. Down near the front, I found this wonderful life-size statue of a nun who looked

203

just like my cousin Doris. It said "Saint Therese." Good enough. I gave a donation of a dollar, what the heck, and lit my candle. And I prayed. I really did. I said, "Dear Saint Therese, tell God to make me a success in the fashion world. After all, He must have given me the idea in the first place, right? Well, tell Him to follow through."

And that's when it hit me! The miracle! I remembered my psychic reading with the Contessa Cafone, Lucchio's mother. She'd not only said I'd be successful, but she'd written down a name and number to call. How could I have forgotten? Where was that number? I raced back to the Y, rummaged through my meager wardrobe, and found the scrap of paper folded twice and tucked into an inside pocket of my fabulous mink. It said, "Lulu Touché, 444-4444."

I called the number. A woman's voice at the other end said, "Adoro," which meant nothing to me.

I said, "Lulu Touché, please." We were connected. A woman with a broad Italian accent answered the phone. I said, "You don't know me, my name is Diana Hunt, but a mutual friend of ours, the Contessa Cafone, told me to call you about a job."

"I don't know no Cafone." Lulu Touché was playing it safe. I didn't blame her. My last memory of the Contessa Cafone, that alluring beauty, soaked in her own blood, had hardly been pleasant. Somewhere, as they say in Hollywood, there were guns in the night. Lulu knew it. And I knew it. I figured I should try being honest for a change. I said simply, "The Contessa Cafone read my cards the night before she died. She told me that someday I would be very successful and powerful in the fashion world, and that I should start by calling you."

The unexpected happened. Lulu broke down in tears. Apparently, she, too, believed in the occult, and the

Contessa Cafone had predicted that one day a young woman, out of nowhere, would call her up for a sewing job, that she would be that young woman's mentor and guide, and that the young woman would take Lulu with her when she rose up in the fashion world.

I said, "Wow! Am I crazy about you crazy Sicilians! You're the most incredible people I've ever met? What style! What support! What imagination! And by the way, I can sew."

"Good," she said. "You start here. You get three dollar per hour."

"Three dollars an hour!" I gasped. "That won't keep me in pantyhose!"

I had underestimated the Sicilian mind. For all its emotion, it is a very shrewd and calculating instrument. Lulu said it very well. "Look, honey, if you are who your fortune say you are, you get rich quick. If you some kind of rotten, no-good liar, who care what you are, right?"

"Right," I said, figuring I'd at least gotten my foot in the door. I wrote down all the necessary information and grabbed my sweater, ready to start a new life.

The House of Adoro, on East Sixty-Sixth Street, as I was soon to discover, was and is a top couturier house, a controversial fashion design center, a mecca for the Beautiful People, and above all, a sweatshop for down-and-out Howard Johnson hostesses from Beavertown, Pennsylvania, who can sew a little and dream a lot. East Sixty-Sixth Street, off Madison Avenue on Manhattan's East Side is probably the toniest residential area in America. It's not that the townhouses are better than Georgetown's or Nob Hills, although many of its brownstones are far larger and better constructed than they look, it's just that no city in the world has New York's creative combination of energies and finance, the arts, fashion, publishing, and media. These high-powered energies feed off each other, producing new styles and new products and fortunes for the people who create them.

The Adolfo Adoro complex, four large brownstones end to end, were painted a kind of squirrel gray. The effect was that of gray suede, with gleaming brass carriage lights and polished brass door knockers for contrast. Each window had a wrought-iron window box with a row of miniature boxwoods. Each brownstone had a separate wrought-iron fence in front, and a tiny front yard planted thick with English ivy.

As it turned out, the backs of the four brownstones were as modern as the twenty-first century. They had been replaced with four-story-high panels of double-pane glass. In other words, with Adolfo Adoro, there were surprises in store, or "You can't always judge a brownstone by its window boxes."

Adolfo Adoro himself lived on the top two floors of the brownstones. It was to be several long weeks before, under the most unusual circumstances, I would be given a special tour of his private quarters. For the moment, my principal interest was in fashion: what was it? why was it? where was it? who was it?

The first three floors of all four brownstones were the Adoro showrooms. They included a small theater with the classical runway for the models displaying the new gowns. In these grand rooms, a woman customer could be fitted, measured, tailored, adjusted, and accessorized while she was served an elegant repast prepared by a French chef. There were a certain amount of "off the rack" gowns and accessories for sale, although the bulk of the Adolfo Adoro ready-to-wear label clothes, bags, belts, swimsuits, furs, perfumes, etc., designed by Adoro in his studio, were manufactured elsewhere, principally in the Orient, and sold in department stores all over the world, much like items bearing the name of Halston, Cardin, and Yves St. Laurent.

East Sixty-Sixth Street was an Adoro show place. The public rooms were a monument to Northern Italian workmanship and design. Simple and full of light, with the finest geometric carpets, hand-made glove-leather sofas, and desks made of mahogany burl. Everywhere, there were vases of tree orchids from Adolfo Adoro's Connecticut country retreat. All the public rooms were elegant studies in subtle, monochromatic grays: French grays, pearl grays, gray flannels, gray suedes, gun-metal grays. This was deliberate. Nothing in the showrooms was allowed to distract from the clothes themselves.

And what clothes! Adoro was the leader in sensuality. His fabrics boasted colors so rich they had an almost Arabian feeling. He freely mixed patterns and designs, combining gold and silver as easily as he used silk and tweed in the same evening gown. His greens were like emeralds, his reds like rubies. His sequins glowed like precious jewels. His business day suits were made of rich, nubby corals and rose-reds trimmed with thick gold braids, or buttons carved from tortoise shell or taken from old nineteenth-century French military uniforms. His fabrics came from Tunisia, from Bangkok, from the Outer Hebrides, from the silk mills of France. Everything Adolfo Adoro touched was full of magic, romance, and sensuality. The House of Adoro was, in every way, a work of art. I was like a schoolgirl discovering the world.

So where was I escorted the first time I rang the front doorbell of the House of Adoro? To the basement workrooms! Those definitely nonglamorus spaces took up the subground level of three of the townhouses. The fourth basement housed the business offices. The workrooms were designed solely for the design, creation, and repair of what are called original couturier gowns; these included suits, coats, and sports wear. About fifty women, mostly Hispanic and Oriental, were involved in sewing on sequins, bugle beads, and semiprecious stones. Several German women, refugees from Hitler, seemed to be the master cutters and sewers. There was no sign of Adolfo Adoro himself.

Lulu Touché. Clearly from the same background and bloodlines as the Contessa Cafone. An Italian princess, a perfectionist, a woman in her late sixties, who would never retire. She was short, stocky, with dyed auburn hair, a slash of coral for a mouth, horn-rimmed glasses, overly made-up eyes that looked wonderful, and exquisite birdlike hands. Her eyes were chestnut brown. They were strong and compassionate and strictly "no nonsense."

"You are Diana Hunt?" she asked, taking off my sailor cap for me as I entered her main workroom.

"Yes," I answered.

"Let me see your palm," she said. I held out my outstretched hand, and she took it and held it under a desk lamp. "Yes. *Si. Si,*" she muttered.

"What are you looking for?" I asked.

"I don't know who to believe anymore," she answered, "but this much I can tell you, you will not be a seamstress for long. My poor Contessa. She read the cards. I read the palms. What can I say? She always loved the Mafioso. She was a Borgia and a Medici, both by blood and in her past life. It was karma. We will meet again in another life. Can you sew buttons on coats?"

"Oh yes!" I cried. "I'm terrific at buttons. I used to make all the cheerleader's outfits at Beavertown High. I can even make buttonholes."

"Buttonholes come later," she cut in. "First, do buttons."

For the next three weeks, every day from eight a.m. to six p.m., with overtime twice a week, I sewed buttons onto coats. And shirts. And blouses. By now, I had moved to a woman's hotel on the Upper West Side. Another version of the plain beige room with the single cot, desk, and chair. Aside from that, in my personal life, nothing happened. I was too scared to put on makeup or take my hair out of braids or put on a skirt. I still looked twelve years old, and that's the way I wanted it.

Then, something happened. I call it The Lulu Touché Delayed Reaction Syndrome. One day, I think it was an ordinary gray Wednesday, as I was minding my own business, sewing hand-carved whalebone buttons onto a hot-pink cocktail suit, Lulu Touché sauntered over, waving a half-eaten chicken sandwich in my face. "Hey!" she said, "were you the girlfriend of Lucchio Cafone, or what?"

"Girlfriend?" I asked, playing as dumb as I could.

"You know what I mean," she said, "you fuck Lucchio Cafone?" Her Italian eyes were piercing black like coals.

"Alright, yes," I blurted out. "Yes, I guess so. I don't want to get into it." And then, I burst into tears, sobbing for the death of that terrific hunk of mutilated, abused, and wayward masculinity.

Lulu ignored my tears. She couldn't abide softness, especially in a woman. She started waving the chicken sandwich again. "Hey! Lucchio, he like the most beautiful girls in the world. So how come you look like you look? Where your hair? Where your body, huh? What's wrong with you?"

I tried to answer her. "I just . . ." I couldn't finish my sentence.

"You just what, huh? What? What you just?"

"Lulu," I said, "when I look pretty, so many men come after me, I cause trouble."

"Oh," she said, "you think you pretty? Huh?"

I said, "I cause trouble."

"You think you pretty enough to cause trouble, huh?" Lulu was really stuble. Then, she turned to the whole workroom and shouted to about fifty people, "Hey! This is Diana Hunt, she think she some piece of ass. She think she stop traffic!" And with that, she took my sailor

209

hat off my head, and tossed it across the room. Then, she called on the intercom for Rosalie and Felice, the hair and makeup experts, as she undid my braids and started combing my hair out. Rosalie and Felice were ordered to make me up for evening, to make me look sexy, "If that were possible."

The truth is, I never wear much makeup, just a smear of red on my full lips, and some gray eyeliner and shadow on my eyes and a dab of blusher on my cheeks. But with just the minimum of color and contrast I have to say that I can look like a dazzling, movie star. That is exactly what I did not want.

Lulu started muttering, "I don't believe it," as the girls in the workroom were beginning to "ooh" and "aah." Rosalie and Felice really overdid it. I normally don't try to look sophisticated, just "girl-next-door" pretty.

"Now, let's see the body," Lulu said. "How much do you want to bet she's got a lousy body, huh? Huh?"

By this time, I was so dispirited I just didn't care anymore. I felt like a worthless object, a piece of ridicule. "Stand up and take off your clothes," she said. So I stood up, as ordered, and took off my shirt and pants and stood there with no bra and just a little pair of bikini briefs. There was shock in the workroom. The girls looked like they'd been slapped in their faces. Not one of them was smiling.

Lulu's jaw dropped. "Oh my God!" she said. "Oh my God!"

"What's wrong?" I blurted out. "I'm a woman. That's what's wrong, isn't it?"

Then, Lulu did it again. "Oh my God!" she said.

Blinded with shame and tears and a feeling of utter worthlessness, I ran from the workroom. I never wanted to see any of those people again. Then, realizing I was almost stark naked, I ran back into the workroom, screaming, "I'm naked! Where are my clothes?"

Well, it seems that Lulu had deliberately burned

them. Not only that, she was furious at me for crying. "Your eye makeup," she said, as if I cared about black smudges underneath my eyes.

"Where are my clothes?" I demanded to know.

"You are a beautiful woman!" she screamed.

"I don't want to be a beautiful woman!" I screamed back.

"Here, wear this!" she ordered, handing me a flesh-colored satin evening gown that looked like a nightgown.

"That looks like a nightgown," I protested.

"It's an evening gown," she said," a nightgown evening gown. Put it on."

It was sewn in such a way, empire fashion, like Napoleon's Josephine, that my breasts were pushed up and looked like soft globes of pink, quivering flesh, with my already prominent nipples most evident through the thin fabric. "Is this really an evening gown?" I asked.

"Put your shoes on," she ordered, ignoring my question. A pair of matching flesh-colored satin pumps were at my feet. "Put your shoes on," Lulu ordered again.

"But how did you know my size?" I asked.

"Put them on."

Finally, I obeyed. "Christ!" I thought to myself, looking at the "glamorous" me, "I can see my belly button right through the dress."

Worse, Lulu hadn't finished. "Go upstairs to the third floor, Room C," she ordered. "Mrs. Von Bartolin wants to see this dress."

"You want me to model this dress?" I asked.

"Never mind 'model'; just stick your stomach in, hold your shoulders back, push your tits out, and smile. I call Mrs. Smithwick, fashion advisor. I tell her I send you. Okay? Felice, you bring Diana Hunt to third floor, Room C."

In the elevator going up, Felice, who looked like Betty Crocker on the back of the cake mix box with her prim graying hair and her unmade-up face, said to me, "Sometimes I wish I were a lesbian."

"What do you mean?" I asked, playing dumb, fearing the worst.

"If I were," she began, "I'd really like to put my mouth all over you, especially your incredible breasts. Oh, Diana, I had no idea..." And with that, she reached for my breasts and scooped her hand in under them, feeling my nipples. Her breathing was labored, and she started repeating, "Oh, thank you, Diana. Thank you."

At that very moment, we arrived at the third floor with an abrupt jolt. Felice quickly pulled her hand away, and as the elevator doors opened on a showroom salon, three very upper-class women, all still attractive, turned and stared at me as I walked toward them.

And then, a man turned around. And so did my destiny. It was Adolfo Adoro himself, but at the time, I thought it was some tailor, unless I was deliberately kidding myself. Powerful men don't have to speak. His face and body said it all. A tough, deeply tanned Italian, the original Godfather, with his air of peasant authority, his thick, workingman's hands, his sun-creased eyes—not to forget his simple beige linen slacks accentuating what looked like a perpetual hard-on. I could feel this "tailor" staring at me. I could feel his strange and powerful energy, even though, as far as I knew, tailors are simple men.

Suddenly, I felt a warm, familiar ache in my crotch, and I thought to myself, "Oh my God, what's happened to me? Oh no, not again!" and I resolved to do my work, to have nothing to do with the other employees on a person level. Then, to my great shock, I discovered that, thanks to Felice, who was nowhere to be seen, one of my nipples had popped out of my empire gown. So, red-faced, I carefully tucked my nipple back into my flesh-colored gown, and, to remedy the situation, kept gently pushing my breasts down into the dress in soft, stroking motions, so as not to call attention to myself. I suppose I must have looked like I was fondling myself, because I could actually hear that "tailor"'s heavy breathing. I'd heard that kind of breathing before, even in Beavertown.

The women were looking at me like they were in shock, but I proceeded to model the dress for them anyway. "What are you doing here?" the "tailor" asked me in his sophisticated Roman accent.

"Here I go again," I thought. "Trouble." "Sir," I said, in my best high-school bravado, "Lulu Touché said Mrs. Von Bartolin wanted to see this evening gown."

"Evening gown!" cried one of the women. "It's a negligee!"

"That's what I said!" I cried, "but Lulu Touché..."

A stout Germanic woman who was about fifty pounds overweight in her tight, white wool suit began to laugh, cutting me off in mid-sentence. "Don't be upset, my dear," she advised, "somebody's clearly playing a joke."

"A joke?" I shrieked. "I'm only a button sewer. I have no interest whatsoever in becoming a clown. Or is the joke on me?" I felt like the original royal fool. For the second time that day, I bolted the room.

The "tailor" shouted, "Young woman! Come back!"

"What for?" I shouted back at him.

"Because I told you to!" he answered.

"This place is worse than a whorehouse," I yelled.

"How would you know," he yelled back. "Are you a whore?"

"I will be, if I stay around here," I answered. Then, like a ten-year-old in tears, I ran for the elevator. The "tailor" ran after me, determined to catch me. So, I turned and fled in the direction of the stairs.

As luck would have it, my heel caught at the top of a short flight and broke clean off the shoe. I careened headlong onto the landing, carpeted, thank God. In the process of falling, my gown caught on the edge of the steel bannister and completely ripped down one side. I lay in a heap on the landing, my entire left side exposed, nipple showing, honey-blonde pubic hair in sight, my entire thatch, in fact, dazzling in that particular light, before I quickly and modestly covered it with my hand. I lay there in tears, feeling used and broken, a laughingstock. Lulu had, for all practical purposes, raped me.

I felt so defeated. The "tailor" was muttering softly in Italian. Then, in a compassionate tone of voice, new to me, he said, "Wait, let me help you. Let me cover you." And with that, he took off his beige turtleneck shirt and wrapped it around me, but not before kissing my raw, exposed breast with his soft warm lips, and not before I glimpsed his torso: stocky, square, and rock-hard, covered with soft, black hair. Not the muscles of a weight lifter, but the perfect torso of a Southern Italian tough guy, who'd loaded freight on the docks in Naples for twenty years.

He reminded me in every way of Lucchio Cafone. The next thing you know, his mouth was in my mouth, his strong peasant tongue, hot and muscular like a young boy's cock, was exploring the pink, raw meat in the back of my throat. He was eating me, drinking me, driving me down. At last, somebody cared. Really cared. I thought to myself, "Thank God," and then I passed out.

When I awoke, I was in a large, dark mahogany-paneled room in a large double bed with a red velvet awning over it and a red velvet spread. I knew instantly that I was naked under the covers. When I peered through the surrounding dark, I could see very little, mostly signs of luxury, like the warmly polished brass sconce lights and the antique armoires with their carved wooden doors. At first, I thought I was back in Muffie's apartment in the Village, but then I remembered that it had been blown up. Besides, this room was different. It was like something I'd seen in movies about lovers in medieval Italy. Yes, *The Taming of the Shrew* with Elizabeth Taylor and Richard Burton. Then I felt weak again, and I lay my head back.

"Don't worry, you'll be fine." It was a soft voice. A man's voice. Then I remembered. The "tailor."

"Are you the tailor?" I asked feebly.

"Yes, I guess I must be," he answered.

"Tell me, what am I doing here?" I said.

"I brought you here to rest," he said. His voice was so gentle, his bedside manner so responsible.

"To rest?" I asked. "What for?"

"The doctor was here," he said. "He said you bumped your head. There was no concussion. Everything is fine."

"Thank you," I said.

"I feel so sorry," he remarked, sounding very sad.

"Sorry for what?" I said.

"This is all my fault," he said. "I frightened you."

"No, it's all my fault," I said. "I've been so afraid."

"Afraid of what?" he said.

"Of everything," I replied. "It seems that every time I dress like a woman is supposed to dress, I get myself into trouble."

"I will show you how to dress," he said.

"You will?" I replied, quite astounded at his kindness and generosity. "Yes, I will show you everything," he said.

"Thank you," I replied, "you're very kind; I'm sorry for shouting at you. I'm sorry for making a fool of myself."

"You poor dear girl, you have been under so much pressure, I can tell," he said.

"Yes, yes," I replied. "Terrible, terrible pressure."

"So much suffering," he added.

"Yes, yes," I said.

"Poor dear, poor darling," he cooed, stroking my naked breasts with one large, forceful hand.

I didn't mind. After all, he had earned the right to

215

touch me. "You're so good to me," I said. And with that, his other hand, so large and muscular, was guiding my own little naked hand to the huge bulge in his pants. No, actually, it wasn't his pants. My little "tailor" was naked, too. And he wasn't so little! I was absolutely unprepared for the size of him; a big lead pipe, hard and heavy, obviously created for women who wanted the real thing—and that meant me. The head of his erection was the size of a small apple, and just about as red. Then, to my utter delight, he climbed into bed with me.

"Please forgive me," he said, "but I wanted to make you feel safe." I could hardly contain myself, I wanted him so badly. He began to suck on my full-bodied, creamy breasts with the caramel-colored nipples he obviously enjoyed so much, and with his strong, hairy, peasant arms he began to explore my body, stimultaneously kissing my inner thighs and cradling my ass in his muscular hands, all the while speaking to me, "My darling *cara mia*, you are the most gorgeous woman I have ever seen!"

By now, his hands were on my tummy and I was mad with desire, almost on fire from the aching in my loins. I cried out, "I love you! I love you! Fuck me! Fuck me!"

Adolfo ruled me. He didn't ask. He took. And I loved it. Every minute of it. "There is too much beauty here," he cried, "too much for one man, too much for one day. You overwhelm me. I need four hands. I need two penises." And with that, he put his hand on my cunt, that tropical pleasure cave, that prime vacation spot, that oasis of the Arabian Nights, and he began to explore its treasures and its mysteries.

In the dim light I saw his stalwart cock in all its confident glory sticking up from his lap like a flagpole, its swollen head already spurting little drops of shimmering ooze. I looked at him and said, "Can I have it?"

He laughed in his rich Roman baritone, obviously

amused at my bawdy innuendo. "You, Diana," he said, "you are the most incredible woman I have ever met, and I began making love at age twelve."

"What a con man you are," I said, teasing him.

"Cunt man," he said, stroking me like a priceless work of art.

I could not wait. I put my hand over his and guided him down my soft hairy opening, up and down, to the silky prepuce around my clitoris. I took my two hands and enveloped his hard, bony, muscular, hairy fingers with my raw flesh. I think I was losing my mind. I was coming, and I had not even been entered!

Suddenly, his face was on top on my vulva, in an instant buried in my hot flesh as I bucked and arced and he rode with me. I was insensate, out of control, this animal demon all fire and blackness. Then, I felt strong hands grasp my buttocks, and, with his massive arms, he lifted me up like a little rag doll and brought me down on him, his strong penis cleaving into me like a mortar shell dividing a battleship in half.

I shuddered and gasped. We were a perfect fit. He was a bullfighter in his thrusts that dug into every delicate nerve-ending in my hypersensitive cunt. Transported with a kind of madness, I grabbed his black curls and closed my eyes as he pumped his hot lust into my loins. His hot mouth was inside my mouth, wrestling to keep it in a state of surrender, in a state of "Yes! Yes! Yes!" My body had lost its form, its shape; I was a mass of uncontrolled feelings. I was being controlled. I was desired. I was held down. I was a willing slave.

At the last minute, I guess he pulled his massive instrument out of me. I don't know. I could not tell where I let off and he began. I only remember that he cried out, and then I felt like I was in a tranquil sea with the warm waves lapping over me. My belly button was full of a thick warm liquid, which I rubbed all over my breasts and face and cunt. I was still tingling. I could hardly believe what had happened to me. At last, I knew passion.

We lay there for an hour, not speaking, just holding each other, warm and secure in each other's arms. "I'm in love with you," I said, finally. I couldn't help myself. True, this man was not my beloved Angelo, who I loved like my first-born son, even though he was much older than I. This man in my arms was my god. So why compare? "You've been so good to me," I said.

"No one is better than you," he replied in his incredible, gravelly baritone voice.

"I've never met a tailor before," I said.

"Oh?" he said.

"Are we still in the House of Adoro?" I asked.

"We are upstairs, in Mr. Adoro's private apartment. It was the only place to take you," he explained.

"You must thank Mr. Adoro for letting us use these rooms," I said. He didn't answer.

"You did get his permission, didn't you?" I said.

"This is Mr. Adoro's bedroom," he replied.

"Please, please," I cried, beginning to get very upset, "don't tell me we don't have his permission. I can't afford to get fired. I really need my job." Then it struck me. The utter absurdity of what I was saying. "To hell with Adolfo Adoro!" I cried.

"What do you mean?" he said, shocked.

"I don't need this job, and neither do you. You can start your own design house. I'll go with you anywhere. We don't need more than a room. You design the clothes, and I'll sew them. I even know how to design lingerie. I'll work overtime, I promise. I promise."

My man began to laugh—a warm laugh, but a laugh, nonetheless.

"Why are you laughing?" I said.

"Because, among other things, I have just had the best fuck of my life, you have proposed I start my design house and you'll devote your life to me, and I don't even know your name!"

218

With that, I began to laugh, too. "Guess what?" I said, "I don't know yours, either."

"You go first," he said.

"My name is Diana Hunt. I am a Sagittarian, and I come from Beavertown, Pennsylvania. And I really will help you start your own design house. I've been working in the basement, and I've learned a million things about how to put a dress together, but never mind me, tell me your name."

With that, he rolled on top of me and looked deep into my eyes. "Promise me, Diana, you won't be mad at me."

"I don't care what you are," I said.

"Diana, I don't know how to tell you."

"Oh, no!" I cried, "you're married!"

"No, not that," he said.

"You've got to go back to Italy! No, you don't have to, marry me and you can stay here forever."

"Don't worry," he said, "if I had to go back to Italy, I would come back to you, I know I would."

I looked deep into his eyes and said, "If you're in the Mafia, I don't care. They will have to kill me first."

"Diana, I am not in the Mafia," he said.

"You're not?" I answered, relieved.

"No, Diana, I am Adolfo Adoro, and I am in love with you."

There was a long silence. I could see the face of Lucchio Cafone. I saw the Tabernacle Witness Church. I saw my mother. I didn't know what to say. I just knew it was time to come down to earth. I pushed Adolfo off of me.

"What are you doing?" he cried.

"I'm doing what I do best," I answered, sucking on his nipple, my hand massaging his large meaty balls.

With that, the door flew open and the lights went on. I looked up. I couldn't believe my eyes. It was Glorianna Bronx, Angelo's live-in love. There was a look of rage on her magnificently beautiful face. Then, I remembered where I had first heard of the House of Adoro, in Angelo's hospital room, when I first met Glorianna Bronx. That's right; Glorianna was supposed to be Adolfo's right hand. Of course, when the fabled Ms. Bronx saw yours truly in Adolfo Adoro's arms, she let out a piercing scream that must have been audible at Lincoln Center halfway across town. In that one moment, I knew I would have to put Beavertown and playing dumb behind me. I knew I would have to fight, or I would lose everything.

Chapter Fourteen

"That slut! It's that slut!" Glorianna had found her forked tongue.

Adolfo got out of bed, his python cock hanging dangerously between his legs like it could strike and kill at any time. "What is the matter, Glorianna dear?" he asked the shrew in the doorway.

"It's that slut! She's fucked Angelo! She's fucked the nurses at the hospital! She's fucked the doctors! I heard she went to Africa for Mary Chrysler and fucked a whole tribe! Mary had to fucking blackball her in all the fucking modeling agencies in fucking New York!"

"What are you doing here, Glorianna?" I cried, figuring I needed some basic information.

She gave it to me pronto. "I'm Adolfo's mistress, you dumb cunt, and I have been for the past ten years!"

Naturally, I turned to Adolfo for his version of their

relationship. "If she's your mistress, how come she's shacked up with Angelo O'Shaughnessy?" I demanded to know.

"*Cara mia,*" he said, "she's not my mistress. She's just crazy about money and power, and most of all, clothes." Then, he turned to me with such depth and longing in his eyes. "I'm like you, Diana. I make love to everyone in sight, but why not? Is that not why people are for? Glorianna thought if she lived with Angelo, the king of the pornographic movie stars, she'd make me jealous. She knows too well there are too many fishes in the ocean for Adoro to be jealous of a man who takes his clothes off in front of a camera."

Glorianna didn't know what to say. Adolfo, in his own way, was every bit as handsome as my beloved Angelo, although Angelo's copper-colored chest hair and flaming bush certainly gave him a certain edge in the looks department. On the other hand, money and fame can make any middle-aged man seem much more exciting than he probably is.

As far as Glorianna and I go, up to that moment in time I had never seen her naked. She was certainly on the long and lean side. Some men prefer that, the animal athletic Amazon, to the sex kitten like me. What I'm trying to say is, my smooth pink flesh and my frankly incredible boobs that bounce like a water bed do not suggest to anyone that I could run a four-minute mile or lead troops into battle. Glorianna was another animal altogether. If she never won the gold medal for the javelin throw, she more than made up for it as Adolfo's top model. She wore clothes like they should consider themselves privileged to sit on her back. She challenged every woman in her show-room audiences to dominate the clothes, and not the other way around.

I don't know why she was so mad at me. At first, I thought it was because I sucked off Angelo in her presence in his hospital room. Then, I found out she was

Adolfo's mistress. Well, I may have lost Angelo to her, but I wasn't going to lose Adolfo Adoro. I could plainly see he desired me more than Angelo ever had. And like I always say, a man's desire for me is what turns me on. What I desire in men is the man who desires me. I have never carried a torch. It's too easy to get burned. That's why I calmly decided to forget Angelo O'Shaughnessy and go with Adolfo Adoro. Besides, Adolfo had a very pleasant apartment, and he loved his work. What more can a girl ask for? And to think I'd known this Perfect Person for so short a time.

Adolfo rose up to his full height, his hairy stomach taut and lean, his cock thicker and shorter as sexual passion gave way to anger. "Goddamn you, Glorianna, this little girl, she have warm heart!"

Glorianna began to sob. "Warm heart! Warm heart! Adolfo, you poor fool! Can't you see you're looking for a mother? If all you want is a warm heart ... well, I may not have a warm heart, but I've got a warm cunt. What's wrong with a warm cunt?" Then, Glorianna turned on me, in a manner of speaking. She lifted her skirt and exposed herself. Her cunt was a long scarlet gash. Her labia hung down from her cave. What a turn-on! But, unfortunately, she had more to say. "The inner muscles of my vagina can practically thread a needle, not to mention what they can do with a cock!" And with that, she burst into tears, dropped her upraised skirt, turned on her heels and ran.

My heart went out to her. For the first time, I felt so sorry for her. Poor Glorianna. She had so much appetite and so much pride. Tragically, she could not reconcile the two.

Adolfo said, "Never mind. Shut the door." I shut the door. "Lock the door," he said. I locked the door. He phoned his associates downstairs and told them he would be indisposed for the rest of the day. "Please send Mrs.

Von Bartolin a dozen pink carnations and invite her to lunch next week. Have the French chef send up Supper Number One for Two to Adolfo Adoro's quarters as soon as possible. That will be all. I am taking my phone off the hook. Good night." Then, Adolfo looked at me and said, "When the food arrives, I promise you the most exciting meal you have ever had."

One hour later, after we had rested in one another's arms under Adolfo's warm slik sheets and red velvet comforter, the door buzzer sounded. "Ah!" he exclaimed, "our dinner, she arrive." He jumped up to answer the door. What happened during the next hour was my first experience with true luxury. After checking out the door with closed-circuit television, Adolfo opened it. In that split second, "Tarzan" and "Jane," the servers, who had been standing there in leopard-skin loincloths and sarongs, let their clothing drop to the floor. "Tarzan" was a blonde Nordic god who looked like a professional full-back with an uncircumcized tool on him that proclaimed instant sexual authority. It was mushroom-shaped, and must have weighed a pound. "Jane" was small and dark, and looked like she might have come from India, which as it turned out, she had. She had little, pointed cone-shaped breasts with nipples like dark fudge caramels. And her snatch! Fantastic! It was shaven. It was coffee-colored, and each side of her dark little vulva looked muscular and ready to grapple in complete lust and abandon the biggest cock or tongue she could find. This woman looked obscene and sinful. I wanted to run over, grab her tight, dark little buttocks in both hands, and grind my pink apple-blossom fuck-flesh against her and sink my mouth into one of those dark, sweet caramel nipples, but I knew I was much too civilized for that kind of behavior.

"I don't know if I like that girl," I said to Adolfo. "She looks like she might be a lesbian."

Adolfo laughed long and hard. "We are all lesbians under the skin," he said. "You Americans. Such hypocrites."

I was irate. "Adolfo," I said, "I have nothing against her. I just said I don't know if I want her. I mean, I don't know if I *like* her." I was beginning to sound confused, and was terrified I'd give my true feelings away.

"Shush, you button-sewer," he said. "This is Carmella, originally from Bombay. She works in my kitchen. And this is Nicolai. He just arrived from the Kirai Ballet in Leningrad. He is a great dancer. He is presently in love with Carmella, but I have heard he is the rogue bull of Leningrad. Nicolai is a defector."

"I don't see any defects," I said, getting out of bed. I wanted to see how quickly that big Russian kilbasi would straighten up and fly right at the sight of me.

Adolfo was right about the rogue bull. At the sight of me, "Tarzan" Nicolai's blue Russian eyes practically bulged out of his head. I guess the girls in Leningrad are a little thicker around the middle, or maybe they don't shave their legs. In any case, I could tell by his expression he considered me a luscious piece of meat, and I couldn't wait to see what Signor Adoro had in mind in terms of satisfying my sexual appetite, which he had succeeding in whetting like few men ever have.

Adolfo nodded to Tarzan, and Tarzan nodded to Jane. This was obviously a well-rehearsed routine. Jane walked around to the front of the serving cart and bent over to get a folded white linen tablecloth, which she unfolded on the bed, which it covered perfectly. Her pussy, up close, was much deeper and fuller than I had expected. When she bent over, a huge portion of sweet dark meat hung down between her slender legs, a purple slit running through its center. I could just imagine her hot vaginal juices simmering in her cunt, hoping for contact with an eager, exploring tongue of either sex. She was absolutely obscene. There is nothing worse than a woman with sex on the brain, but what can you expect from the people who gave us the *Kama Sutra*? She was entirely too feminine for my taste, much too sweet, much too dark, and much too rich.

It was my own fault for having come to New York in the first place. Adolfo's personal rooms were too small. They were beginning to get to me. The air was too close. It was too late. I thought I was going to pass out.

Thank God, it was almost time to eat. Adolfo snapped his fingers. The great Slavic Tarzan touched that obscene woman on the shoulder, and she lay down on top of the white linen tablecloth and spread open her legs and then tilted her pelvis upward like she was about to give birth, her hot-pink hole layered with what looked like folds of raw salmon. The whole thing, no pun intended, was inescapable. I could see Adolfo's thick, muscular snake begin to stir and awaken. Tarzan, his blonde cock throbbing in front of me, his pale gold dancer's body covered with its mist of blonde fuzz, took a sterling silver bucket filled with what turned out to be about two quarts of the freshest, juiciest, Chincoteague raw oysters and ladled them into our little Jane's choice cunt, pushing them back and tucking them in. When he finished, he took a smaller, silver vessel, which was evidently full of hot pepper sauce, and, as best he could, he dipped the first three or four inches of his cock into it.

"What do I do?" I asked Adolfo, playing dumb again, barely able to catch my breath.

"I thought you were hungry," he said. "Watch, Diana, I'll show you how."

Adolfo knelt before Tarzan, put one hand on the man's well-developed buttock, and, with the other, grasped the thick root of his blonde cock. Then, as if receiving communion in church, he bent down to put that magnificently designed knob into his mouth.

225

"Stop!" I screamed.

"What's the matter? he said, with a look of horror on his face.

"If you're gay, Adolfo," I pleaded, "I don't want to know about it. Please, go into another room and do that kind of thing." I was so upset and confused. I kept thinking about that maddeningly delicious cunt on the bed, just lying there, unattended. It just grew larger and pinker and more irresistible in my imagination the more I thought about it. I was sure my vulva had turned purple from the strain, and my vaginal juices were practically running down my legs.

But they weren't, not really. I was just hot and moist and tingling and ready to explode. It's all because of Beavertown and the evangelical tabernacle—my sexual repression, I mean.

Adolfo just looked at me and smiled. "In Europe, my little firebird, there have been so many wars, so much death, we are more sophisticated about sex."

"What does that mean!" I shrieked.

"We tell the truth." And with that, he put the glans with the hot pepper sauce into his mouth and licked it and licked it until there was no more sauce. Tarzan seemed pleased. Then, Adolfo went over to that Indian slut, and, with his hands under those ripe-melon buttocks, put his face smack into her raw cunt and began to slurp up the oysters, which were runny and juicy and full of sea brine.

By this time, I had my hand inside my own hole, and I was almost senseless with passion rubbing my hand up and down, ready to go into a seizure and foam at the mouth. The Indian slut was going into orgasm. I couldn't stand it any longer. I just snapped. I threw myself onto the bed on top of Adolfo, and, riding him, spread my legs and ran my open cunt up and down on his black-haired, muscular back, as I crammed my face into her hole.

Adolfo acted shocked. "Where are your manners, my sweet?"

"I'm not sweet, I'm sweet and sour," I said, as I, ravenous and uncontrolled, ran my tongue in and around the precious pink folds of her dazzling, never-to-be-equalled cunt, sucking up oysters and labia, the labia far more delicious.

When I was done, I looked around for Adolfo, looked around just in time to see Tarzan on the bed grease his farm tool with globs of homemade butter from a little silver bowl, ream my Adolfo up the ass, then begin to jerk him off at the same time with both massive blonde hands, which were in startling contrast to that dark Italian cock-meat. Adolfo, in turn, reached out and grabbed our Princess Delicious by her nut-brown ankles and draw her under him, so that her cunt was within shooting distance of his humongous instrument.

Thanks to Tarzan's practiced hands, Adolfo came quickly in thick spurts of come, which his obedient server aimed directly into the world's most tasty piece of meat, Jane's matchless cunt. "Quick!" shouted Adolfo. The King of the Jungle withdrew his big tool from my lover's ass and ran to serve the next course, black caviar. Again, he ladled the little fish eggs into my favorite serving dish.

"Wait," said Adolfo, "these eggs are too salty; we need a final topping of white sauce."

Now it was Adolfo's turn. Taking more globs of soft, yellow-white butter, he greased Tarzan's throbbing pole, working the ultrasensitive cylinder of flesh. "Help me, my love," he said to me.

And so, trying to be the perfect helpmate I had promised him I would be, I joined him, our two hands clasped in love, friendship, and excitement over one big fucking hunk of living flesh, Tarzan's erection. As soon as I so much as touched his skin, my hard nipples brushing against the tough muscles of his arm, he began to moan and shudder. Since I was hungry for caviar, I figured I

227

could do better, so, kneeling, I spread my legs and rubbed on his thigh until my cunt-lips opened and I was smearing my juices on his leg and making sure my soft, pendulous globes stroked his own hard breasts. Tarzan's cock, in the meantime, swelled in our hands, and he began to spurt come. It was like a big firehouse out of control.

As his orgasm mounted, I had to lean against him to make sure his abundant come struck home. Like I say, my mind was on the caviar, which is to say, the cunt. He kept coming and I massaged his balls, which made me think of tennis balls. What a physical specimen! And what a devoted employee! I was certain he would make a great American. By the time he had finished his orgasm, Jane's vagina was full of glistening black caviar topped by a generous portion of the smooth white sauce Adolfo was talking about. It looked indescribably delicious. Adolfo said to me, "You first."

This time, I had a better idea. I stretched out on top of Princess Jane of Pleasureville, so that my own inflamed and aching cunt was directly on top of her practiced mouth, and my mouth in turn was on Treasure Island, that glorious mound crammed full of come and caviar and a clitoris nesting in fuck-flesh, bejeweled with drops of precious ointment. It was a feast beyond belief. And to think she was eating me out at the other end! My heart was beating so fast I was afraid it would stop beating. But so what? At least I would die in Paradise.

Adolfo, God bless his grand soul, joined me in the feast, as he met me head to head, his tongue lapping at mine, his lips as eager to wrap themselves around her button of desire as mine, with an impassioned kiss of love and tenderness to let her know she was wanted, yes, wanted, yes, desired.

Oh God! Adolfo, my Santa Claus! What woman wouldn't be head over heels in love with him? My orgasm? Tidal wave after tidal wave, and when I lost all

228

bodily control, my head collapsed into the center of her living flesh, with my nostrils revived by her odors; the sweat, the oil, the body itself. Musk, salt, sugar, each flavor more subtle than the one before, her sweat so piquant, like baby sweat. Just the suggestion of effort, the merest hint of strain.

And when the orgasms were over, all four of us lay together on the bed hugging and kissing and nibbling each other's ears. It turned out that Tarzan, true to form, knew practically no English, whereas Jane, in what had to be the biggest shock of my life, spoke in an upper-class English accent, clipped and precise. It totally destroyed my vision of her as the Goddess of Sensuality. From the minute she began to speak, it was as if a cold knife cleaved into my brain, dividing it in half. From that moment on, she was two people, and I could not put the two together again. If I had known beforehand of this problem, I would have paid a million dollars (ha!) to her never to speak in my presence, but, as it was, I had no warning and very little money, so after eating what seemed like a ton of delicious, cold, sliced filet mignon sandwiches with green mayonnaise and cold shrimp vinaigrette, and tomato aspic made from scratch with vintage champagne, and fresh strawberries for dessert, Adolfo and I kissed our servants good-bye.

Then, silently, he took me by the hand into his pink marble bathroom where a sunken tub, much like Lucchio's, had been mysteriously filled with warm, soapy water. I realized in that warm, foggy room that Adolfo was in love with me. He treated me like a rare jewel, so tender, so attentive, so respectful. And so horny! His was the greatest desire I have ever known before or since. During our first weeks together, he could not keep his hands or his mouth off me. He said that normally one orgasm a night was enough, but that with me his cock would not stay down. He apologized for fucking me so much. My response, whenever he talked like that, was

229

to reach out, unzip him, grab his big cock, and stick it in me.

What can I say? Adolfo Adoro marked my life and shaped me forever afterward. I do not know what Karma means, not really, or the true meaning of body chemistry. I do know that I loved his body, and he loved mine. I was at peace with him, but our story was far from over. After all, he was an Italian, and I was in many ways still a kid. Together, we had much to celebrate and much to learn.

Chapter Fifteen

Next, I learned the Ropes. The Business. Fashion. The Big Time.

For the next several months, Adolfo taught me everything there is to know about fashion. I learned how his simple sketches are translated into exact technical drawings, both for original gowns and for mass-market copies, where one slip of the cutter's hand can ruin hundreds of pieces of expensive fabric. On separate buying trips, Adolfo took me to Paris, Hong Kong, and the Outer Hebrides, where he purchased the best silks and woolens he could find. In New York, where I had already learned about how a fine garment is constructed and sewn from Lulu Touché, Adolfo instructed me in the art of accessories: shoes, handbags, hats, jewelry. I observed how he brought in experts in a given field to help him make choices with respect to mass-produced products bearing his name. I learned, moreover, about marketing, advertising, television commercials. I met thousand-dollar-a-day models. And I met many of his regular customers, among them some of the wealthiest women in the world. These women had beauty, brains, and sex appeal. Some of them even came upstairs with us. If our days were full, our nights were even fuller.

As for my personal self, I became an expert in the art of makeup, the wearing of perfume, the pouring of fine wine, the names of the best decorators, and the best places to have my shoes resoled. I met the best travel agents and the best hairdressers. By spring, I had achieved a more subtle look. My hair had lost its hint of brass, my lips seemed more rose than orange, my walk had become a little straighter, my fingernails a little bit shorter. In short, I was learning the ways of the world.

Of course, in some respects, the wise ol' world still had a few things to learn from me. I guess we become experts in the things we love, and, of course, unlike most people, I have never been afraid to admit my greatest love is sex. My cunt had never been better or more active. Adolfo, at the age of fifty-two looked thirty-five, and fucked me all day long, whenever he could; in bed, across tables, on piles of fabric, in his basement supply room, in his sunken tub, in the backs of taxis, on planes, and once, in the back row of a synagogue during the funeral of one of his dearest and oldest customers. I grew to love every line and mark on his body, every fold in his skin, every scar from every wart that had ever been removed. I found out about his early life: he'd been born in Rome, the grandson of a princess of the Orsini family, who had served the Church for generations. His father had been a self-made rug merchant from Marseilles, who made a fortune importing Oriental carpets from the Middle East. Besides his Italian bloodlines, his ancestry was part Armenian Jewish and part Maltese. Consequently, he had no real allegiance to any god or flag, except the absolute here and now. Better yet, he had never

231

known a place like Beavertown, Pennsylvania, so I was never a country hick to him. I was always the Goddess of his Waking Dreams. It's true. He told me. Many times.

By the time he was fifty, Adolfo had been married and divorced three times, and I knew it would not be long before he asked me to be the fourth Signora Adoro. That was okay by me. At least I had no hang-ups about premarital sex for either him or me. I suspected that the three previous wives had bolted the door once they discovered that Adolfo was ready and willing to fuck the Thanksgiving turkey, if he felt like it. As for myself, I did not care where he got his pleasure; in fact, I hoped he got as much cunt as he could from wherever he could, and I knew he felt the same way about me. Getting cock, that is. Why would I ever want a cunt? I keep asking myself that question.

Anyway, Adolfo and I loved each other deeply because we wanted the best for each other. Consequently, neither one of us was about to get involved with a man or woman who was liable to become jealous or possessive. Strange how some man who can fall into a woman's arms or slip into her cunt, or, likewise, a woman who can greedily sink her open mouth onto a gentleman's stalwart cock an hour after they've met, can then take it upon themselves to decide that the act of intercourse signifies that they now exclusively belong to each other.

In light of all the many changes in my life and the changes that were undoubtedly about to come, I mean happen, I had one overriding mental obstacle, namely, my beloved Angelo, who I knew loved me more than Glorianna, indeed, more than life itself. Indeed, after lighting a grand total of forty-seven candles at St. Patrick's Cathedral, I decided that if Angelo admitted he wanted me rather than Glorianna Bronx to live with him, I would immediately vacate the House of Adoro and see Adolfo only on alternate weekends, or when Adolfo was out of town. I mean, there was no reason why

Adolfo could not be Number Two if Angelo truly needed me and wanted me. With these upsetting considerations constantly in my mind, I had no choice but to trap Angelo into admitting the truth about his feelings for me before I made the wrong decision, married Angelo, and completely ruined my chances for happiness.

My plan was simple and devious. I would hire a hungry actress for five hundred dollars to impersonate a New York social worker, supposedly in the hire of the New York hospital system, to visit Angelo at home when Glorianna was out. She would ask him questions relating to his hospital stay. Was he satisfied? How was the food? How was the noise level at night? What about the bedside manner of the different physicians? Were any of the hospital personnel offensive? Then, after he began to offer information, she would say that it had come to the attention of the hospital staff that he had been severely depressed. Was this true? If so, was he taking medication? Was he seeing a psychiatrist? If so, what did the psychiatrist say? Did he have a happy home life? Did he think this helped his recovery? Did he have a satisfactory sex life? Did his wife come to visit him? If he was not married, was he living with someone? What did his woman think of the care given him in the hospital? Then, after the actress had gotten him talking about personal sexual feelings, she would slyly get around to the main point, which was that there had been reports, in some cases complaints, that he had been seen and heard having frequent sexual relations with, among others, a magnificent-looking, voluptuous blonde woman in her early to mid-twenties. Some people had reported that this young blonde woman worked on him like a miracle drug and that afterward, the medical personnel noted marked improvement, not only in his depressive moods, but in all his systems, especially the circulatory and nervous systems.

I figured that Angelo's reproductive and execretory

systems had always a functioned pretty well, so I told the actress, whose name was Hilda Hopper, a tall skinny redhead with glasses, to stick to the main topic, which was Angelo's overwhelming love for me. My secret plan involved letting myself into the back kitchen door of Angelo and Glorianna's apartment with keys made from a wax impression of Glorianna's. While Angelo talked about me in the living room, around the corner, in the kitchen, I would be undressing. When Angelo finally got to the part where he admitted he loved me and wanted to spend the rest of his life with me, shazaam! I would appear naked in front of him, and order Hilda Hopper from the house. She would exit from the kitchen, where another five hundred dollars would be waiting for her. By the time she exited I would be impaled on my favorite cock, squirming like a salmon on the end of a spear, perfectly happy to die in the cause of my favorite lover's ravenous appetite.

The appointed hour arrived. I quietly let myself into Angelo's kitchen. I could hear a man and a moman talking in the next room. I couldn't make out what they were saying, exactly. But wait—yes, it was definitely Angelo's voice. Yes, I definitely heard him mention my name. I slipped out of my Burberry trench coat and Papagallo flats and my Adoro custom-made black silk shift I'd picked out especially for the occasion. I wore no underwear, no hosiery, no jewelry that morning. I'd poured bottles of scented oil and rare perfumes into my morning bath so that my skin would be soft and sleek for my beloved Angelo. I'd dried myself briskly with a thick turkish towel to stimulate the circulation near my skin and to give myself a rosy, glowing look. Since I'd been at the House of Adoro, I'd started using the exercise machines and working out with the weights, so that my muscles were better-toned than ever. Not only that, I began to take better care of myself, trimming my wild, overgrown bush, for example, so that it formed a perfect inverted triangle of dark honey which pointed directly down to my luscious secrets below. Except that with Angelo there were no more secrets. Maybe that was the trouble. Maybe I should have teased him or played hard to get.

I couldn't believe what happened next. I stood in the kitchen for at least ten minutes waiting for Hilda to give me the sign and make her exit. Except that Hilda never came. Worse, I heard nothing more in the living room. Not a peep. Then, I heard tittering. Then giggles. Then full-throated belly laughs. It was worse than odd. Something was definitely wrong! I peeked around the corner to see what Miss Hilda Hooper was saying to Angelo. What I saw was such a shock to my central nervous system that I'm afraid I went beserk. I was facing Hilda, who was stark naked and not as thin as I had thought. As it so happened, she was monumentally stacked! She was on her knees, leaning over an equally naked Angelo, who was tit-fucking her with his wide, blue-veined super-cock. She must have brought K-Y jelly in her purse, because she had created a soft and sensuous fucking channel between her mammoth mammaries. In one glance I saw that her nipples were so erect from her raunchy, desgusting desire for Angelo that they were almost an inch long, only to be outdone in the absurdity of their proportions by the tennis ball swelling at the end of his cock.

I had never seen Angelo so sexually aroused. Yes, Hilda Hopper had definitely made a play for him. What a cheap slut! I couldn't believe my eyes! He was squeezing her breasts together, kneading them, burying his cock in them, as she tickled and stroked his pendulous testicles and the broad underside base of his ivory shaft where the root was so rock-hard and the skin there so loose and sensitive and vulnerable. Worst of all, they were

235

kissing each other on their mouths, a definite sign of emotional closeness, which has nothing to do with raw sex.

And to think they had just met! Something in me snapped. I grabbed a long wooden spoon off the kitchen counter and raced into the living room, screaming like a crazed banshee.

"I'll kill you, you filthy slut!" I yelled, and began to beat her on her breasts and buttocks with the back of the spoon, while Angelo, to my utter humiliation, instead of helping me fight our common adversary, began to laugh at me like I was some kind of hired clown!

Hilda's reaction was far worse. My whipping aroused her! Instead of protecting herself, she clutched at her *mons veneris*, fingering her clitoris, yanking her bush, stroking her inner thighs, begging me to hit her some more. "Please, Miss Hunt! Hit me, I deserve it! Please hit me! I'm no good! I'm a naughty girl!" And she rolled over on her stomach, as I, still in a fury, continued to strike her with the long-handled spoon. "Please, pretty please, Miss Hunt!! Hit me on my pussy! Beat my pussy! It's a baddy!" Worse, she smiled every time I hit her, and her smiling absolutely infuriated me, enraged me, made me go beserk. I threw away the wooden spoon and lunged at her with both fists. I struck at her repeatedly in her perfect, even face until at last, thank God, her nose began to gush bright, pink blood. The blood aroused my killer instinct. I turned into a wild animal and attacked the slut savagely with my long fingernails. I bit her on her pretty little lips with my teeth, tearing the skin and drawing more blood.

Then, I decided on the ultimate: I would bite off her nipples and then go for the clit! When I sank my teeth into her nipple, it was Hilda's turn to snap. I had gone too far. In an instant she returned to reality. "You bitch! You fucking bitch!" she screamed, smashing me in the face with her right hook.

To my horror, I enjoyed it! Hilda was streaming with blood from the wounds I had inflicted. Red shiny rivulets ran down from her chiseled nostrils over her perfect unmarked skin onto the white masses of her breasts. The blood from the tear on her lower lip stained her teeth, and blood was spurting onto me, warm blood, wonderful blood. "Oh Christ," I thought, "this is ridiculous. I better go back to the suburbs and marry an engineer or product manager. I'm a sadist. I'm perverted. I'm sick." And what was worse, I loved it! I loved the torn skin, the gushing blood, the red stains, the threat to life, the intimacy of violence.

By now, Angelo had stopped laughing and was whacking himself off with both of his strong, golden-haired fists. I wanted to be there to relieve him, that poor vulnerable man, in that quiet moment after ejaculation when I knew he would feel alone and friendless. Most men do feel that way, and so few women understand, but I couldn't do anything. I couldn't move. I was being beaten up by a woman I had trusted, an actress I had paid a small fortune to. I felt so powerless and so betrayed, I burst into tears and fell on the floor, sobbing and miserable. Angelo could not bear to see me suffer. He was far more sensitive than I had given him credit for, and to prove it he stopped whacking off and told Hilda Hopper to go home.

That was the final slap in her face. "But you're attracted to me!" she muttered.

"Get out of here," he ordered her.

Her reaction was predictable. "Goddamn porn stars, you think just because you got a big cock, you can abuse women. I hope you go to hell and take your fucking cock along with you!" Then, she turned on me. "You're nothing! Your hair's too blonde and you're too fat; that is, unless a man wants to fuck a pig!"

"Get out of here, and I'm telling you for the last time," Angelo said.

Hilda Hopper grabbed up her clothes and left through the kitchen door, presumably dressed, but not before she had grabbed up the second five hundred dollars I had stupidly left on the kitchen counter and a sterling silver pitcher Angelo's maternal grandmother had left him and which took several weeks to recover. Talk about throwing good money after bad!

Now, Angelo and I were alone. I felt manipulative and perverse, and I probably was. And a thousand dollars poorer. To prove his absolute sensitivity to my extreme plight, he laid me out on his carpet and spread-eagled me. Instantly, I wrapped by legs around his waist and dug my heels into the small of his back. He expertly entered my tight, warm pussy with his lethal weapon of love and surrender and absolute desire. I had forgiven him everything. I had forgotten all his petty mistakes, and I hoped he had forgotten mine. This, after all, was my beloved Angelo, with whom I had always found absolute emotional peace.

Who would have believed, even now, that the world's most popular porn star would ignore Hilda Hopper for me? Her breasts were bigger than mine. She was taller. Her skin was so lustrous in its whiteness, her hair so close to the color of gold gleaming in the Acapulco sun, that she literally took one's breath away. I guess I looked warmer and friendlier, and certainly more comfortable. Angelo must have thought so. If I had not completely forgotten Hilda Hopper, he certainly had. Or at least he had the good grace to pretend he had! Such rare sensitivity! His body said it all as his pork prod slammed back and forth inside my tight, slippery tunnel. I was exultant! I got what I came for: Angelo.

"Yes! Yes! Yes!" I cried, "I'll never leave you again!" The muscles in his washboard stomach rippled with ever-present energy, and the backs of his arms stood out like a longshoreman's. He was a hardened athlete in top form. He plunged back and forth all the way to his oversized balls, which slapped softly against the underside of my ass. He plowed into my raw meat, massaging every nerve ending, every sensitive fiber in my cunt.

"Diana, I'll give you anything! Anything! Tell me what you want!" Then, before I could answer, the combination of blood lust and physical friction triggered his machine gun. The bullets exploded inside me. His marble hard phallus erupted, a geyser of milk-white come.

"Angelo, you've come home!" I cried, as waves of electricity pumped through me; I let go, released into orgasm, knowing that when it was over, I would be safe in my beloved Angelo's arms.

That's exactly what happened. Afterward, we were at peace. There was solitude. There was an all-pervading warmth, just the right atmosphere to make plans for the rest of our lives. I decided it was the best sex I had ever had. In any case, I was centered and at peace. That was all I cared about. I knew, at last, that Angelo was My Man. He had to be. No one had ever loved me as much. If Adolfo Adoro loved me more than Angelo, I din't want to know about it. Adolfo frightened me. He was a take-charge person, the original self-made man. It was hard for me to sense Adolfo's vulnerability, to play mother to his little boy. But Angelo! He was my father, my mother, my baby, my friend! I had decided all these things the very hour I met him, when he was driving me to Muffie's apartment from the Port Authority and I went down on him and almost totaled the car.

"Oh, Angelo," I mused, "tell me, where shall me live?"

"We will always be friends," he said, with typical understatement.

"I know, my darling," I insisted, "but tell me, where shall we live, in the Village?"

"If we're not in the same city," he kidded, "we'll have to arrange to meet."

"Why?" I kidded back. "Are you interested in long-distance marriages?"

"Don't worry," he said, "the longest distance between me and Glorianna is the telephone cord!"

"What does Glorianna have to do with this?" I asked. I knew Angelo was still kidding, he had such a British wit, but when it came to Glorianna, I had to be sure. I wanted Basic Information.

This time, I got it. I got it good. "Glorianna and I are getting married. You already knew, right?"

"Knew!" I shrieked.

"What do you mean?" he said. "I thought you were marrying Adolfo Adoro."

"Who told you that?" I screamed. "I assumed it," he said.

"Angelo, don't be a fool!" I said.

"What do you want me to do?" he protested.

"If you marry me, I'll never see Adolfo Adoro again!" I meant every word of what I said.

So did Angelo. "Diana, I'm marrying Glorianna."

"Angelo, you can't marry Glorianna."

"I love her, Diana."

"Angelo, you don't love her. You can't possibly love her. How can I forget you just made love to me?"

Then, Angelo handed me a dose of my own medicine. "Diana, love and sex, as you well know, are not necessarily the same thing."

That really hurt. If I had come in my cunt, I had egg on my face. I decided to make one final try. "But you love me!" I wailed.

Angelo tried to be gentle and understanding. "I love Glorianna, Diana. I make love to her far more often than I make love to you, with far more passion. But, no matter what, you must believe me when I tell you, you are a great gal and a great piece of ass. Glorianna, however, despite what you may think, reaches deep down into the center of my soul."

"And?" I said. That was all I could say. "And?"

240

I never should have said that. Angelo's reply killed me on the spot. "And you don't."

That was all. "And you don't."

"Eeeeeeeeeeeeeeeehhhh!!!!!" I could not speak. My cry was that of a wild animal, wounded in the jungle, in its death throes.

Within minutes I had left the apartment and returned to Adolfo Adoro, determined never to think of Angelo O'Shaughnessy again. Moreover, I determined that I would do everything in my power to get Glorianna fired. I was stung to the quick. I was destroyed. I had nothing to look forward to but nights of passion and days of wealth with a man who adored me. The trouble was, he was Number Two on my list. In time, I came to my senses and made the best of the situation. After all, it was my Destiny. Like my Granddaddy always told me, "Diana, you have to take the cards life deals you and play with them." I decided that Adolfo would become the greatest passion of my life.

Chapter Sixteen

Adolfo Adoro and I were married at City Hall on the first of April, April Fool's Day, which turned out to be an omen of things to come. I carried a sprig of cherry blossoms and wore a knubby white Chanel suit trimmed in gold braid and gold buttons from an old British military uniform of the late Lord Mountbatten, an old drinking buddy of Adolfo's. Adolfo wore one of his own raw-silk beige suits. We were a stunning couple; bright, energetic, and beautiful. Lulu Touché and one of the doormen, a part-time law student named Rafael we had grabbed at the last minute, were the witnesses. Afterward, we drove to Connecticut to a simple country inn northeast of Ridgefield, where we spend our wedding night. Our suite smelled of daffodils and onion grass. It was, after all, the beginning of spring, and for all the gray fog caused by the constant rain, the air was crisp with a sharp, invigorating chill.

I was now Diana Adoro. It fit. Adoro meant "I adore." Perfect for me; I had always been in love with love. I decided to keep my new name forever, no matter if I lived to be a hundred and five.

There were a few small problems, to be sure, at least in my head. Adolfo had already been married three times, making me a precarious Wife Number Four. Furthermore, he was, as I later found out from secret enemies, all of fifty-seven, not fifty-two as he had claimed, even though he still looked a vigorous thirty-five. It turned out his previous marriages had lasted about five years apiece. The divorce proceedings had taken another two years. The resuming of bachelor patterns and the courtship of each subsequent wife took another three. I wondered sometimes how long it would be before he tired of me, but I really didn't care. Every minute with him was rare and valuable time.

Adolfo could read my mind, particularly when I was staring wistfully at the spring rain through the window of our bridal suite. "Diana Adoro," he said, softly, "in some respects you will always be a little girl, but in other ways you are already a genius."

"A genius? Me?" I couldn't imagine what he was talking about.

"Sh-h, my pussy, let me finish. A genius, yes. You know fabric design, color, workmanship. Your instinct for cost and marketing is not to be believed. You learned it in a

242

week. Besides, if you really have a serious financial problem, you can always hire the best financial managers, just as you hire the best person to sew on buttons. It's all the same."

"What are you talking about, my love?" I said, not understanding what he was getting at.

"Please, Diana," he implored, "you must let me finish. There is not much time."

I was shocked. "What do you mean, not much time?" I asked, incredulous. "Not much time for what?"

"Diana," he said, "if I were twenty years younger, I could pretend we'd be married forever, knowing in my heart of hearts I'd fall in love again in five years. In other words, if I were younger, I could play the game of love until the game, she is over. But I am older than you think, and the sad truth is, I may not have long to live."

"What?" I shrieked.

"Diana, you must learn to be calm. Death is not so terrible. We all die. Even you."

"But Adolfo . . ." I started to say, and couldn't finish. I was dissolved in tears.

"It's my heart, Diana. My doctors tell me it could go any time. It's true. It's in the family. My father. My grandfather. My uncles. No one lived past sixty."

My stomach was in knots. Our honeymoon was ruined. Our marriage was ruined. "Adolfo, don't you understand," I pleaded. "I love you."

"Diana," he said, "I'm leaving it all to you."

"All of what?" I didn't know what he was talking about.

"Adoro International. The House of Adoro," was his answer.

"Nooo," I wailed. "Don't leave anything to me. If you die, I die."

"That's too bad, Diana. The one thing I have lived for is the House of Adoro. If you love me, you will live for The House of Adoro. In fact, you will *be* the House of Adoro." Then, Adolfo told me about my special wedding present. It seems he had discovered my private sketch books with all my fantasy drawings of gowns and dresses and suits and even lingerie. Unbeknownst to me, he had sent my sketches, which he said were fabulous, to Lulu Touché's workrooms in the basement. The mock-ups were almost ready for my critiques, my comments, my changes. Six months hence the House of Adoro would present me as a major designer, with my first collection in the Colosseum in Rome. Adolfo had already hired publicists in Rome, plus a theater director and a lighting designer. Everything. Gloriana Bronx was to be the executive in charge, and if she gave me any trouble, I was empowered to fire her immediately.

That night, and for the next two months, we made frequent and violent love. Adolfo was aften short of breath and had to take digitalis. Sometimes, he seemed to become deathly pale. The plans for my first international show in the Colosseum proceeded on schedule. Glorianna was a bitch. I often wondered if she'd undermine me at the last minute, and have my evening gowns sewn with surgical catgut. I could just picture the gowns dissolving under the hot lights of the Colosseum as the models turned my show into a strip-tease contest, with all the Beautiful People laughing, and me back in the arms of Adolfo determined never to design another dress. But Adolfo understood my fears, and he accepted me the way I was. I guess the man loved me.

On three separate occasions, I was ushered into his lawyers' offices to sign papers to the effect that if he died I would agree to run his business. He told me that when Christian Dior died, he had willed everything to the twenty-one-year-old Yves Laurent, and here I was, almost twenty-three!

"But Yves St. Laurent is a genius!" I protested.

"Only because he decided to be one, and you must be the same," Adolfo admonished me.

244

"Oh, Adolfo," I said so many times, "you just can't ever leave me."

"And you, you just can't ever leave the House of Adoro! You must make it greater than ever!" Three times I nodded "Yes," and three times I had to be led sobbing from the lawyers' offices.

The end came at the end of spring, the end of May. It was the most mind blowing sexual experience of my life.

Imagine my profound shock on that bright afternoon, when Adolfo returned home from his annual check-up at Lenox Hill Hospital to tell me that his doctor and four consulting physicians had informed him that he had the worst kind of degenerative heart disease and that if he wanted to see sixty he'd not only have to stop drinking, smoking, and drugs, and yes, sexual activity, but that he'd have to undergo a triple-by-pass heart operation immediately.

I was absolutely stunned. I said, "But my Italian angel, what will happen to your favorite customers while you are ill?"

He looked at me with those black smoldering eyes, which reminded me of night, and, nibbling my bottom lip, whispered, "Cara mia, you can do it all."

Running my tongue around the top of his teeth, I protestd, "But I am a nobody." I could see the tears running down his cheeks, and I knew I better stay several feet away from him before I gave him a heart attack.

"That's alright," he said, struggling against his tears, "you can touch me. Nothing will happen. I am under medication." I embraced him, weeping.

But he had something important to say to me. "I have to tell you, my darling, that last night I had a dream where you were in charge of the House of Adoro and making a fortune. I am certainly not a superstitious man, but this time I think I have had a message from the gods."

245

I didn't know what to say to him. I didn't want to contradict his deepest insights. I figured that whatever happened to me would happen to me. In my whole career I have never gone after anything but the people who turned me on, and that's the gods' honest truth.

Without elaborating on the gory details of Adolfo's bypass operation and his subsequent recovery, which included taking medication which made him groggy and sedated, just let me say that even the most glamorous lives have limits and boundaries. We must seize our pleasure while we can. During the tragic weeks of Adolfo's illness, much like the events in his dream about me, and much to my own dismay, I pretty much had to direct the day-to-day operations of the Adoro empire with the salutary help of Adolfo's best friend, lawyer, and financial counselor, Maxey von Fuchs, an imperious German with ice-blue eyes and a voice like gravel. Maxey, sooner than I expected, was to become an important part of my own career. Without his constant guidance and deep personal attention, I wouldn't have been able to continue. The truth is, he worshipped my body; how could I callously reject someone whose very personal happiness and mental health depended on me? But more about Maxey von Fuch later....

Five weeks after Adolfo's triple bypass, he made one of the most fateful decisions of his life; namely, to discontinue the heart medication and resume the high-powered personal preferences he had put aside. His doctors warned him that his decision could prove fatal. Adolfo protested that he could not live at a slower pace, and that, above all, if he could not make love, especially to me, he would rather be dead. I sobbed when he told me. "If you die, Adolfo, I could not bear to continue living, and I certainly couldn't continue living in Manhattan!"

Upstairs in our private quarters, we disconnected the telephones, locked all the doors, pulled down the shades, closed the shutters, and informed the servants that we were not to be disturbed. Then, we began what was to be the most climactic love scene of his life or mine, up to that time. Adolfo, as I implied, had not had an orgasm in five weeks, and I, not being under doctor's orders, had, nonetheless, not seen Maxey von Fuchs for at least a week. We were both ravenous. Race horses straining at the gate.

When Adolfo touched me, I shivered from sheer excitement. He said, "Your skin is like gold satin; I want to rub my cock all over it."

I told him I wanted to put my tongue and lips on every gorgeous inch of his strong workman's body. We must have taken half an hour to undress each other. He loved it when I ran my tongue around his dark nipples until they stood up erect, which gave him an instant erection. By the time I managed to work his briefs over and around his magnificent throbbing tool and oversized balls hanging in their dark down-covered sac, I had pink passion flowers all over my neck from his passionate sucking. Adolfo, at once my puppy and my executioner, gazed at me with such longing, such intense desire, I was overwhelmed. I threw myself down on his inflamed sceptre so large from his excitement I could scarcely get my mouth around the head, but was glad to taste his sweet white ooze once more and to place both my hands over the loose outer flesh of his erection, working it up and down over the steel-hard inner core. Silently I licked and sucked his glans as he massaged my nipples with his strong tongue until they stood out taut, half an inch long, and I could feel what seemed like electrical charges passing between my crotch and the tips of my breasts.

We ate each other out like starving cannibals, I being careful to squeeze the base of his enormous shaft from time to time to prevent him from coming too soon, since I suspected he would not dare come more than once his

247

first time back in the saddle. His tongue, like his cock, was huge and fully capable of exploring the deep recesses of my honeyed cave, causing my vaginal muscles to contract into spasms as I came and came what seemed like a thousand times. Then, he gently spread open my legs and unfolded and mounted me, and I cried out, "Oh please, Adolfo, let me get on top. Don't overexert yourself. It will be less of a strain for you," but he protested, "No, no, *carissima,* my lovely one. If I cannot be like I was before, I would rather be dead."

What could I say? Like the Germans invading France, his rocket cock rammed into me, causing my complete and total surrender. Then, he rode me, the eager lips of my cunt clinging to his divine rod like my life depended on it. We were both drenched in sweat, gleaming, glistening, hugging onto each other. I was exploding inside. As his shaft began to swell larger and larger within me, and his glans began to feel like an apple, I knew he was starting to come. I wanted to squeeze the base of his cock again, but Adolfo screamed out, "No, no, my angel, I am coming! I am coming!"

He was absolutely right, poor lovely one. Suddenly, I felt a load of warm, caressing fluid splatter against my insides with the force of a small cannon, and Adolfo cried out with exultation, a wonderful glow on his face, his dark eyes shining like beacons in the surrounding dark. I felt his bottomless energy rippling through every corpuscle of his magnificent body as he came and came again.

Then, a terrible thing happened. Without warning, he suddenly went rigid, and, with a sweet sigh, fell on top of me, still smiling and absolutely dead. It was the most awful moment of my life up till then, because, in trying to get out from under him, in trying to wrest his enormous cock out of me, I couldn't help being stimulated. I kept coming and coming, and all the time I knew he was dead. My grief and my sorrow were inextricably mixed with sexual excitement. In that moment I learned one of life's eternal truths that has stayed with me since that day I lost him, namely, that things never get so bad that you can't find someone, living or dead, to get off on.

And I must confess, although I have never before publically admitted this, that after I had gotten out from under Adolfo, I turned him over to look at his chiseled body for one last time, and horrors! I could not restrain myself from going down on him once more. His cock was still rigid, and so I sucked him off until he came again, licking and squeezing his balls, magnificent jewels that they were, until he came once more, and I swear I could feel his body shudder from deep within and the smile on his face widen just a little bit more. After that, I lay on top of him, tears streaming down my face, rubbing my clit furiously against his cock and balls, massaging his cock until it grew hot and hard, with my desperate lips smothering his still-warm mouth. I came and came again, exploding in feverish excitement, as my heart was breaking within me. It was the most satisfying spiritual experience of my life up till that time. It gave me the courage to call the police and make plans for the funeral.

And to think that just one year earlier I had been little Diana Hunt, ex-cheerleader from Beavertown High, a hostess at the local Howard Johnson's, with dreams that seemed too big to come true! Now I was Diana Adoro, bereaved widow of one of the world's most beloved men. Somehow, even then, I knew that Adolfo's love for me would continue beyond the grave, just as he had promised. I am here to tell you it has. God bless Adolfo Adoro.

Chapter Seventeen

What followed upon Adolfo Adoro's tragic death, namely, his funeral and the reading of his will, which left The House of Adoro and the bulk of his million-dollar estate to me, is really the beginning of another story, which I call *Diana's Debut*. The sad truth was, Adolfo's death put the spotlight on my triumphal debut as an international fashion designer and has allowed me to travel all over the world as a welcome guest visiting the factories which produce the Adoro products: the perfumes, the scarves, the leather goods, the men's line, the toiletries.

In my first months of mourning, I learned more about marketing and advertising. I also learned how to make commercials and how to star in them myself. Most importantly, I learned how to invest my money in real estate, mining, utilities and municipal bonds. Today with the help of my wonderful financial advisor and dear friend Maxey von Fuchs, it seems I know half the successful men and women in the world. God bless Maxey.

In my next book, *Diana's Debut*, I will explain the best way for young widows to deal with their untimely grief. I will also make suggestions as to how the concerned friends of young, attractive widows can contribute to their well-being and their great need for emotional comfort and security. Using the story of my international debut in the sensual city of Rome, I will tell all about the many wonderful men and women, including some fantastic international studs and playboys who were so kind to me in my first year of struggle and grief.

And now I must finish the story of my first year in New York which brought me from poverty to unparalled wealth. I must finish the story of how Desire brought me to Discovery.

I have promised myself that I wouldn't dwell on the mournful and tragic aspects of My First True Love's funeral, except to report the basic facts: since Adolfo was, at heart, such a devout Roman Catholic, who always kept a crucifix over our bed, I made sure that he was given a wonderful celebrity funeral at St. Patrick's Cathedral on Fifth Avenue, where so many attractive and exciting men like Bobby Kennedy had their final farewells. After all, at the time of his death, Adolfo Adoro was already a household name in America, where *Women's Wear Daily*, in a reader's poll, estimated that at least half the women in America under fifty owned at least one item in the Adoro line. Keeping this in mind, and since I had been informed that Roman Catholics had taken to wearing white at their funerals, I designed for myself a body-hugging white jersey dress—with long sleeves and a high neck, to be sure, to show my respect for the Church—but with a big heart-shaped cut-out on the bosom cut right down to the edge of my cinnamon aureoles to show off my full, ripe, golden globes that my dear departed husband had prized so much. And out of absolute devotion to the memory of his glorious and never-fading cock I made sure that the crotch was as tight as possible. I wanted my Adolfo to be so proud of me, even though I knew that some typically jealous and mean-hearted souls would callously remark that I was just looking for attention.

I was so grateful that Senator Ted Kennedy could be present, along with so many handsome, virile, and deep-feeling American male celebrities who so respected

Adolfo and who always came to his parties. Unfortunately, certain of the top box-office movie stars who came to Adolfo's funeral, along with the brilliant and most compassionate Senator Kennedy, have privately asked me not to write about our brief and nodding acquaintances at this time in my life, so for now, I shall respect their wishes. I shall only say that it was during the abject and soul-wrenching loneliness of Adolfo's funeral Mass that I first saw my beloved "Vanni," otherwise known as Monseigneur Giovanni Caro, Adolfo's best boyhood friend, who had flown in from the Vatican to say his funeral mass. It is Vanni who figures so prominently in the next segment of my life in Rome, the story I call *Diana's Debut*. Note: I have had to slightly alter Vanni's last name to protect his career, since a great many bishops are jealous of his fantastic cock, as I later discovered in Rome when I was so desperately seeking spiritual consolation and an ultimate meaning to my vulnerable young life.

Vanni, even though he was almost fifty, didn't have an ounce of surplus fat on his tall, stocky, extremely muscled body, which was as pale as a Swede's. He was from Northern Italy and a former professional soccer player. His fat white cock with its throbbing blue veins looked like it had been carved from the finest Carrara marble, and in all the times he was to console me with his overwhelming love, I don't think his tool of passion ever completely relaxed, at least not with me. As Vanni so often told me in his deep, rich, paternal tones, which made my cunt grow warm and moist just hearing him, and my clitoris tingle when I felt his hot compassionate breath on my cheeks, the two of us had a profoundly spiritual destiny, and if we loved the Almighty, we should respect our God-given feelings and give in to them. Totally.

Later, in Rome, when we were together for the first time, an episode I will describe in detail later on, Vanni confessed to me that all during the funeral Mass at St. Patrick's, he could scarcely concentrate on God or death, and certainly not on Adolfo, since he had a raging hard-on because of me and was grateful that his priestly robes covered his passion. He said he had wanted to race down from the altar, grab my tits, pull them out of their heart-shaped window, and suck on them. Of course, I had to admit that despite my tremendous grief, I had known all along that Vanni's constant looking up at me from his holy texts was more than a stranger's concern for a young and admittedly attractive widow, but at the time I had my grief to think about.

Then, again, there was Maxey von Fuchs, The House of Adoro's lawyer and financier, who kept accidentally stroking my thigh and brushing up against my ass all during the service, and who, to put it frankly, fucked me in the back seat of the limo on the trip between the church and the cemetery. Even though I trace the development of my relationship with Maxey in the next stage of my life in *Diana's Debut,* I think Adolfo has been dead a long enough time now for me to tell what happened between St. Patrick's Catherdral and the cemetery on Long Island.

Thank God the limousine had dark windows. As soon as we had closed the doors and pulled away from St. Patrick's Maxey tipped the driver and made him close the partition window between the front and back seats. Then, without saying a word, he began kissing me all over my tear-stained cheeks while his hands were pushing my white jersey dress up over my thighs. I decided that the only way to avoid a scandalous scene and to avoid hurting his feelings was to give in to him. After all, Maxey was a foreigner, who had to struggle so hard with an unfamiliar language. His cock, moreover, was obviously straining in his pants, and I knew he must be suffering great pain because of me.

When I finally was able to wrest his ramrod free of

its constraining prison, I felt such an overwhelming longing for my dear Adolfo that I bent over and kissed Maxey's love knob, which made it swell even more. Maxey stopped feeling me for a moment, looked deep into me with his ice-blue eyes with such an expression of gratitude, that if our time had not been so short I would have burst into instant tears. Then, I have to say that Maxey went beserk, unfortunately, tearing at my dress and moaning, "Oh, Diana, Diana, I can't bear to be without you!"

I was so grateful to Maxey for being so consistently considerate of my feelings that I was overwhelmed with affection for him. I couldn't help myself. I raised my legs up over his shoulders and wrapped them around his tanned and muscular neck, as he dove into the fur-covered entrance of my lover's cave, pushing my legs apart, stroking my inner thighs, whispering in his wonderful Teutonic accent, "We are alive, my *schotzie*, alive! We must live for today!" as he began to eat me, telling me my cunt was so fabulous I deserved all the success and all the love in the world. He told me my thighs were like thick, clotted English cream, and my cunt was like honey candy to him. I started to get very hungry, and the strong, thick muscle of his tongue, which must have been at least six inches long, explored my tunnel of love, sucking up my juices. I grew ravenous. I wanted him in my mouth. All of him. I kept exploding inside, again and again, the deepest reaches of my vagina convulsing involuntarily, causing my whole body to heave in an ecstasy I never thought possible, as I saw white light and heard inner music; I remembered nothing until we were out of Manhattan and in Queens. He pushed his golden ramrod, so hard and disciplined, straight into me, his deep thrusts clean, direct, almost violent. I felt like taking his cock out and rubbing his uncircumcized foreskin against my clitoris, which was standing up, hot and pink.

254

I was ravenous. I felt like I was being raped, like I had no will, like I was being taken out of an airplane and we were free-falling, wrapped around each other as we fell to our deaths, which is why just before we landed, so to speak, I could stand it no longer. Like an Amazon, I grabbed his massive, swollen cock and his loose sack of jewels, massaging them, running his thick dark fore-skin up and down over the rigid iron core, as Maxey shivered in delight, murmuring like a baby as the sticky ooze which precedes ejaculation started bursting through the tiny gaping mouth in his purplish glans, causing him to heave his whole torso as I went down on him.

Like I have always said, here is nothing I like better than to have a sexually powerful man, especially a rich and successful one, empty a huge load of rich creamy seed-laden come into my sucking, slurping mouth. When he came, his whole body heaved up and down with such an electrical charge, like he'd been struck by lightning, I thought the car was going to go off the road. I held onto his cock like an anchor.

If sometimes I wonder why I never became a prosti-tute, I finally realize that its because I, unlike many women, have never been able to separate sex and love. And every night I thank God that He has given me the capacity for so much love.

My dear Adolfo's tragic funeral was the most moving event of my life up until that time. God bless those caring and sensitive men, Monseigneur Vanni Caro and Maxey von Fuchs, as they lowered my Adolfo into the cold, cold ground.

My lesson? I realized that at tragic events we feel closer than ever to other members of the human race, especially to those of the opposite sex. From that day forward, I have had no fear of tragedy or loss, because I know that no matter what happens to me, I can always find someone who's looking for a little passion in his life and a woman like me who desires to be desired.

For Your Pleasure
from Warner Books